THE BOOK

"Irving is one of the best. In this novel he applies his extraordinary gifts and holds—knowledge and imagination—to battle royal, Greco-Roman relationship, all the Australian tag team theatrics of body contact and love."—Stanley Elkin

THE AUTHOR

"John Irving, it is abundantly clear, is a true artist. He is not afraid to take on great themes."—*The Los Angeles Times*

THE ACCLAIM

"The action takes them into the shower, to a summer house on the Cape, into various complicated positions, and into shock. . . . Mr. Irving develops this theme in a deft, hard-hitting style, breaking cleanly at the clinches."

—*The New York Times*

Books by John Irving

The 158-Pound Marriage
Setting Free the Bears
The Water-Method Man
The World According to Garp

Published by POCKET BOOKS

John Irving

The 158-Pound Marriage

PUBLISHED BY POCKET BOOKS NEW YORK

Portions of this book appeared in considerably different form in *Viva* and
Works in Progress.

POCKET BOOKS, a Simon & Schuster division of
GULF & WESTERN CORPORATION ·
1230 Avenue of the Americas, New York, N.Y. 10020

First Pocket Books printing October, 1978

10 9 8 7 6 5

POCKET and colophon are trademarks of Simon & Schuster.

Printed in the U.S.A.

for JMF

There were four of us then, not merely two, and in our quaternion the vintage sap flowed freely, flowed and bled and boiled as it may never again.
—John Hawkes, *The Blood Oranges*

It was a most amazing business, and I think that it would have been better in the eyes of God if they had all attempted to gouge out each other's eyes with carving knives. But they were "good people."

Ford Madox Ford, *The Good Soldier*

1

The Angel Called
"The Smile of Reims"

My wife, Utchka (whose name I some time ago shortened to Utch), could teach patience to a time bomb. With some luck, she has taugh me a little. Utch learned patience under what we might call duress. She was born in Eichbüchl, Austria—a little village outside the proletarian town of Wiener Neustadt, which is an hour's drive from Vienna—in 1938, the year of the Anschluss. When she was three, her father was killed as a Bolshevik saboteur. It is unproven that he was a Bolshevik, but he was a saboteur. By the end of the war, Wiener Neustadt would become the largest landing field in Europe, and the unwilling site of the German Messerschmitt factory. Utch's father was killed in 1941 when he was caught in the act of blowing up Messerschmitts on the runway in Wiener Neustadt.

The local *SS Standarte* of Wiener Neustadt paid a visit to Utch's mother in Eichbüchl after Utch's father had been caught and killed. The SS men said they'd come to alert the village to the "seed of betrayal" which obviously ran thick in Utch's family. They told the villagers to watch Utch's mother very closely, to make sure she wasn't a Bolshevik like her late husband. Then they raped Utch's mother and stole from the house a wooden cuckoo clock which Utch's father had bought in Hungary. Eichbüchl is very close to the

Hungarian border, and the Hungarian influence can be seen everywhere.

Utch's mother was raped again, several months after the SS left, by some of the village menfolk who, when questioned about their assault, claimed they were following the instructions of the SS: watching Utch's mother very closely, to make sure she wasn't a Bolshevik. They were not charged with a crime.

In 1943, when Utch was five, Utch's mother lost her job in the library of the monastery in nearby Katzelsdorf. It was suggested that she might be foisting degenerate books on the young. Actually, she was guilty of stealing books, but they never accused her of that, nor did they ever find out. The small stone house Utch was born in—on the bank of a stream that runs through Eichbüchl—connected to a chicken house, which Utch's mother maintained, and a cow barn, which Utch cleaned every day from the time she was five. The house was full of stolen books; it was actually a religious library, though Utch remembers it more as an art library. The books were huge poster-sized records of church and cathedral art—sculpture, architecture and stained glass—from some time before Charlemagne through the late Rococo.

In the early evenings as it was getting dark, Utch would help her mother milk the cows and collect the eggs. The villagers would pay for the milk and eggs with sausage, blankets, cabbages, wood (rarely coal), wine and potatoes.

Fortunately, Eichbüchl was far enough away from the Messerschmitt plant and the landing field in Wiener Neustadt to escape most of the bombing. At the end of the war the Allied planes dumped more bombs on that factory and landing field than on any other target in Austria. Utch would lie in the stone house with her mother in the blacked-out night and hear the *crump! crump! crump!* of the bombs falling in Wiener

Neustadt. Sometimes a crippled plane would fly low over the village, and once Haslinger's apple orchard was bombed in blossom time; the ground under the trees was littered with apple petals thicker than wedding confetti. This happened before the bees had fertilized the flowers, so the fall apple crop was ruined. Frau Haslinger was found hacking at herself with a pruning hook in the cider house, where she had to be restrained for several days—tied up in one of the large, cool apple bins until she came to her senses. During her confinement, she claimed, she was raped by some of the village menfolk, but this was considered a fantasy due to her derangement at the loss of the apple crop.

It was no fantasy when the Russians got to Austria in 1945, when Utch was seven. She was a pretty little girl. Her mother knew that the Russians were awful with women and kind to children, but she didn't know if they would consider Utch a woman or a child. The Russians came through Hungary and from the north, and they were especially fierce in Wiener Neustadt and its environs because of the Messerschmitt plant and all the high officers of the *Luftwaffe* they found around there.

Utch's mother took Utch to the cow barn. There were only eight cows left. Going over to the largest cow, whose head was locked in its milking hitch, she slit the cow's throat. When it was dead, she unfastened the head from the milking hitch and rolled the cow on her side. She cut open the belly of the cow, pulled out the intestines and carved out the anus, and then made Utch lie down in the cavity between the great cow's scooped-out ribs. She put as much of the innards back into the cow as would fit, and took the rest outside in the sun where it would draw flies. She closed the slit belly-flaps of the cow around Utch like a curtain; she told Utch she could breathe through the cow's carved-

11

out anus. When the guts that had been left in the sun drew flies, Utch's mother brought them back inside the cow barn and arranged them over the head of the dead cow. With the flies swarming around her head, the cow looked as if she'd been dead a long time.

Then Utch's mother spoke to Utch through the asshole of the cow. "Don't you move or make a sound until someone finds you." Utch had a long, slim wine bottle filled with camomile tea and honey, and a straw. She was to sip it when she was thirsty.

"Don't you move or make a sound until someone finds you," said Utch's mother.

Utch lay in the belly of the cow for two days and two nights while the Russians wasted the village of Eichbüchl. They butchered all the other cows in the barn, and they brought some women to the barn too, and they butchered some men in there as well, but they wouldn't go near the dead cow with Utch inside her because they thought the cow had been dead a long time and her meat was spoiled. The Russians used the barn for a lot of atrocities, but Utch never made a sound or moved in the belly of the cow where her mother had placed her. Even when she ran out of camomile tea and the cow's intestines dried and hardened around her—and all the slick viscera clung to her— Utch did not move or make a sound. She heard voices; they were not her language and she did not respond. The voices sounded disgusted. The cow was prodded; the voices groaned. The cow was tugged and dragged; the voices grunted—some voices gagged. And when the cow was lifted—the voices *heaved!*—Utch slipped out in a sticky mass which landed in the arms of a man with a black-haired mustache and a red star on his gray-green cap. He was Russian. He dropped to his knees with Utch in his arms and appeared to pass out. Other Russians around him took off their caps; they appeared to pray. Someone brought water and washed Utch. Ironically, they were the sort of Russians who were kind to children and in no way thought Utch was a woman; at first, in fact, they thought she was a *calf*.

Piece by piece, what happened grew clear. Utch's mother had been raped. (Almost everyone's mother and daughter had been raped. Almost everyone's father and son had been killed.) Then one morning a Russian had decided to burn the barn down. Utch's mother had begged him not to, but she had little bargaining power; she had already been raped. So she had been forced to kill the Russian with a trenching spade, and another Russian had been forced to shoot her.

Piece by piece, the Russians put it together. This must be the child of that woman who didn't want the barn burned down, and it was because . . . The Russian who'd caught the slimy Utch in his arms as the putrid cow was thrown up on a truck figured it out. He was an officer, too, a Georgian Russian from the banks of the eely Black Sea; they have queer phrases and lots of slang there. One of them is *utch*—a cow. I have asked around, and the only explanation is that *utch*, to various offhanded Georgians, imitates the sound a cow makes when she is calving. And *utchka*? Why, that is a calf, of course, which is what the Georgian officer called the little girl who was delivered to him from the womb of the cow. And it is natural, now, that a woman in her thirties would no longer be an *Utchka*, so I call her Utch.

Her real name was Anna Agati Thalhammer, and the Georgian officer, upon hearing the history of Utch's family in the good village of Eichbüchl, took his Utchka with him to Vienna—a fine city for occupying, with music and painting and theater, and homes for orphans of the war.

When I think of how often I told Severin Winter this

13

story, I could break my teeth! Over and over again, I told him he must understand that, above all, Utch is loyal. Patience is a form of loyalty, but he never understood that about her.

"Severin," I used to say, "she is vulnerable for the same reason that she is strong. Whatever she puts her love in, she will trust. She will wait you out, she will put up with you—forever—if she loves you."

It was Utch who found the postcards. It was the summer we spent, ill-advised, in Maine, ravaged by rain and biting insects, when Utch was bitten by the bug of antiques. I remember it as a summer littered with foul furniture, relics of Colonial America—a kick which Utch was soon off.

It was in Bath, Maine, that she found the postcards in some grimy warehouse advertising "Rare Antiques." It was near the shipyard; she could hear riveting. The owner of the antique shop tried to sell her a buggy whip. Utch implied there was a look in his old eyes that begged her to use it on him, but she's European, and I don't know if many Americans go that way. Perhaps they do in Maine. She declined the whip and kept herself near the door of the warehouse, browsing warily with the old man following behind her. When she saw the postcards in a dusty glass case, she immediately recognized Europe. She asked to see them. They were all of France after World War I. She asked the old man how he got them.

He had been an American soldier in World War I, a part of the army which celebrated the victory in France. The postcards were the only souvenirs he had left—old black-and-white photographs, some in sepia tones, poor quality. He told her that the photographs were more accurate in black and white. "I *remember* France in black and white," he told Utch. "I don't think France was in color then." She knew I'd like the photographs, so she bought them—over four hundred postcards for one dollar.

It took me weeks to go through them, and I still go through them today. There are ladies with long black dresses and gentlemen with black umbrellas, peasant children in the traditional *costumes bretons,* horse carriages, the early auto, the canvas-backed trucks of the French Army and soldiers strolling in the parks. There are scenes of Reims, Paris and Verdun—before and after the bombardments.

Utch was right; it's the kind of thing I can use. That summer in Maine I was still researching my third historical novel, set in the Tyrol in the time of Andreas Hofer, the peasant hero who turned back Napoleon. I had no use for World War I France at that time, but I knew that one day I would. A few years from now, perhaps, when the people in the postcards—even the children in *costumes bretons*—will be more than old enough to be dead, then I might take them up. I find it's no good writing historical novels about people who aren't dead; that's a maxim of mine. History takes time; I resist writing about people who are still alive.

For history you need a camera with two lenses—the telephoto and the kind of close-up with a fine, penetrating focus. You can forget the wide-angle lens; there is no angle wide enough.

But in Maine I was not pondering France. I was nursing infected fly bites and worrying with the peasant army of Andreas Hofer, the hero of the Tyrol. I was despairing over Utch's despair at the jagged Maine cliffs, the hazards of Maine water; our children were then in dangerous phases (when are they *not?*)—they were both nonswimmers. Utch felt they were safest in the car or in antique shops, and I would not encourage another bite from a black fly, a greenhead or a saltwater mosquito. A summer on the Maine coast, spent hiding indoors.

"Why did we *wont* to come here?" Utch would ask me.

"Why did we *want* to come here," I'd correct her.

"*Ja,* why did we *wont* to?" Utch would say.

"To get away?" I'd venture.

"From *vut?*"

It's ironic to think of it now, but before we met Edith and Severin Winter there was really nothing we needed to get away from. That summer in Maine we did not know Edith and Severin.

An example of the close-up lens occurs to me. I have several before-and-after photographs of the Cathedral of Reims. There are two close-ups, from the left doorway of the western porch, of the angel called "The Smile of Reims." Prior to the shelling of the cathedral, the angel was indeed smiling. Next to her, a forlorn Saint Nicaise held out his arm—his hand gone at the wrist. After the bombardment the angel called "The Smile of Reims" was headless. Her arm was gone at the elbow, and a chunk of stone was fleshed out of her leg from thigh to calf. The forlorn, forewarning Saint Nicaise lost another hand, one leg, his chin and his right cheek. After the blasting, his wrecked face described them both, much as her smile had once outshone his gloom. After the war, there was a saying in Reims that the *joie de vivre* in the angel's smile had actually attracted the bombs to her. More subtly, the wise people of Reims implied, it was her morose companion, that sour saint, who could not abide glowering alongside such ecstacy as hers; it was he who drew the bombs to them both.

It's commonly said in that part of France that the moral of "The Smile of Reims" is that when there's a war on, and you're in it, don't be happy; you insult both the enemy and your allies. But that moral of "The Smile of Reims" isn't very convincing. The good people of Reims haven't got eyes for detail like mine. When the angel has her smile and head intact, the saint beside her is in pain. When her smile and the rest of her head leave her, that saint—despite new wounds of his own—seems more content. The moral of "The Smile of Reims," according to *me,* is that an unhappy man cannot tolerate a happy woman. Saint Nicaise would have taken the angel's smile, if not her whole head, with or without the help of World War I.

And that goddamn Severin Winter would have done what he did to Edith, with or without me!

"Haf patience," Utch used to say, in the early rounds of her bout with English.

Okay, Utch. I see the close-ups of the shelling of Reims. The telephoto is still unclear. There's a long, broad view taken from the cathedral of the fired quarters of the city, but neither I nor the clever people of Reims have extracted a moral from it. As I advised, forget the wide-angle. I see Edith and Severin Winter only in close-ups, too. We historical novelists need time. Haf patience.

Severin Winter—that simple-minded ego, that stubborn Prussian!—even had some history in common with Utch, for all that it mattered. History occasionally lies. For example, the decapitation of the angel called "The Smile of Reims," and the rest of the damage done to the great Reims cathedral, are considered among the *human* atrocities of World War I. How flattering to an angel! How bizarre for sculpture! That the loss of art should be considered as similar to the rape, mutilation and murder of French and Belgian women by the Boche! The damage to a statue called "The Smile of Reims" doesn't quite compare to the shishkebabbing of children on bayoncts. People regard art too highly, and history not enough.

I can still see Severin Winter—that schmaltz lover, that opera freak—standing in his plant-festooned living room like a dangerous animal roaming a botanical garden, listening to Beverly Sills singing Donizetti's *Lucia*.

"Severin," I said, "you don't understand her." I meant Utch.

But he was only hearing Lucia's madness. "I think Joan Sutherland carries this part better," he said.

"Severin! If those Russians had not tried to move the cow, Utch would have stayed inside her."

"She'd have gotten thirsty," Severin said. "Then she'd have climbed out."

"She was already thirsty," I said. "You don't know her. If that Russian had burned the barn down, she would have stayed."

"She'd have smelled the barn burning and made a break for it."

"She could have smelled the cow *cooking*," I said, "and Utch would have stayed until *she* was done."

But Severin Winter did not believe me. What can you expect of a wrestling coach?

His mother was an actress, his father was a painter, his coach said he could have been great. More than ten years ago Severin Winter was runner-up in the 157-pound class at the Big Ten Championships at Michigan State University in East Lansing. He wrestled for the University of Iowa, and runner-up in the Big Ten was the closest he ever came to a major conference or national championship. The man who beat him in the finals of the Big Ten tournament was a lean, slick, leg wrestler from Ohio State named Jefferson Jones; he was a black with a knuckle-hard head, bruise-blue palms and a pair of knees like mahogany doorknobs. Severin Winter said Jones put on a figure-four body scissors so hard that you were convinced his pelvis had that strange spread of two sharp bones like a woman's pelvis. When he rode you with a cross-body ride—your near leg scissored, your far arm hooked— Severin said Jones cut off your circulation somewhere near your spine. And even Jones wasn't good enough for a national championship; he never won one, though he was the Big Ten champion for two consecutive years.

Severin Winter never came close to a national title. The year he was runner-up in the Big Ten, he placed sixth in the national tournament. He was pinned in the semifinals by the defending national champion from Oklahoma State, and pinned again in the second round of the consolation matches by a future geologist from the Colorado School of Mines. And in the wrestle-off to decide fifth from sixth, he lost another convincing decision to Jefferson Jones of Ohio State.

I once spent some time trying to interview the wrestlers who had beaten Severin Winter; with one exception, none of them rememberd who he was. "Well, you don't remember everyone you beat, but you remember everyone who beat you," Winter was fond of saying. But I discovered that Jefferson Jones, the wrestling coach at a Cleveland high school, remembered Severin Winter very well. Altogether, over a three-year period, Winter had wrestled Jefferson Jones five times; Jones had beaten him all five.

"That boy just couldn't get to me, you know," Jones told me. "But he was one of those who kept coming. He just kept coming at you, if you know what I mean. You'd break him down on his belly and he'd work like a stiff old dog to get back up to his hands and knees again. You'd just break him down on his belly again, and he'd get up again. He just kept coming, and I just kept taking the points."

"But was he, you know, any *good?*" I asked.

"Well, he won more than he lost," said Jones. "He just couldn't get to *me.*"

I sensed in Jefferson Jones an attitude I'd often felt radiating from Severin. A wrestler's ego seems to stay in shape long after he's out of his weight class. Perhaps

19

their history of cutting weight makes them tend to exaggerate. For example, to hear Winter describe the exploits of his ancestors is to be misled.

His mother was the Viennese actress Katrina Marek. This much of his story is true. Katrina Marek's last performance in Vienna's Atelier was on Thursday evening, March 10, 1938. The papers claim she was an "astounding" Antigone, which seems a suitable role for her to have played at the time; she would have required loose garments for her costume, for she was eight months pregnant with Severin. The Friday performance was canceled due to her failure to show up. That would have been Black Friday, March 11, 1938, the day the Anschluss was decided, the day before the Germans marched into Austria. Katrina Marek knew the news early and got herself and her fetus out of the country in time.

She took a taxi. Apparently, even this much of Winter's story is true. She actually took a taxi—herself, her fetus and a portfolio of her husband's drawings and paintings. The paintings, oil on canvas, had been taken off their stretchers and rolled up.

Severin's father, the artist, didn't come. He gave Katrina the drawings and paintings and told her to take the taxi to the Swiss border, to take a train to Belgium or France, to take a boat to England, to go to London, to find the two or three painters in London who knew his work, to ask them to find a theater in London that would employ the Austrian actress Katrina Marek, and to show the drawings and the rolled-up canvases to anyone demanding proof of who she was. She was to say, "I am Katrina Marek, the actress. My husband is the Viennese painter Kurt Winter. I am Viennese too. You see, I am pregnant . . ." But clearly, even dressed as Antigone, anyone could see that.

"Don't drop that baby until you're in London," said Kurt to Katrina. "You won't have time to get it a passport." Then he kissed her goodbye and she drove out of Vienna on Black Friday, the day before the Germans drove in.

Incredibly, in Vienna alone, the first wave of Gestapo arrests took seventy-six thousand. (Katrina Marek and the unborn Severin Winter were boarding a train in St. Gallen, bound for Ostend.) And the father who stayed behind? To hear Severin tell it, his father stayed behind because he was devoted to the revolution, because there was still something a hero could do. Someone, for example, drove the daring, criminal editor Herr Lennhoff across the Hungarian border at Kittsee—after having been turned away by the Czechs. Another taxi was used. Kurt Winter could have been reading Lennhoff's editorial about the German *Putsch* as late as noon and still have gotten away with it; Hitler was in Linz only at noon. "That was cutting it close," Severin Winter has admitted. The first time he told the story, it sounded as if his father was the driver of the cab that drove Lennhoff to Hungary. Later this became confused. "Well, he *could* have been the driver," Winter said. "I mean, he needed a big reason to stay behind, right?"

And the business about the zoo. I checked the facts on that, and it's at least recorded. In 1945, just before the Russians got to Vienna, the entire zoo was *eaten*. Of course, as the people got hungrier, small raiding parties had escaped, mostly at night, with an antelope or a zebra here and there. When people are starving, it seems silly to be taking care of all that game. Yet the Army reserves were on guard duty, day and night, in the great sprawling zoo and botanical gardens on the grounds of the Schönbrunn Palace. Winter has implied that the reserves were rationing the animals to the poor people, one at a time—a kind of black-market zoo, according to him. But then the story gets cloudy. Late on the night of April Fool's Day, 1945, twelve days before the Soviets captured Vienna, some fool tried to let all the animals out.

"My father," Winter said once, "loved animals and was just the right sort of sport for the job. A devout antifascist, it must have been his last act for the underground . . ."

Because, of course, the poor fool who let those animals out was eaten right away. The animals were hungry too, after all. The freed animals roared so loud that the hungry children woke up. It was as good a time as any for butchering the last meat in Vienna; the Soviets were already in Budapest. Who in his right mind would leave a zoo full of food for the Russian Army?

"So the plan backfired," Winter has said. "Rather than set them free, he got them killed, and they ate him as a favor."

Well, if there ever was such a plan, and if Winter's father had any more to do with that zoo bust than with Lennhoff's escape. If he stayed behind, why not make heroics the reason?

Utch says she can sympathize with Severin's impulse. I'll bet she can! I once had a thought of my own about their similar ancestors. What if Utch's father, the saboteur of Messerschmitts in Wiener Neustadt, was something of a two-timer and led a double life? What if he knocked up this actress in Vienna, where he posed as a brash young artist, bought off a paternity suit with a bunch of drawings and paintings, blew up the Messerschmitts, got caught but not killed (he somehow escaped), had no inclinations to return to a raped wife in Eichbüchl, felt especially guilty on April Fool's Day, 1945, and tried to atone for his sins by liberating the zoo?

You see, we historical novelists have to be as interested in what might have happened as what did. My version would make Severin Winter and Utch related, which would explain parts of their later union which remain curious to me. But sometimes it calms me down to think that they just had their war stories in common. Two heavies from Central Europe with their bundle of shrugs! When she was cross, Utch was fond of reducing the world to an orgasm. Severin Winter rarely gave the world credit for much else. But when I think of it, they had more than a war in common.

For example, those rolled-up canvases and drawings that Kurt Winter gave to Katrina Marek are very revealing. All the way to England she never once looked at them, but at British customs she was obliged to open the portfolio. They were all nudes of Katrina Marek, and they were all erotic nudes. This surprised Katrina as much as it surprised the customs official, because Kurt Winter was not interested in nudes, or in any other form of erotic art. He was best known for rather spectral colorist work, and for some unsuccessful variations on Schiele and Klimt, two Austrian painters he followed and admired too much.

Katrina stood embarrassed at the British customs desk while an interested customs official looked carefully at every drawing and painting in her husband's portfolio. She was approaching a full-term pregnancy and probably looked very harassed, but the customs official who smiled at her and graciously let her into England (for the bribe of one of the drawings) probably saw her more as Kurt Winter had seen her—neither pregnant nor harried.

And the painters who were to help Katrina find theater work in London were never meant to feel obliged to perform this service out of their respect for the *art* of Kurt Winter. He did not send art to England; he sent an Austrian actress with poor English, pregnant, graceless and scared, into an English-speaking country without anyone to take care of her. What he gave her in the portfolio were advertisements for her-self.

Painters and gallery directors and theater directors said to Katrina, "Uh, you're the *model* here, aren't you?"

"I'm the painter's wife," she would say. "I'm an actress."

And they would say, "Yes, but in these paintings and drawings, you're the *model,* right?"

"Yes."

And despite her nine-month growth, which was Severin Winter, they would look at her appreciatively. She was well taken care of.

Severin was born in London in a good hospital in April of 1938. I attended his thirty-fifth birthday party and overheard him telling Utch, when he was quite drunk, "My father was a lousy painter, if you want to know the truth. But he was a genuis in other ways. He also knew that my mother was a lousy actress, and he knew we'd all starve in London if we went there to-gether. So he set up my mother in the best light he could imagine her in and removed himself from the overall picture. And it *was* her best light, too," he told Utch. He put the palm of his hand flat against Utch's belly, a little under her navel. He was as drunk as I've ever seen him. "And it's *all* our best lights, if you want to know the truth," he told her. At the time I was struck that Utch appeared to agree with him.

Severin's wife, Edith, would not have agreed with him. She had finer bones. She was the classiest woman I've ever known. There was so much natural good taste about her—and about what you imagined about her—that it was always a shock to see Severin beside her, looking like an awkward, maltrained bear beside a dancer. Edith was a relaxed, tall, graceful woman with a sensuous mouth and the most convincing, mature movements in her boyish hips and long-fingered hands; she had slim, silky legs and was as small- and high-breasted as a young girl, and as careless with her hair. She wore all her clothes so comfortably that you could imagine her asleep in them, except that you would rather not imagine her sleeping in any clothes. When I first met her, she was almost thirty—the eight-year wife of Severin Winter, a man who wore *his* clothes as if they were all hair shirts of the wrong size; a man whose shortness stunned you because of his width, or whose width stunned you because of his shortness. He was five feet eight inches tall and maybe twenty pounds over his old 157-pound class. The muscles in his back and chest seemed to be layered in slabs. His upper arms seemed thicker than Edith's lovely thighs. His neck was a strain on the best-made shirt in the world. He fought against a small, almost inconspicuous belly, which I liked to poke him in because he was so conscious of it. It was as taut and tough-skinned to the touch as a football. He had a massive, helmet-shaped head with a thick dark-brown rug of hair which sat on the top of his head like a skier's knit hat and spilled like a cropped mane just over his ears. One ear was cauliflowered, and he liked to hide it. He had a cocky boy's smile, a strong mouth of white teeth with one weird bottom tooth knocked askew—a V-shaped chip taken out of it, nearly as deep as the gum. His eyes were large and brown and far apart, and there was a knot on the bridge of his nose that was only noticeable when you sat to the left, and a crook where his nose had been broken another time that you saw only when you looked at him straight-on.

He not only looked like a wrestler, but wrestling was a constant metaphor to him—one he frequently mixed, being both romantic and practical. His gestures were those of a trained wild man; he was crude and chivalrous; he made much of dignity but often seemed foolishly out of place. At our faculty meetings he had a reputation for bilingual oratory, a belligerent belief that education was going to the dilettantes and "the Now-ist Dogs," a principle that "knowledge of the wretched past" was essential and that at least three years of a foreign language should be a requirement for *any* college graduate. (He was an associate professor of German.) Needless to say, he was a baited man, but he was baited cautiously. He was too athletic a debater to be recklessly provoked; he had developed sarcasm to a point of fine pain, and he had the dubious ability to outlast anyone in a world (like the academic committee) where tediousness is a virtue. Also, despite his affiliation with the German Department, it was well known that he was the wrestling coach. In fact, he was stubborn about that, especially with strangers. When introduced, he would never admit that he taught in the German Department.

"Are you with the university?"

"Yes, I coach wrestling," Severin Winter would say. Once I saw Edith cringe.

But he was never a physical bully. At a party for new faculty members he had an argument with a sculptor who threw a substantial uppercut into Winter's misleading football of a belly. Though a head taller than Winter, and ten pounds heavier, the sculptor's punch caused his own arm to fly back like dead weight off a trampoline. Winter never budged. "No, no," he told the sculptor impatiently. "You've got to get your shoulder into a punch, get your weight off the back of your heels . . ." There was no hint of retaliation; he was playing the coach, a harmless role.

His insistence on the sporting life—to the boredom of more than a few friends—once led me to suspect that he'd never been a good wrestler at all, so when I was asked to lecture on the historical novel at the University of Iowa, I thought I might try to look up Winter's old coach. I had a sudden notion that Jefferson Jones of Ohio State might have *invented* an opponent he'd beaten five for five.

I had no trouble finding the coach, retired to some honorary job of fussing in the Athletic Department, and I asked him if he remembered a 157-pounder named Severin Winter.

"*Remember* him?" the coach said. "Oh, he could have been great. He had all the moves, and the desire, and he kept coming at you, if you know what I mean."

I said I did.

"But he blew the big ones," the coach told me. "He didn't psych himself out exactly. You wouldn't call it clutching up—not exactly. But he'd make a mistake. He only made *big* mistakes," the coach decided, "and not too many. In the big matches, though, one mistake's enough."

"I'm sure it is," I said. "But he *was* the runner-up one year, in the Big Ten, at 157 pounds?"

"Yup," the coach said. "But the weight classes have changed since then. That's actually the 158-pound class now. It used to be 123, 130, 137, 147, 157 and so on, but now it's 118, 126, 134, 142, 150, 158 and so on— you know."

I didn't, and I certainly didn't care. Everyone says the academic life is one long prayer to detail, but it's hard to match athletics for a life of endless, boring statistics.

Occasionally I would chide Winter about his great love. "As a former 157-pounder, it must be nice, Severin, to involve yourself in a field that's changed one pound in ten years."

"What about history?" he'd say. "How many pounds has civilization changed? I'd guess about four ounces since Jesus, about half an ounce since Marx."

Winter was an educated man, of course his German was perfect, and evidently he was a good teacher—

27

though there is some evidence that native speakers of a foreign language don't always make the best teachers. He was a good wrestling coach, but the way he got the job was a fluke. He was hired to teach German, but he never missed a wrestling practice and rather quickly became an unofficial assistant to the head coach, a thunkish heavyweight from Minnesota who'd been both a Big Ten and national champion at the time Winter wrestled for Iowa. The ex-heavyweight shortly dropped dead of a heart attack while he was demonstrating a setup for the fireman's carry. (Winter said, "I thought he looked like he was setting it up all wrong.") Caught in midseason without a coach, the Athletic Department asked Winter to fill in. He told Edith it had been his secret ambition. His team finished the season so strongly that he was salaried as head coach for the next year, creating only a small, unuttered scandal among the more petty faculty who were envious of his double pay. It was only his enemies in the Division of Language and Literature who made any claim that Winter gave less than enough time to his German students because of his new work load. Naturally this disgruntlement was never expressed to his face. Enrollment in German actually soared, since Winter required every member of the wrestling team to take his language.

Winter claimed that wrestling helped him as a German teacher (but he would claim that it helped everything he did—indeed, he claimed it aloud and in various company, his hand on Edith's sleek bottom, shouldering her off-balance and jarring her drink: "It makes everything work a little better!").

Their affection for each other seemed real, if strange. The first night Utch and I had dinner with them we drove home very curious about them.

"God, I think he looks like a *troll*," I told Utch.

"I think you like how *she* looks," Utch said.

"He's almost grotesque," I said, "like a giant dwarf . . ."

"I know you," Utch said; she put her heavy hand on my thigh. "You go for her kind, the bones in the face —the breeding, you would say."

"He has almost no neck," I said.

"He's very handsome."

"You find him *attractive?*" I asked her.

"Oh *ja,* more dan dat."

"More than that," I corrected her.

"*Ja,*" Utch said, "and you find *her* attractive, too?"

"Oh *ja,* more dan dat," I said. Her strong hand squeezed me; we laughed.

"You know what?" she said. "He does all the cooking."

I will say that Severin was no savage at preparing food—only at eating it. After dinner we sat in their living room; their sofa curved around a coffee table where we had brandy. Winter was still ravaging the fruit and cheese, popping grapes, slashing pears—gobs of Brie on bread and chunks of Gorgonzola. He continued with his dinner wine, to chase his brandy. Utch was sleepy. She put her bare foot on the coffee table and Winter seized it at the ankle, looking at her calf as if it were meat to be deboned.

"Look at that leg!" he cried. "Look at the width of that ankle, the spread of that foot!" He said something to Utch in German which made her laugh; she wasn't angry or embarrassed at all. "Look at that calf. This is peasant stuff," Winter said. "This is the foot of the fields! This is the leg that outran the armies!" He spoke more German; he clearly approved of Utch's sturdy body. She was shorter than he—only five feet six inches. She was rounded, full-hipped, full-breasted, with a curve at her belly and muscular legs. Utch had a rump a child could sit on when she was standing up, but she had no fat on her; she was hard. She had that broad face of Central Europe: high cheekbones, a heavy jaw and a wide mouth with thin lips.

Utch spoke some German to Severin; it was pleasant listening to their singsong Viennese dialect, though I wished I could understand them. When he let go of her leg, she left it on the table.

I picked up the candle and lit Edith's cigarette, then my own. Neither Utch nor Severin smoked. "I understand that you write," I said to Edith.

She smiled at me. Of course I knew, then, where her smile was from and where we all were going. I had seen only one smile as confident as Edith's before, and Edith's smile was even more heedless and alluring than the one on the postcard of the angel called "The Smile of Reims."

2

Scouting Reports: Edith [126-pound class]

Edith Fuller left prep school in her senior year to go with her parents to Paris. They were the New York Fullers and there was no strife connected with the move; Edith was happy to leave, and her father said that she should not waste her time on education when she could live in Paris. She went to a good school there, and when her parents returned to New York, she chose to travel in Europe. When she returned to the States to go to college, her mother registered disappointment that Edith was "suppressing her natural beauty in an unnatural way, just to look like a writer." For two years at Sarah Lawrence, Edith looked like a writer— causing the only friction with her parents that ever existed. Actually, she really looked as if she was still traveling in Europe; being a writer had nothing to do with it. When her father died suddenly she left Sarah Lawrence and joined her mother in New York. Seeing no reason to upset her mother further, she took up the cause of caring for her "natural beauty" again, and found that she could still write.

Edith was instrumental in finding her mother a job —not that any of the New York Fullers ever needed a job, but her mother needed to have something to do. One of Edith's boyfriends directed the New Acquisitions Department at the Museum of Modern Art, and since both Edith and her mother had been would-be art history majors (neither of them ever finished college) and there was interesting volunteer work in the New Acquisitions Department, the matter was easily arranged.

All of Edith's boyfriends had interesting jobs of one kind or another. She had never dated a college boy when she was in college; she enjoyed and appealed to older men. The boyfriend at the Modern was thirty-four at the time; Edith was twenty-one.

She spent six months in New York keeping her mother company. One night she asked her to come see a movie with her, but her mother said, "Oh, I really couldn't, Edith. I have much too much to do." So Edith felt free to go back to Europe.

"Please don't feel you have to *look* like a writer, dear," her mother told her, but Edith was over that. There were friends in Paris from the Fullers' year there; she could have a room in someone's nice house; she could write; and there would be interesting things to do at night. She was a serious young girl who had never worried anybody, she was leaving behind no serious boyfriend in America, and she wasn't rushing to Europe to meet one. She had never had a serious boyfriend, and though, as she later told me, she did think —in the back of her mind as she left New York— that this might be the time to "have the experience of really falling in love with someone," she wanted to finish a good piece of writing first. She admitted that she'd had no idea what that piece of writing was going to be, any more than she'd "bothered very hard to imagine what that first real lover would be like." She had slept with only two men before, one of them the man who was at the Modern. "I didn't do it to get Mommy the job," Edith told me. "She would have gotten the job all by herself." He was married, he had two children, and he told Edith he wanted to leave his wife for her. Edith stopped sleeping with him; she didn't want him to leave his wife.

It took her one day in Paris to be invited to use the sumptuous guest room and studio in the house of one of her parents' Paris friends for as long as she'd like to stay. Her first day out shopping she bought a fancy typewriter with a French-English keyboard. She didn't look like a writer, but at twenty-one that's how serious she was.

In the beginning she spent a lot of time answering her mother's letters. Her mother was excited about all the research projects she was given to do. She was in charge of "rounding out" what was called the Modern Movement Series. The Museum of Modern Art had most of the major representatives of every major and minor movement in the twentieth century, but they were still missing some minor painters, and Edith's mother was seeking available paintings by minor artists of more or less major schools. Edith had never heard of any of the painters her mother was so absorbed in. "But my own writing felt so minor," she told me, "that

I had a pathetic sort of sympathy for all these unknowns."

We must have had similar parents. My mother began developing a keen interest in minor fiction simultaneously with the publication of my first historical novel. Most historical novels are pretty bad, of course, but my mother felt compelled to "keep up" with my field. I'd never read any historical novels before, but she began her habit of sending me her rare discoveries; it goes on to this day.

When I went home to see my parents shortly after my first book was published, my mother met me at the door in what was to become a ritual for all my publications. She had just finished my book, she told me, wringing my hands; she was surprised at how much it moved her, and (as we tiptoed through the hall) my father was just this minute finishing it. She thought he had liked what he'd read "so far." And we would creep through the old house, approaching my father in his den as one might sneak up on an unpredictable beast who was said to be "just finishing" his raw meat. It wouldn't do to arrive while he was still eating.

We would surround my father's sunken reading chair. Standing behind him, I could tell that he was asleep. He had a way of pinching his Scotch between his thighs when he fell asleep; somehow, he never relaxed his muscles and the drink never spilled. And all around him books would be splayed open, books he was "just finishing." There were usually at least two in his lap. One of them would be mine, but it was impossible to tell which book had put him to sleep. I never saw a *finished* book in his house. He told me once that the endings of all books left him overwhelmingly sad.

He was a historian; he had taught at Harvard for thirty-six years. When I was a student there I made the mistake of taking one of his courses. It was one of those Intellectual Problems courses, of which Harvard was very proud. The problem in this one was deciding whether or not Lenin was necessary to the Russian Revolution. Would it have happened anyway? Would it have happened *when* it happened? Was Lenin really important? Like most of the Intellectal Problems courses, you weren't really supposed to come up with the answer. About fifteen of us speculated on the question. My father speculated in his lectures, too. In the last class (I called him "sir"), I asked him if he would just state his own opinion, since he must have one: *Was* Lenin necessary?

"Of course not," he said, but he was angry that I had asked; he gave me a C. It was the only C I ever got anywhere. And when I asked him how he felt about my writing—I said I assumed that he thought the historical novel was bad for both history and literature, but in my particular case . . . "Quite," he said.

My first historical novel was about one year of the great plague as it was decimating France. I focused on one small village, and the book was a terrifyingly accurate, if clinical. account of how all the seventy-six inhabitants of the village eventually died of the Black Death. There were a lot of gibbet images. "I like it so far," my father said. "I haven't finished it yet, but I think you were wise to select a *small* village."

My mother was the far. She sent me one bad historical novel after another, with a trail of notes saying, "I think your books are so much better!" And after each of my publications, the ritual would repeat itself. There I would be at the door on Brown Street, Cambridge, the only house I ever grew up in or went back to. At first I was alone, and then with Utch, and then with our children and my mother would whisper us all inside, saying, "I just loved it so much, and your father's liking it a great deal. Better than the last, he says. In fact, I think he's just finishing it now . . ."

And we would creep down the hall, approach the den, see my father sleeping with his Scotch held tight between his thighs. My book, along with all the others, lay culprit around him, possibly responsible for his stupor.

I never saw him finish a Scotch, either. It was my mother, like Edith's mother, who took her work—however minor—seriously.

I think that, as a rule, mothers are more serious than fathers. Once I sat down to dinner, patted Utch on her thigh and topped up my son's half-empty milk glass with wine. "Have you even looked at your children today?" Utch asked me. "Shut your eyes and tell me what they're wearing." But my theory breaks down with Severin Winter. *He* was the mother in their family.

Not more than a week after Utch had caught me mixing milk with wine, we were in Winter's active kitchen; everyone's children were everywhere, and Severin was making his bouillabaisse for us all. Edith and I were talking at the kitchen table; Utch was tying someone's shoe; and the younger Winter daughter was staring fixedly at her mother's earring. I hadn't heard the child say anything, either, but suddenly Severin turned at the stove and hollered, "Edith!" She jumped. "Edith," he said, "your daughter, who looks at you all day as if you were a mirror, has asked you the same question four times. Why don't you answer her?" Edith looked at her daughter, surprised to see her sitting there. But Utch knew; she, too, heard everything the children ever said.

Utch said, "No, Dorabella, it doesn't hurt very much." Edith still stared at her daughter as if she'd just learned that she'd had a part in the child's lovely flesh.

"Does it hurt to have your ears pierced, Mommy?" Severin boomed from the stove.

And Edith said, "Yes, a little, Fiordiligi." Right name, wrong daughter; we all knew; we waited for Edith to catch her own slip, but she didn't.

"That's *Dorabella,* Edith," Severin said; Dorabella laughed, and Edith stared at her. And Severin, as if to explain to Utch and me, said, "It's understandable. About four years ago Fiordiligi asked Edith the same question."

But suddenly it was very quiet in that energetic kitchen; only the bouillabaisse was speaking. Perhaps to break the tension we always felt when we recognized the peculiar alliances we felt toward each other, Severin said (but what a queer thing to say!), "Does it hurt to have your tongue nailed to a breadboard?"

We all laughed. Why? I thought about the four of us, but what I remembered was my father's reply to an interviewer from the *Times* who had asked him to say a few words about some new gesture in American foreign policy, "with some emphasis on the subtleties we laymen may have missed."

"It's about as subtle as the Russian revolution," my father said. No one knew what he meant.

My father's creepy wide-angle lens. I never agreed with him about Lenin. Lenin *was* necessary. People are necessary. ("How nice for you," Severin said to me once. "Edith's a romantic too.") And my mother's terrible books, I sometimes think, were closer to the truth than my father ever came close enough to see. Edith and I were brought up unsure of ourselves as snobs—in love with our mothers' innocence.

In Paris, Edith went out and read everything she could find about all the minor painters mentioned in her mother's letters. There wasn't much to find out about some of them, but she tried. She didn't get much writing done, and just when she mastered enough research to respond knowledgeably to her mother's interests, she was proposed to by the father of the household in which she was a pampered guest. He was always very polite and fatherly to her, and she'd never suspected. One morning he struck his soft-boiled egg too hard; it catapulted out of its eggcup and landed on the Persian rug in the breakfast room. His wife ran to the kitchen to get a sponge. Edith stooped next to his chair and dabbed her napkin into the yolky mess on the rug. He put his hand into her hair and tilted her surprised face up to him. "I love you, Edith," he croaked. Then he burst into tears and left the table.

His wife returned with the sponge. "Oh, did he rush off?" she asked Edith. "He gets so upset when he makes a mess."

Edith went to her room and packed. She wondered if she should write her mother and try to explain. She was still wondering what to do when the maid brought the mail to her room. There was a new letter from her mother about minor painters. Could Edith tear herself away from her work in Paris just long enough for a business trip to Vienna? Her mother's boss was interested in rounding out one of the Modern Movement Series. Of course, they had something from the Vienna Secession; they had Gustav Klimt, who (Edith's mother said) did not really belong to Vienna's Late Art Nouveau, since he was really a forerunner to the Expressionists. For Viennese Expressionists, they had Egon Schiele and Kokoschka, and even a Richard Gerstl (a *who?* Edith thought). "We do have a dreadful Fritz Wotruba," Edith's mother wrote, "but what we want is someone from the thirties whose work is random and imitative and transitional enough to represent it *all*."

The painter on whom this dubious distinction was about to fall had been a student of Herbert Boeckl's at the Academy. He had appeared to be "peaking" at about the time the Nazis marched into Austria in 1938. He was twenty-eight at the time he disappeared. "All his paintings are still in Vienna," wrote Edith's mother.

"There are four on loan to the Belvedere, but most of them are in private homes. They are all owned by his only son, who apparently wants to sell as many of them as he can. We only want one—two, at the most. You'll have to get slides made, and you're not to promise anything in the way of a price."

"Leaving today for Vienna," Edith wired her mother. "Delighted to take a break. Perfect timing."

She flew from Orly to Schwechart. She'd been in Vienna in December three years ago; she'd hated it. It was the most Central European city she'd ever seen, and the cold slush in the streets seemed to belong with the city's squat Baroque heaviness. The buildings. like the men, had seemed to her to have an unhealthy color and ill-cut, elaborate clothes. It was not as friendly as a village, but it had none of the elegance she associated with a city. She felt that the war was just barely over. Throughout the city she kept seeing signs indicating the few kilometers to Budapest; she had not realized she was almost in Hungary. She spent only three days and saw only one opera *Der Rosenkavalier;* it bored her, though she thought it shouldn't have, and at intermission a man made a vulgar pass at her.

But now when her Paris flight landed in Vienna, it was a different season: early spring weather. wet-smelling with a sunny wind and a hard-blue Bellini sky. The buildings. which had all seemed so gray before, now shone in such rich and subtle shades; the fat putti and the statuary everywhere seemed like a stone welcoming party hanging off the buildings. People were out walking; the population seemed to have doubled. Something in the atmosphere was changed, felt chiefly by the sight of baby carriages; the Viennese were feeling fit to reproduce again.

The taxi driver was a woman who knew the English word "dear." "Say to me where you want to be gone, dear," she said. Edith showed her the addresses in her mother's letter. She wanted a hotel which was near the Belvedere; more important, she wanted to know where the painter's son lived. The son had graduated from an American university a few years ago and had gone back to Vienna because his mother was dying; afterwards he inherited all the father's paintings. He was staying in Vienna just long enough to complete a degree at the university, and he wanted to sell as many of the paintings as he could. He had written a very literate and witty letter to the Museum of Modern Art. He had begun by saying that the people at the Modern had probably never heard of his father, which was forgivable because he wasn't a very important painter and they shouldn't feel they had missed anything. The son was twenty-seven, five years older than Edith. She found out that his address was a two-block walk from the Belvedere.

Her driver took her to a hotel on the Schwarzenberg Platz. Outside the hotel waiters were setting up big redwhite-and-blue Cinzano umbrellas for the café. It was still too brisk to sit outside for long; the sun was weak, but Edith had the feeling that she was arriving early to a party still in the preparation phase. She thanked the cabdriver, who said, "Okay, dear."

Edith had one more thing to ask; she didn't know how to pronounce the son's first name. "How do you say this?" she asked the driver, holding out her mother's letter. She had the name underlined: *Severin* Winter.

"*Say*-vah-rin," the cabdriver crooned.

Edith was surprised how she liked to say that name. "*Say*-vah-rin," she sang in her hotel room as she took a bath and changed her clothes. There was still sunlight on the west faces of the buildings on the Schwarzenberg Platz. Behind the spuming fountain was the Russian War Memorial. It no longer felt like the afternoon of the same day a man had put his hand in her hair, said,

39

"I love you" and then burst into tears. She would send them both one of those Dresden pieces of great delicacy; she caught herself smiling at the idea that it might arrive smashed.

She put on a sleek, black, clingy blouse and a soft, gun-gray cashmere suit. She wrapped a bright-green scarf twice around one wrist and knotted it; she did things like that and got away with it. "*Say*-vah-rin *Vin*ter?" she said to the mirror, holding out her hand, the bright scarf like a favor.

She hated the telephone, so she would not call; she would just take a walk and drop in. She tried to picture the son of a minor artist. She had no idea whether he would buy her a drink, invite her to dinner, suggest the opera, make a phone call to have the Belvedere opened at night—or whether he would be poor and awkward and she should really offer to take him to dinner. She did not know whether to be smart and businesslike and say she had come to Vienna representing the Museum of Modern Art, who in response to Herr Winter's letter about his father's paintings . . . or whether she should confess just how unofficial her visit really was.

She'd been so glad to leave Paris that she hadn't thought about what she was doing here, and now she even began to have doubts about what she was wearing. She put on kneehigh glossy-green boots and decided to leave it at that. Few enough people in Paris dressed the way Edith did, and she assumed that no one in Vienna did. Severin Winter had been in America, after all. Edith always thought of New York when she thought of America. She didn't know that Severin Winter had spent most of his time in *Iowa,* dividing his time between wearing headphones in a language lab and earguards on a wrestling mat (for these reasons and reasons in his genes, his ears lay flat against his head).

"*Say*-vah-rin," she said again, as if she were tasting soup. She pictured a thin. bearded man who looked more in his thirties than twenty-seven. She had not looked twice at a single graduate student in America, and she could not imagine a Viennese graduate student at all. A degree in what? A doctorate in minor painting?

The sun now struck only the top row of cupids on the old buildings along the Opernring. She would need to wear a coat. She felt like buying one, but she remembered Austrian clothes as being either leather or thick, scratchy loden, so she put on her black Paris cape. It was a little dressy: when she saw herself in it, she decided she *was* representing the Museum of Modern Art in New York—just flown in from Paris. What was the harm?

After a short walk she was standing outside the Schwindgasse address. just around the corner from the Belvedere. Somehow. it was already dark. The street was small and cobblestoned: the apartment building was opposite the Bulgarian embassy and next-door to something called the Polish Reading Room; there was a dim coffeehouse of faded elegance a half-block down the street. She read the brass nameplates in the lobby of the Schwindgasse apartment house, then walked up a marble flight of stairs and rang a bell on the first landing. "*Say*-vah-rin," she whispered to herself. She poised her chin, expecting to look up when he opened the door; she had decided he would be thin, bearded and tall. To her surprise. she had to look down a little. The boy in the doorway was clean-shaven, and wore sneakers, jeans and a T-shirt: he looked like the rawest of American tourists in Europe. He wore a blatant college letter-jacket. black with leather sleeves and a thick, oversized gold "T" on the breast. American Baroque, Edith thought. Obviously he was a young friend from Severin Winter's college days.

"Does Severin Winter live here?" Edith asked, not at all sure.

"I sure do," said Severin; he bounced backward in the doorway, more like a boxer teasing an opponent to come after him than like a man inviting anyone in. But his smile caught her completely off-guard. It was boyish, but it wasn't, and she noticed the one askew tooth with the V-chip sliced deep to the gum. In the light behind him, she saw that his dark hair was thick and fluffy and clean. It's a baby bear, she thought, stepping inside.

"My name is Edith Fuller," she said, and was surprised at how self-conscious she felt with him. "I'm here to look at your father's paintings. You wrote a letter to the Museum of Modern Art?"

"Yes, yes." He smiled. "But I never thought they'd actually *want* one."

"Well, I'm here to look," she said, and embarrassed herself by sounding cool.

"At night? Don't they look at paintings in daylight in New York?" he asked. She felt flustered; then she saw he was teasing her; he was all fun, this bear, and she laughed. She stepped into a living room with so many paintings everywhere that she didn't see one of them. It was a room with at least four doorways, leading off everywhere, and it was crammed with books, photographs and objects of a most peculiar taste. She suspected that the living room was only the tip of an iceberg—one hill of a continent. There was so much stuff in the room that she didn't notice the people, and when she realized that he was introducing her, she gave a little leap. There was a woman who could have been forty-nine or sixty-two; she wore a blowzy off-the-shoulder dress which was gathered and belted and slit in a way Edith couldn't fathom—as if it had been hastily made from an Art Nouveau bedsheet. This was Frau Reiner. "A friend of my mother's," said Severin

Winter. "She was a model too." Frau Reiner's deeply lined face, her huge mouth and dusky skin were all that Edith could evaluate in terms of what Frau Reiner had to model; her body was lost in the art of her dress.

Then came two almost twin men whose names were as baffling as their appearance. Their names were something on a menu you wouldn't dare to order without advice. They were in their sixties and looked like spies, or gangsters, or retired prizefighters who'd lost more than they'd won. Edith didn't know then that they were like loving uncles to Severin Winter. They were Zivan Knezevich and Vaso Trivanovich, old Chetnik freedom fighters who'd fled Tito and the Partisans at the end of the Yugoslav civil war; like a lot of others, they'd found that Vienna was close to the East. They'd had as much to do with Severin Winter's upbringing as Katrina Marek. They'd taught him how to wrestle; they'd told him to go wrestle in America and one day beat the Russians. They were former members of the Yugoslav freestyle wrestling team. Vaso Trivanovich had won a bronze medal in the Berlin Olympics in 1936; Zivan Knezevich had been almost as good.

Like two old knights out of armor, Vaso and Zivan each kissed Edith's hand. But Frau Reiner held her hand up; Edith dimly realized she was supposed to kiss it and did so. The hand was a jewel box of rings; the perfume, Edith realized with a shock, was the same as her own. One of her tastes must be suspect.

And around a heavy hardwood table with a large tile chessboard in its center, Severin Winter restlessly moved with the grace and the spring of a bizarrely muscled deer. "Will you have some Kremser Schmitt?" he asked Edith. "Or a beer?"

She did not like beer, and Kremser Schmitt sounded like a kind of sausage to her, but she dared it and was relieved to find out that it was a nicely chilled and decent white wine.

The old Chetniks babbled at each other in Serbo-Croatian. Even Edith could tell that their German was halting; one of them was slightly deaf and needed to be shouted to. Frau Reiner smiled hugely at Edith, as if she were an hors d'oeuvre. She felt most comfortable looking at Severin, who in relation to his friends was changing radically in her eyes. He seemed like their Darling Prince; she had never seen anyone less self-conscious. Mozart was playing on a terrible phonograph, and Severin could not sit still. He swayed in his chair; he tossed his head. Why does he wear that awful jacket, Edith thought, imagining scars on his arms.

Frau Reiner asked Severin one question after another, which he translated to Edith. "Frau Reiner thinks you never got that cape in Vienna," he said.

"I got it in Paris," Edith told him, and Frau Reiner nodded.

"And your boots could only be from New York?" Right again.

None of the colleges Edith could think of began with a garish yellow "I".

Somehow, they all went out together. Edith thought they must look like a circus act. The two old wrestlers in their dark spy-suits and the kind of trench coats for concealing weapons; like the old locker-room boys they still were, they jostled and shoved and batted each other as they walked. Frau Reiner took Severin's arm on his right, and Edith found herself naturally holding his left. He walked them along bilingually. He would say to Edith, "Schiele liked to eat lunch here, on occasion," and Frau Reiner would pick up on the word "Schiele" and hum her rich German into his ear.

"She says," Severin told Edith, "that she was a child model for Schiele in the last year of his life."

"He died when he was only twenty-eight," Edith offered, then felt like a fool because he looked at her as if she'd just said, "When it rains, things get wet."

"But I don't believe it and neither should you," Severin said.

"What? He wasn't twenty-eight? He didn't die?"

"I don't believe Frau Reiner was ever a child model for him. No painting or drawing of her exists among Schiele's workbooks and unfinished canvases, and everything he painted in that last year has been looked over. Unless it was something so bad that he destroyed it, which was not his habit. Frau Reiner has modeled for a lot of people—though not so many as my mother modeled for—but she has always regretted that she could only be a child model when Schiele and Klimt were alive."

Frau Reiner said something and Severin said, "She's admitting she never modeled for Klimt."

Frau Reiner said something else.

"But she claims he spoke to her once," Severin whispered to Edith. "This could be true, but she would hardly have been old enough to remember it."

Edith was struck by how close he moved toward her when he talked. He couldn't talk without touching, squeezing and coming very close. but she felt there was nothing sly or sexual about it. She noticed that he also touched the old Chetniks when he talked to them.

This is true: Severin could never keep his hands off anyone he spoke to. Later it irritated me how he would be all over Utch—I mean in public. at large parties. He would be mauling her in conversation. Of course, Edith and I were more discreet But I confess Severin mauled *me* in conversation too There was always an arm around you, or he would seize your wrist in his hand and squeeze it between sentences. Sometimes he pinched; I even remember that he used to touch my beard. But it was just a way he had, a part of his restless movement. I don't think I agree with Edith that he was unselfconscious—whether he really was, or whether he might have been so self-conscious that you assumed no one could be *that* self-conscious and decided he was completely natural.

Anyway, he struck Edith as a friendly animal. When he talked he seemed much older, and when he smiled she found herself liking his boyishness.

I think, when we meet people, we can like them right away if we see how much their friends like them. Most of all, Edith said, she was aware of how much Frau Reiner and the two Chetniks adored Severin.

"But I'd have loved him anyway," Edith told me, "because he was the first man who treated me lightly. I mean, he was comic. He wasn't the sort of awful comic who tries to make everything funny, either. He was a *pure* comic. He simply found the comic ingredient in most things—even in me, and I took myself very seriously, of course."

Well, I won't split hairs. I think that what really got to Edith is what can get to any of us: she discovered jealousy.

They went to a Serbian restaurant where the whole crowd knew that Vaso and Zivan were heroes and clapped their backs and threw celery stalks at them, and where Edith and Severin and Frau Reiner were treated as partial heroes themselves. There was torturous string music and too much spice in everything, and too much of everything, but Edith had a wonderful time.

Severin Winter told her stories about his mother and father (I'm sure the zoo fantasy must have been a part of it); he told her stories of Zivan's and Vaso's escape from Yugoslavia; he told her stories about Frau Reiner when she was the hottest model in the city (Edith was beginning to believe it.). "She learned everything she knew from my mother," said Severin. And he told her that the "I" on his jacket was for Iowa, and that the closest he'd ever come to winning a major conference or national championship was when he was runner-up in the Big Ten at 157 pounds.

"What do you weigh now?" Edith asked. He looked so much bigger, though he was lean in those days.

"One fifty-eight," he said. She wasn't sure if this was a joke. With him you never knew.

Then he leaned across the table and said, "In the morning, then? We'll see the Belvedere, I'll take you around to a few apartments—old friends of my parents have some of the best ones. I don't believe my father ever *sold* a damn thing; at least, he didn't make any money. I can't tell you how glad I am that you came here." Edith looked at his eyes, his hair, that one weird tooth. "I'm dying to leave Europe," he told her. "Everything and everyone is dying here. I want to go back to America very much, but I've got to unload some of these paintings first. This is a break for me, I must tell you." And it suddenly struck Edith that he was talking about *money;* he was talking to the representative from the Museum of Modern Art in New York, just flown in from Paris to give old Kurt Winter a second look. She realized she had no idea how much money the Modern would pay, but she didn't think it would be much. God, maybe they would only consider a Kurt Winter as a *gift!*

Wasn't that the way it usually happened? And only one—two at the most—her mother had said.

For some reason, she touched his hand; his damn physical habits were catching. But before she could say anything, Frau Reiner leaned against Severin; she bit his ear, took his chin in her hand, turned his head toward her and kissed him lushly on the mouth. Edith could see where Frau Reiner's tongue went. Severin didn't seem surprised, only interrupted. but Frau Reiner gave Edith a very clear look which Edith wilted under. She felt like a very young girl. *His mother's friend,* indeed. So she blurted, "I've been looking at your dress all night and I still can't figure out how it works." Frau Reiner was surprised that Edith spoke to her; she couldn't understand, of course. But Edith was saying all this for Severin. "I wonder if Gustav Klimt designed that dress for you," she said; Frau Reiner stiffened at the word "Klimt" while Edith went on, "I mean, it looks like a Klimt: the shiny gold gilt, the little squares, the Egyptian eye forms. But the way you've got it wrapped around you, it doesn't seem to show itself quite right." She stopped, embarrassed; she couldn't remember ever showing off before.

And Severin replied in his boy's face but with the same irritating fatherliness she was used to from other men. "I don't think you want me to translate for you," he said. But he was smiling; he showed her his teasing tooth. "I *will* translate, though, if you wish."

"Please don't," she said. And in a burst of candor, "I think she's too old for you." That got to him; he looked self-conscious for the first time. But she felt uneasy that she had said it; Why do I care? she almost said aloud.

They all rode home in the same cab. Frau Reiner sat on Severin's lap; twice, she licked his ear. Edith was crammed between them and either Zivan or Vaso —she still couldn't tell them apart—the other one rode up front.

They dropped Edith off at her Schwarzenberg Platz hotel. "Ah, *Geld,*" said Frau Reiner, regarding the hotel. Edith knew enough German to know that meant *money.*

"Well, you know the Museum of Modern Art," Severin said in English. It was to Edith—not to Frau Reiner—that he spoke, and Edith knew that he knew *she* had a lot of money. Possibly the Museum of Modern Art was just another thing he found funny.

She felt terrible. But as she was slipping out of the

cab—one old Chetnik wrestler holding the door for her, like a bodyguard—Severin picked Frau Reiner up off his lap, put her down in the back seat, came around the cab and said to Edith, "I agree with you. And I'll meet you at the Belvedere at ten." He shook her hand so quickly that she did not have time to firm her grasp before he bounced back into the cab. The old wrestlers shouted something to her in a chorus, and she was inside the hotel lobby, seeing herself in twenty gold-edged mirrors, before she realized that she wasn't sure what Severin Winter agreed with her about. Frau Reiner's Gustav Klimt dress? Or that Frau Reiner was too old for him?

Edith went to her room and took another bath. She was angry at herself. She decided that she had felt so much out of her element that she had performed. She decided they were all very odd people, dwellers in a city, as her mother had written, that "never took the twentieth century seriously." The remark is quite true. Once I asked Severin if he regarded the new so-called Sexual Freedom as a fad. "I regard the twentieth century as a fad," he said. But there was his tooth winking at you. He never told the truth!

Before Edith went to bed she went through all her clothes trying to decide what to wear to the Belvedere. Then she got angry at herslf about that too; she had never been self-conscious about what she wore. In bed she watched the city lights struggle through the high windows and the rich cream-colored drapes. Why do I wear black so much? she brooded. Before she fell asleep, she wished that Severin Winter would not wear that awful letter-jacket to the Belvedere.

I saw that letter-jacket only once. By the time Utch and I met him, he had outgrown it—physically, I mean. I assumed that it was thrown out or packed away. Then one day Utch and I were sitting on the steps of our house when Edith came along the side-

walk alone and sat down between us. Severin was upset about "the whole thing," she told us. Utch and I
had just been talking about that. This was at a time
when Edith had already expressed her fears to me that
she doubted whether "the whole thing" could work.
We all knew Severin was unhappy, but our relationship was very new and Severin had never made it
clear what he was unhappy about. "I thought we all
ought to talk," Edith told us. "I mean, all four of us
—together." We sat on the steps waiting for Severin.
He was driving his daughters to some friend's house
to play. Our children were out. It was early spring,
and in the sun's warm hours, it was barely possible to
sit on the steps.

"Does Severin want to talk?" Utch asked Edith. "I
mean, all together."

"Well, I thought we should," Edith said. We sat
there.

Severin parked his car in front of us, then sat in the
car after he shut the motor off and looked at the three
of us together on the steps. He was grinning. I realized
I was holding Utch's and Edith's hands. He sat in his
car like a smiling camera. and when he got out and
started toward us, I felt Edith's grip spasm in my
hand. Then I saw that he was wearing that goddamn
letter-jacket. The sleeves stopped halfway down his
forearms and the jacket's waist barely reached below
his chest. The T-shirt and jeans and sneakers were
familiar, almost a uniform. but though I'd never seen
it, I knew about that jacket. Even the fucking weather
that day must have been like it had been in Vienna!

He never reached the steps. Edith jumped up and
ran to him while he was still on the sidewalk. "Where
did you find that?" she cried; she seized him by the
jacket. She had her face toward him, away from us, so
that we couldn't see whether she was angry or happy.
She shook the jacket, then hugged him. It was im-

perceptible, but I think he steered her to the car—or maybe she turned toward the car herself and he simply supported her. She sat in the passenger seat in severe profile, so I couldn't read her face. Severin bounced into the driver's seat and waved to us hurriedly; I don't think he actually looked at us. "Later!" he called. Edith never moved as he drove off.

"Severin will not easily relinquish the driver's seat," Edith told me later.

"How do you feel about that?" I asked.

And Edith said, "I always felt, from the first, that he was a pretty good driver."

A firm believer in the past, Severin Winter dug up his old letter-jacket and stole our scene before we could have it.

3

Scouting Reports:
Utch [134-pound class]

On July 9, 1945, the Allies quartered the city of Vienna for occupation. The Americans and British grabbed up the best residential sections, the French took over the markets and the major shopping areas, and the Russians (who had long-term, realistic plans) settled in the worker-industrial districts and within the Inner City, nearest to the embassies and the government buildings. During the carving of the great game bird, the dinner guests revealed their special tastes.

Everyone knows that the Soviets could not quite

work in Vienna what they had worked in Berlin; perhaps not everyone knows how hard they tried. Sixteen out of twenty-one districts had Communist chiefs of police, a kind of Russian magic. During the ten-year occupation, as many as a third of the anti-Soviets in Vienna ended up missing: perhaps they never understood whose zone of occupation was whose and got lost. Whatever, Chancellor Figl was prompted to confess: "We have had to write down against a very long list of names simply the word 'disappeared.'" More magic.

Unless you were a Communist, or were untroubled by rape and machine-gunning, you would not have chosen to live in the Soviet zone of occupation. Utch, of course, had no choice. Only seven years old, she had good reason to be a Communist; if her guardian Captain Kudashvili was not a hero to many of the good women of Eichbüchl, he was at least her savoir. If not her father, he was at least the available midwife who'd delivered her from the cow where she'd been kept so safe.

Captain Kudashvili, of course, moved into a district in the Russian zone, the fourth. It is fortunate for Utch that he was an idealist. He had never seen a postwar orphanage before. Utch had never seen Vienna. The day that Captain Kudashvili walked up Argentinierstrasse (the orphanage was near the Südbahnhof) was the first day she could remember being outside a barracks or a barn. I imagine that if you've spent two days inside a cow, being outside anywhere is uplifting. And the buildings along the Argentinierstrasse were so ornamental that they reminded her of her mother's stolen books.

Utch had her birth certificate pinned to the lapel of her coat. Kudashvili had given her a dead soldier's scarf; it wrapped around her neck four times and still dragged on the sidewalk. When they got to the orphanage, Utch somehow knew she'd been brought here to stay. Kudashvili had been telling her, of course, but she didn't understand Russian yet.

Inside the building they were holding a demonstration of a generation gap—the gap being the generation that was missing. There were grandparents galore, giving children away; it was the parents' generation that had lost (and been lost in) the war. Utch remembers that Kudashvili was the only member of his generation there; everyone stared at him. One old woman came up to him and spat on his chest, but that was because of the Russian uniform. One grandmother was trying to free herself from five or six children. An orphanage attendant was restraining one child, and another attendant was handling two, but there were always two or three the grandmother couldn't get free of. Just as she'd get to the door, one of them would get to her and cling. All her grandchildren were screaming, but it wasn't the screaming ones who impressed Utch, it was the children who'd already been left. They were not crying; they were not even moving. They were mute voyeurs, and Utch somehow inferred that they would never have any expressions on their faces again.

Kudashvili was trying to sign something, but Utch grabbed his writing hand. She wouldn't let go, she bit him, and she tried to tie him up in the long scarf he'd given her. Kudashvili did not protest; it's possible he never had his heart set on the idea of an orphanage anyway. He picked her up and carried her out of there. To this day, she claims that she shouted, *"Auf Wiedersehen!"* to everyone.

As they walked back down the Argentinierstrasse into the fourth district, Kudashvili unpinned Utch's birth certificate from her coat lapel and put it in his leather folder with his own papers. On his chest, under his medals, the old woman's spittle shone like a gob of

53

cold chicken fat. Kudashvili cleaned himself with a handkerchief. He removed one of his medals and pinned it on Utch's coat lapel. She has it to this day: a Medal of Excellence, signifying—as nearly as anyone has been able to tell me—Captain Kudashvili's valorous participation in the defense of the great city of Kiev, the capital of the Ukraine. But perhaps that's only a symbol.

So Utch went back into the fourth district with her guardian, Captain Kudashvili, and for the ten years that the Allies occupied the city of Vienna she shared the captain's quarters with an occasional housekeeper, baby-sitter and laundress named Drexa Neff. Frau Neff didn't care for the Russians any more than most of the Viennese, but she did care for Captain Kudashvili. She was a sarcastic old woman whose husband had left her before the war and who'd had some fun when a young Austrian boy who was too sickly to be a soldier had paid her twenty schillings a week, when he picked up his mother's laundry, for doing something extra to him in the steam room.

Drexa Neff scolded and teased Utch, but she took care of her. Kudashvili protectively walked Utch to school every day, and Drexa Neff was at school to meet her and walk her home. When the other kids would bully her, Drexa Neff would tell her to say to them: "Captain Kudashvili is a moral man, even though he is a Russian, and a moral man is more than some of you can call your fathers, if you have a father left . . ." Which, of course, Utch never said.

It was Drexa Neff who prepared Utch for becoming a Russian. Drexa thought school was a waste for Utch. *"Ja,* but did they teach you how to do it in *Russian* today?" she'd ask after school. "Because that's where he'll take you, *Liebchen,* if he doesn't leave you here—and *der* Kudashvili is too moral a man to leave you just anywhere, you should already know." So Utch paid attention to her guardian and learned the Russian language from him, as well as a game called *Telephon*. She learned never to go outside without first phoning 06–036–27. In those days there was no direct dialing; Utch would have to tell the operator the number. She learned it by heart: *"Null sechs, null sechsunddreizig, siebenundzwanzig."* It was Captain Kudashvili's office number; she never knew where it was, and the captain never answered the phone himself. She would call and then wait in the apartment or the laundry where Drexa Neff steamed and talked.

Usually, two men came for her. They were never other Russians; they were never in uniform. But they were working for The Russians. Utch remembers that they were very watchful. Sometimes they would follow her at a short distance instead of walking beside her, and whenever someone spoke to her, the two men would come up very suddenly and whoever had spoken to Utch would say that he was very sorry.

It was much later, of course, when she realized who the men were and why she needed to be protected. Most people in the Russian sector needed protection, but Utchhka was "that Russian captain's daughter, or something," and needed to be protected from the anti-Soviets. The men who were her bodyguards were members of the most notorious criminal gang in Vienna: the Benno Blum Gang, a cigarette-smuggling ring and black marketeers of the precious nylon stocking, to mention only their lighter trades. What they were really responsible for was the "disappearance" of that famous one-third of the anti-Soviets in Vienna. They were allowed to flourish in their petty crimes, protected from the police in the Russian zone for the services they rendered the Russians in return. They killed people. It is likely Captain Kudashvili was in partial charge of them, and of course it's likely that people in Utch's neighborhood knew this. Any Viennese knowing her story would not wish her harm, but she was a link to Kudashvili and they certainly wished him considerable harm. The Benno Blum Gang smuggled more than cigarettes and nylon stockings; they transported people—forever. Utch may have been the best-guarded child in the fourth district.

Severin Winter, who has never enjoyed being a runnerup, had said that Utch was not the best-guarded child in the forth district; he claimed that *he* was. Of course, he was being protected from the Russians, not by them; his situation was more typical. His mother had brought him back from London at the end of the war; she still had many of Kurt Winter's paintings left, and many had been left in Vienna. She came looking for Kurt Winter, on the slight chance that she'd really find him, and insisted on reoccupying her old apartment on the Schwindgasse, even though her friends told her that it was in the Russian district. She insisted. Where else would her husband look for her?

Katrina Marek had not been an actress in London during the war, and she never returned to the stage again. She had been an artist's model in London, and she took that up in Vienna in 1945. She was quite well known by the time Severin was marched off each morning to a boy's academy. She did not want her son to forget his English. "It's your ticket out of this old horse stable, this greasy *Küche*," she told her son, and she insisted that he be marched each day out of the Russian sector, into an American sector and the American school, and then back home to the Russian zone. It was a feat of beating red tape few could have pulled off, but Severin had escorts who knew the ropes. Friends of his mother, Severin's escorts were the two most sought-after male models of any in Vienna. Severin claims they were nearly as popular as his mother in Guetersloh's classes at the Vienna Academy. Katrina had met them when a painter had asked her to model with them at a joint session. They were, of course, Zivan Knezevich and Vaso Trivanovich, the wrestlers from the '36 Berlin Games. In the years of the occupation of Vienna, Vaso and Zivan were still young and strong. They were also former Chetnik guerrillas, and their abiding contempt for the Russians made their daily sorties in and out of the Russian zone very satisfying to them.

But Severin Winter is full of shit if he wants me to believe that two ex-wrestlers would ever have been a match for the Benno Blum Gang. It is fortunate for him that their paths did not cross. Those former athletes would have been found bloated in the Danube, nylon stockings over their faces and twisted round their necks—a Blum Gang specialty.

It's a wonder, though, that their paths did not cross —Utch off to school each morning with the captain, or out to shop with Benno Blum's hired murderers carrying her chocolate; it's a wonder that she didn't once pass on the street that short, dark, athletic boy in the company of his wrestlers. Perhaps they simply don't remember it. It's likely they saw each other at least once, because for ten years Utch lived in a second-floor apartment next to the Bulgarian embassy, directly across the Schwindgasse from the Marek second-floor apartment. They could have looked in each other's windows.

And they used the same laundress. At least once, while Utch sat listening to Drexa Neff or helped her stack the clean clothes, surely Severin must have walked into the steam, flanked by his wrestlers, and asked if his mother's laundry was ready.

"She didn't have much laundry," Winter said. "Her dress was quite informal."

Such understatement. Katrina Marek went out modeling each morning in her calf-length brown coat of muskrat fur, the gift of an American painter she had modeled for in London. It had a collar that rolled up above the top of her head, and beneath the coat peeked the bottoms of her thigh-high orange stockings. They were the same stockings—that is, the same orange, if not the same pair—that the model wore in Schiele's *Vally with Red Blouse* (1913) and *Woman with Purple Boa* (1915). Katrina Marek had several pairs. Her workday laundry was characteristically light. Central heating was rare in Vienna; when she wasn't modeling, she kept her muskrat coat on. Under the coat, she wore orange stockings and nothing else.

"Mother would dress when she came home," Winter said. "Or if it was late, she might not bother."

Utch remembers hearing about Katrina Marek, but she can't remember ever seeing her. "Was she tall?" she asked Severin. "A blond, yes!" I remember her. She had a very thin face—"

"She was short and dark," Winter said, "and her face was as broad as yours."

But he couldn't visualize Captain Kudashvili either, although he swears he heard the name every day. "*Ja,* of course, *der* Kudashvili. He was the sergeant of the block, the General of the Schwindgasse. 'You watch out, you mind your manners,' the mothers would tell you, 'or *der* Kudashvili is taking you away.' Oh *ja,* he was blonder than a German's German, he was as fat as a Russian's bear. He wore elevator shoes."

"He never did," said Utch. "He was tall and lean, with a long sad face and a mustache like black wool. His eyes were gray-blue, like a revolver."

"Oh, *that* one!" Severin Winter cried. "Of course I remember him." But he didn't; it was just his clever tooth talking again.

But why couldn't they remember? Children were scarce. Out of rarity, alone, all the children must have looked at each other. Children stare at each other—even now, when there are so many.

"There was a lot of forgetting going on," Utch told me.

Yes, and much of it was hers. She must have been uncomfortable about her guardian captain's job. Drexa did not make things easier for him. At supper, Kudashvili allowed her to eat with Utch and himself, despite Drexa's babble.

"Well, Captain, you must have heard," Drexa would say. "Old Gortz is gone—the machine-parts store up Argentinierstrasse? He owned it for years."

"Gortz?" Kudashvili would say; his German was better than he let on.

"Just disappeared," Drexa would say. "Overnight. His wife woke up and the bed was empty. She woke because suddenly she felt cold."

"Men are poor, weak creatures, Drexa," Kudashvili would say. "You have to marry a good one if you don't want him to run away." And to Utch he'd say, "You're going to be lucky. You won't ever have to marry anybody until you want to."

"*Ja,* Utchka will marry a Czar!" old Drexa would cackle. She knew that was old Russia, but she liked it when the captain raised his black eyebrows at her.

"The Czars are gone, Drexa."

"*Ja mein Hauptmann,* and so is Gortz."

"You must have known what was going on," Severin said once to Utch.

"I knew what was going on before too," Utch answered.

"So what's the difference between one Gestapo and another?" Winter asked.

"Kudashvili took good care of me," she said.

We were sitting in our living room late one evening after dinner. It was often awkward when all four of us tried to have a conversation; by then, it was Edith and

I who talked to each other, and Utch and Severin. Still, if such things are ever going to work, it must be thought of as a relationship between four people, not two couples. The whole point was not to be clandestine, but it was Severin who would never give the four of us a chance. He would either be sullen and say nothing, or he would get into these long family-history harangues with Utch and expect Edith and me to listen. He was uncomfortable, so he tried to make us uncomfortable too. Sometimes, at their house, he'd appear holding Utch's coat out to her immediately after supper, in the middle of a fairly relaxed conversation. He'd say suddenly to her, "Come on, we're keeping them from talking about their writing." That was a habit at his insistence too: somehow he always took Utch home, or stayed with her in our house, and I would end up with Edith in their house. He made a Prussian routine out of our relationship, and then made fun of it for being a routine! "Exasperating," he said one night when the three of us were very much aware that he hadn't said a word all evening. "We're just biding time before we go to bed. Why not forget the dinner part and save a little money?"

So we tried it a few times, and he seemed to enjoy the coldness of it. I'd arrive at their house after dinner and he'd slip out the back door as I came in the front. Or when he came to our house first, he sat around with his coat on, mumbling "Yes" and "No" until I left to see Edith. Then he would take his coat off, Utch told me.

But it didn't have to be that way, or like other times when he'd consciously set out to bore us all, engendering a monologue at dinner which he'd carry to the living room afterwards with every intention of making us all fall asleep. One night he talked so long that Edith finally said, "Severin, I think we're all tired."

"Oh," he said. "Well, let's call it a night, then. Let's go to bed, then," he said to *Edith!* He kissed Utch goodnight and shook my hand. "Another time, then. We've got lots of time, right?"

I remember the endless evening which began with his saying to Utch, "Do you remember the riot at the Greek embassy in '52?"

"I was only fourteen," Utch said.

"So was I, but I recall it very clearly," Severin said. "A horde of rioting Communists attacking the Greek embassy; they were protesting the execution of Beloyannis."

"I don't remember any Beloyannis," Utch said.

"Well, he was a Greek Communist," Severin said, "but I'm talking about the attack on the Greek embassy in Vienna. The Soviets wouldn't let the police send an armed force to break up the riot. The funny thing was that the rioters were *brought* to the embassy in Soviet Army trucks. Remember now?"

"No."

"And even funnier is that the Soviets disarmed all the police—in our sector, anyway. They even took away their rubber truncheons. I always wondered if that was Kudashvili's idea."

"I forget a lot," Utch said.

"So does Severin," Edith said.

"Like what?" Winter asked her.

"Your mother," said Edith. Utch and I chewed our food quietly while Winter sat looking as if he was remembering.

"What about my mother?" he asked Edith.

"Her modeling," said Edith lightly, "and the fact that she was naked nearly all the time."

"Of course I remember that!" he hollered.

"Tell the story about her coat and the guard," said Edith. "That's an interesting story." But Severin went back to eating.

I know the story Edith meant. On weekends when Katrina would go modeling, Severin was out of school and had to come along. He sat in various artists' studios painting, drawing and pasting while the real artist attempted to render his mother. One of the studios was in the Russian sector, and the building had a guard. It was normal to tip the guard when he admitted you to the foyer, but Katrina, who had been coming there almost every Saturday for years, would never tip anyone. With little Severin beside her, she would approach the guard. He would put his truncheon down and smile, and just as she was abreast of him, she would fling open her brown muskrat coat for just a few steps, until she was past him. "*Heil* Stalin!" she'd say.

"*Guten Tag,* Frau Winter!" the guard would say. "*Guten Tag,* Sevi!" But Severin would never answer him.

I think Severin thought about his mother too much. The first time I saw those erotic drawings and paintings Kurt Winter did of her, I'll admit I was startled. It was the first time I slept with Edith. She took me upstairs in their house; I had never seen the upstairs before. All of us had agreed to be very careful about the children, so Edith and I tiptoed and she peeked into their rooms. I saw the laundry in the upstairs hall. I went to look at the toothbrushes in the bathroom. Edith's nightgown hung on the back of the bathroom door; I brushed my beard against it, nuzzling it. I saw an open box of hemorrhoid suppositories (those would be Severin's, surely).

Edith's and Severin's bedroom was dark and neat. She lit a candle; the bed was turned back. For some days all four of us had projected this. Severin had quietly taken Utch home, and Edith and I had suddenly realized we were not just alone in the living room; we were alone in the whole house. Later, it surprised me that Utch claimed it never began that way. In her version she and Severin had been talking in the kitchen, and when they returned to the living

62

room to join us they discovered we had gone upstairs, so it was *then* that Severin took Utch home.

What's it matter? I looked at everything in their bedroom. I wanted to see clothes lying about, but there wasn't anything. There were books (Utch and I never read in bed), and evidence that candles were frequently burned—a few hardened puddles of dull, colored wax on the window ledge. I was surprised that Edith was playful when I undressed her; it seemed so unlike her, and I had the feeling that with Severin she roughhoused a bit in bed. I did not roughhouse. It was not until I lay beside her on Severin's high Baroque bed that I saw the goddamn paintings and drawings all over the walls—the erotic dowry Kurt Winter had given his wife for her journey to London. Even as new and exciting as Edith was to me, I had to look at those damn paintings; nobody could have stopped looking at them. At that time I didn't know the full story of Kurt Winter; Edith and I had done most of our talking about ourselves. "What the hell!" I said. "Whose . . ." I meant who had painted them, but Edith assumed I meant the model.

"That's Severin's mother," she said. I thought it was a joke and tried to laugh, but Edith covered my face with her light body and blew out the candle so that I wouldn't see his mother any more that evening.

We historical novelists are somewhat hung up on *what if*'s of this world. What if Utch and Severin had met in those early years? What if her guardian had met Katrina Marek? (One night on the Schwindgasse, past the curfew hour, when Severin's mother was walking arm in arm with one of her admiring painters, who was always enough of a gentleman to walk her home when he'd kept painting her long after dark. Under the light by the Bulgarian embassy, Captain Kudashvili would have stopped them with his sad, official face. "Your papers, please?" he might have asked. "You must have special papers if you're out after the curfew." And the painter would have groped for canvas strips, wet brushes, other signs of identification. And Kudashvili—politely, from all I've heard of him—would have asked Katrina to open her brown muskrat fur coat. Who knows how history could have been altered?)

But Utch and Severin did not meet in those years. "That's a frumped-up idea of yours, anyway," Utch told me once. "I mean, if we had met, we probably wouldn't have liked each other. You assume too much." Maybe.

"It's clear they led different lives. In March of 1953, for example, Utch attended a funeral. Severin was not there. It was a memorial funeral; the body was not in Vienna. She remembers the hearty mournfulness of the Soviet Army chorus and Kudashvili weeping; lots of Russians wept, but Utch thinks to this day that Kudashvili wept more for whatever the Soviet Army chorus evoked in him than for the deceased. She herself didn't weep a drop. She was fifteen and already had the beginnings of the bosom that would later stun so many. She thought that memorial funerals were a rather nice way to die, considering the other kinds of dying she had known.

Severin was fifteen too; he was out with his mother and the former Olympic warriors from Yugoslavia, and they were drinking themselves sodden and hollering themselves hoarse with happiness. There was little chance of crossing paths with Utch that day. Though it was a public and crowded beer hall, Katrina left her coat open a little during the celebration. It was the first time Severin got drunk enough to throw up. I'm told that the Russian radio station played Chopin all day.

The death that had provoked both celebration and mourning was, of course, the death of Iosif Dzhugashvili—a Georgian, better-known as Joseph Stalin—who, speaking of *what if*'s, was himself a figure surrounded by a horde of *what if*'s.

What if, for example, Utch had gone to Russia? And if the world were flat, as the poet says, people would be falling off all the time. The poet knows that people fall off all the time as it is, and Captain Kudashvili was one. It surely was his intention to adopt Utch legally and take her with him to the Soviet Union. But we historical novelists are aware of how carelessly good intentions are regarded.

Kudashvili and the occupying force of the Soviet Army left Vienna in 1955. The day they left is called Flag Day in Austria now; very few Viennese were sorry to see them go. Utch was seventeen; her Russian was excellent; her German was native; she was even making progress with her English, at Kudashvili's suggestion. He was making arrangements for her to become a Russian. He thought she should be a translator, and though German was useful, English was more popular. He wrote her from Russia, closing his letters with: "How goes Utchka's English?" They would live in the great city of Tbilisi and she could go to a university.

Utch had moved out of the Schwindgasse apartment, but she still brought her laundry—considerably out of her way—to old Drexa Neff. In the new *Studentenheim* on Krügerstrasse, Utch was happy, because for the first time people didn't know her as *der* Kudashvili's "something" or a Russian spy. It took her about three months after the Russians left to realize that she was attractive to other people. She realized that it was enviable to have breasts like hers, but that she had to learn what to do with them, and that her legs were the most peasant part of her and she had to learn how to hide them. That she liked the opera and the museums is to Kudashvili's credit; that her clothes were strange is probably his fault. She was the top-rated student at the language school, which was then a part of the Diplomatic Academy, but at times, between letters from Kudashvili, she wished that her second language was English or French instead of Russian. Most of all, she liked walking alone in Vienna; she realized that her view of how the city really looked had been colored by the fact that she'd always seen it in the company of the Benno Blum Gang. She did not miss them, especially her last escort among them, a short bald man with a hole in his cheek. It looked like an impossibly large bullet hole, except that if it had been a bullet, something would have had to come out the other side. It was a crater about the size of a ping-pong ball, like an extra eye socket below one of the man's real eyes. It was gray-black-pink on the edges, and deep enough so that you could not, so to speak, see the bottom. *Der* Kudashvili had told her that the man had been tortured during the war with an electric drill, and that the hole in his cheek was only one slow wound among several.

Since her new liberty, Utch read more than the Communist-supported newspaper. There was something every week about Benno Blum's Gang; every week they captured another old-timer. Benno's boys had a popularity second only to the unearthed ex-ecutioners and experimenters from the death camps. She did not harbor any great nostalgia for her old protectors.

She felt guilty that she did not miss Kudashvili as much as she thought she would, and she made her weekly trips to the Soviet embassy with a little un-easiness, though she signed all the necessary immigra-tion forms and many times gave the oath that she was a member of the Communist Party. She supposed she was, but it occurred to her that she was going to Russia for Kudashvili's sake, not her own. That's the point about Utch: she never once thought about *not* going. Kudashvili had loved her and made himself responsible for her. He had not left her in Eichbüchl, he had not left her among those blank-faced children in the orphanage; she owed him.

I don't think that Severin ever realized what was rare about Utch. She thought that doing something because of a debt was perfectly natural. It was unthinkable that you wouldn't do it; it was unwarranted to complain. And that thought has a complicated sister: when you don't owe anybody anything, you're free. Seventeen years old, Utch wasn't free; what's more, she didn't think it cause for self-pity. She was falling in love with Vienna, but when Kudashvili was ready she would go to Russia.

It was the good people of Budapest who freed her. On October 25, 1956, a lot of people's good intentions were upset. The Hungarians did not feel that because Russia had liberated them from the Nazis they owed the Russians anything as unreasonably large as their country. The Hungarian revolution must have been something of a wonder to Utch; from her peculiar point of view, the notion of "dying for one's own freedom" must have seemed like a terrible self-indulgence. It must have confused her; the refugees streaming across the border seemed almost like another war. Into Vienna, unstuck on barbed wire and unexploded by the former minefields, came a hundred and seventy thousand Hungarians. They were still trickling across two days later, when Vienna celebrated its first Flag Day. It was the first anniversary of the official end to the occupation. Kudashvili had been back in Russia for a year.

The week after Flag Day, Utch went to the Russian embassy and discovered that all her immigration papers had been returned—rejected. She asked why, but no one would tell her anything. She went back to the

Studentenheim and wrote Kudashvili. She had not heard from him when, less than a week later, she received a message from the Russian embassy that a M. Maisky wished to see her.

M. Maisky took her to lunch at a Russian club near the Graben. After the fish course, he told her the news. Captain Kudashvili had been sent to lend his assistance at the disturbance in Budapest, and during a nighttime investigation of a university building, he had been shot and killed by an eighteen-year-old sniper. Utch cried with remarkable control through the main course and dessert. M. Maisky produced a photograph of Kudashvili. "This is for you, my dear," he said. He also produced the slight portion of Kudashvili's leftover wages, which the captain had designated were to go to Utch in the event of his death. It amounted to four thousand Austrian schillings, or one hundred and sixty American dollars. Maisky thumbed through a thick file, which was Utch's life story up to 1956. He said her life had been a model of suffering under facism, which made Captain Kudashvili's rescue of her all the more meaningful—and his death all the more tragic. But he wanted Utch to know that she still had the Communist Party, and some time in the future she could go to Russia if she wanted to. She shook her head; she was confused at the number of uses the word "facism" could be put to. The Russian embassy, Maisky was promising, would help her in any way they could. Utch's translation ability, for example: when there were Russians in Vienna who were in need of an interpreter, he would try to break Utch into that circuit, "though they're a very jealous and competitive group," he warned her.

"Keep up with your English," M. Maisky told her. "That's what *he* would have wanted you to do." Utch knew they had read all her letters, but she also knew that a little Russian money for translating would be helpful. She thanked M. Maisky for lunch and went back to the *Studentenheim,* where she lived—almost alone—until 1963.

In those seven years her English got better, her Russian got practice, and her native German was spoken almost exclusively to two boyfriends who were both in love with her and were roommates down the hall. It took almost three years of knowing them before she decided to have sex with one of them, and when she saw how this affected the other, she had sex with him too. Then she stopped having sex with both of them because it seemed to hurt them, but they continued to court her, perhaps waiting for her to make another decision and start the cycle again. They remained roommates. But Utch decided that it was impossible for her—at least at that age—to make love to more than one person at a time, and she found a third young man, altogether outside the old friendship (he was an understudy for a great tenor in the Vienna Opera Company), and made love to him for a while. When her two old boyfriends discovered her new affair, they waylaid the tenor-understudy one evening in the maze of scaffolding supporting St. Stephen's Cathedral and told him they'd tear out his vocal chords if he saw any more of her without proposing marriage to her. This may seem quaint, but Utch didn't find fault with her old boyfriends' adolescent behavior. They were hurt, and they were going to hurt the tenor-understudy if he didn't pay for something. Utch always felt that there was no reason for any kind of hurting that anyone could stop, so she told the tenor-understudy that he'd better propose to her if he wanted to see her again. He changed opera companies instead, which she thought was a perfectly decent way of not hurting anybody, and she warmly declined the renewed, invigorated courtship from her old boyfriends. "No, Willy, *nein,* Heinrich," she told them. "Someone would get hurt."

Severin, whose perceptions often ran parallel to Utchs, surprised us one evening when we were all trying to talk about what our relationship meant to us. At least Edith and I were trying; Utch rarely said much about it and Severin had just been listening in his irritating, bilingual way. Edith and I said that it wasn't the *sex* so much that made our mutual agreement so exciting; it was the newness of meeting someone—that old romance was eight years old, more or less, for all of us—that was so enhancing.

"No, I think it's sex," Severin said suddenly. "It's *just* sex, and that's all it can be in a thing like this. There's nothing very romantic about hurting anybody."

"But who's getting hurt this way?" Edith asked him. He looked at her as if there were some information between them that was too special for Utch and me to hear, but he'd said nothing to Edith before about "hurting." We'd all agreed that if any of us suffered for any reason from our quaternion, the relationship would end. We'd all agreed that our marriages and children had priorities. And here was Severin (feigning martyrdom?) casting his ambiguities among us as carelessly as gerbil food. We'd all agreed that the relationship was good only if it was good for *all* of us—if it enhanced our marriages, or at least took nothing away.

And we'd all nodded our heads—of course, of course—when, in the beginning, Severin seemed to think it was necessary to say, "Sexual equality between two people is a difficult thing, and among *four* . . . Well, nothing's really equal, but it has to feel pretty equal or it can't go on. I mean, if three of us are having a good time and one of us is having a bad time, then the whole thing is bad, right? And the one person who blows it all shouldn't be made to feel that it's his or her fault, right?" Yes, we had nodded.

"If you're unhappy, we should stop it," Utch told him.

"It's not that, exactly," he said. "Everyone else seems so happy with it."

"Well, it's *supposed* to make people happy," Edith said.

"Yes, *sex* is," Severin said.

"You call it what you want to; I'll call it what I want to," Edith said. He always seemed uncomfortable about her independence of him.

"*Ja,* I think it's just sex too," Utch said. I was surprised at her, but then I thought that she was just trying to help him out. He was always so insistent on setting himself apart from the rest of us.

"Look, Severin, if you're unhappy, we'll stop the whole thing right now," I said. That was *his* loose phrase: "the whole thing." I asked him, "Are you unhappy, Severin?"

But if Severin had ever been questioned by God he'd have found a way to evade *Him.* "It's not that simple," he said. "I just don't want any of us getting in over our heads." I know that Edith was insulted by that. She'd already told him how much in control of herself she was.

"I think we're all pretty stable, Severin," I said. "Nobody's going to leave anybody, or run off with somebody else."

"Oh, I know that," he said. "I don't mean anything like that."

"Well, what *do* you mean?" Edith asked him; he was exasperating to her.

He shrugged her off. "I guess I feel that I have to do the worrying for all of us," he said, "because no one else seems worried about anything. But let's give it time; everything takes time." I felt angry. He seemed

71

so insensitive—to Utch, for example. His way of reducing our relationship to "just sex" must have hurt
her feelings a little. And since he clearly behaved as if
he were unhappy, I know that Utch must have had
thoughts that it was *her* he was unhappy with.

Edith laughed. "Well, we certainly don't have to
worry," she said. "You're doing enough worrying for
everyone." I laughed; Severin smiled, but his smile
was nothing I'd care to wake up to. Utch said later that
she'd been angry with Edith for using a tone toward
Severin that you might use toward a child, but I felt
he'd deserved it. As if Severin were out of the room,
Edith told us that we mustn't worry if Severin appeared unhappy sometimes. "He's more unhappy than
us, anyway," Edith said lightly, "and it's a mistake to
think that he's unhappy *because* of anything. I think
we're all just happier people than Severin," she
said, and looked at him—for confirmation? He'd said
the same thing about himself once, but now he seemed
sullen when Edith said it—as if, typically, he never
took anything he said seriously, but had to believe
Edith.

It was an awkward moment, and suddenly Utch
had her coat on and was standing between Severin's
chair and where I sat on the sofa with Edith. *"Vitch*
one of you is taking me home?" she asked. "Who gets
me tonight?"

Well, we all had to laugh. And I stood up, and
bowed, and said to Severin, "Please, the honor is all
yours," and he stood up and bowed and *hesitated*—
and I thought that he might be on the verge of saying,
"Take your goddamn wife home yourself and let me
have mine!"

But with a look to Edith which was mostly in fun,
he said, "Allow me to do you such a favor sometime."
And he picked Utch up in his arms, easily resting her
over his shoulder, and left with her worrisome laughter
dying away outdoors.

72

In the way Edith and I then smiled at each other, I sensed that *time* was not what Severin Winter needed. I think we felt conscious of him as the driver (any one of us could have asserted ourselves, too, but we didn't seem to have the need for it)—and we knew that he might choose to stop it. (Any one of us could have done that, but we felt that if anyone would stop it, it would be Severin.)

Usually Edith and I talked a long time after we were alone about each other and about writing. I would read her some of my new work; occasionally I gave her latest things a good critique. It was often two o'clock in the morning when we'd realize the time and know that Severin would be home in an hour or so, and then we would go upstairs and always be careful not to be still making love when he returned. Usually we were asleep; he'd knock once on the bedroom door to wake us, and I'd get dressed and go home to Utch.

But that night we went to bed almost as soon as Severin took Utch home. I suppose we may have felt some anxiety that it was going to end. When I told Utch about it, she said, "Don't try to tell me it's not sex."

"Edith and I meant it's not *just* sex," I said. "At least not for *us*." But I think that such distinctions—like self-pity and dying for freedom—were dubious to Utch. She had been brought up, better than any of us, to know the difference between what you are willing to do for someone else and what you do for yourself.

4

Scouting Reports:
Severin [158-pound class]

The new gym included an indoor hockey rink, three basketball courts, a swimming pool, various exercise rooms, men's and women's locker rooms, and an awful hall displaying trophies and photographs of all the old heroes. From the outside, it had the tomblike appearance characteristic of public skating arenas and modern libraries. There was considerable murmuring among the old guard that the place should have at least been made to resemble the old campus—bricks and ivy—but it was clear that ivy could never be encouraged to cling to all that slick concrete and glass. Severin Winter loved the building.

What was left of the old gym was a vast underground labyrinth of squash and handball courts, and the old locker rooms, now used by visiting teams—perhaps to depress them. This maze was connected to the new underground of shiny steel lockers and ingenious shower nozzles by a long tunnel to what was called "the old cage."

The cage was an ominous humped dome of brick; it looked like a crematorium for athletes. It was laced with ivy as thick as a girl's wrist; the roof was a beehive of glass, skylight windows so old and dull that they'd lost their glint. A huge circular space with a hard-packed mud and cinder floor, it was used primarily for indoor track and field events; it smelled like a greenhouse, except that plants don't sweat. ("Everything sweats," said Winter.) To prevent discuses from breaking the skylights during track meets, they'd drop nets all over the inside of the dome, like a see-through shroud. Indoor tennis was played there, too.

Around the inside rim of the cage was an elevated board track so that runners could operate on two levels; the ones below used spikes in the mud and cinders; on the board track, you ran in rubber soles. The track was banked at the curves; it assumed you ran with some speed; if you were just walking around it, you drifted toward the rail. People claimed that if you ran too many laps on that track, one leg would become longer than the other. ("Not if you occasionally reverse your direction," said You-know-who.)

When the cage was busy, it was a noisy place. The track thundered and shook; starting guns sounded for the trackmen on the mud and cinder floor below; the wind and snow made the old skylight windows hum and creak. The only modern addition to the cage was a long rectangular room partitioned off to one side of the board track, up in the rafters under the skylights; it was also glaringly lit with long fluorescent bulbs and had two roaring blow-heaters and its own thermostat. Its walls were padded in crimson matting, and from wall to wall it was carpeted with crimson and white wrestling mats.

Winter claimed that the wrestling room was perfectly situated for "psychological reasons." Prior to a match, the team would assemble in their little wing off the abandoned cage and watch the gym gang take away the mats. They were carried to one of the dazzling basketball courts in the new gym and properly spread out and taped together. There would be a few mats left in the wrestling room, and the wrestlers would warm up on these.

When it was time, Severin would lead them out of the wrestling room and around the creaking board track; he would turn lights off as he went, so the great gloomy cage would grow darker as they left it. (Winter scheduled all his home matches at night.) He would take his wrestlers through the long connecting tunnel to the new gym. To each side of the clammy tunnel, bright slots of light winked at the wrestlers from the squash and handball courts, where, like prisoners in strange cells, a few solitary athletes played those lonely games. Everything echoed in the tunnel. Winter would kill the lights as he went. An occasional squash player would holler, "Hey, what the fuck!?" and open his cell. The effect of the wrestlers in single file, solemn in their robes and hoods (Winter's choice), was quieting. Timidly, the squash and handball players often came out of their cells and followed the procession. It was a rite. The wrestlers had the longest, quietest, darkest walk imaginable; they had a weird way of concentrating. When they came to the light at the end of the tunnel, Winter always paused at the door. He looked them all up and down, as if he could see in the darkness. *"Wie gehts?"* he'd ask them; in the tunnel, his voice boomed. The squash and handball players hung back in the shadows, not wanting to disturb the ritual. *"Wie gehts?"* Severin Winter would holler. They were all his German students, you see.

And in unison the wrestlers would bellow in that tunnel, *"Gut!"*

Then Winter would fling open the door, and like moles emerging into daylight, his wrestlers would blindly follow him into the new gym and startling light and yelling crowd and out onto that shining crimson and white wrestling mat. To the spectators they always looked as if they had been brainwashed in a dungeon and sent out on some grim task into the real world. They *had*.

76

The Viennese are old hands at psychology. Severin didn't get the best material in the country, and he frankly admitted that he was not the best coach, either. The university wasn't what you'd call a wrestling power, but Winter's teams never lost a match at home. Of course he was clever at scheduling.

The lure of the university's old Eastern academic prestige was more responsible for bringing Winter the few good wrestlers he had than anything he was able to muster in the way of recruiting. He did his duty and made himself remembered by a few big high school coaches in the serious parts of the real wrestling country, but though he was remembered by a few coaches of his generation as a former contender, he was not known by the younger wrestlers, who remembered only the champions. And though he did get a few good wrestlers, they were drawn to the university because they were flattered as students; if they'd really wanted to wrestle, they wouldn't have come to New England. In short, he got athletes but not fanatics. "I don't get the ones with the real killer instincts," Severin complained. "I get guys who think. If you think, you realize you can lose—and you're right."

But I pointed out that the effect he got out of his famous tunnel-walk would probably be lost on wrestlers who didn't think. "Why do you think I do it?" he asked me. "All the great wrestlers have tunnels of their own—long, dark, empty walks through their long, dark, empty heads. I'm just creating a little illusion for my intellectuals. I'm just playing Plato."

He didn't pick an easy schedule; he just fostered his illusions at the home matches. He'd take his team on the road at least twice a season, and they'd wrestle three or four matches with the Big Ten and Big Eight schools. He'd always lose out there, of course, but he'd lose respectably. Usually he'd win one or two weight classes, and not many of his losing wrestlers would get pinned. This class of competition was necessary so that his team could win at home. There wasn't another school in New England that could beat him; he routed the Ivy League, and he'd usually schedule one home match a year with one of the big Eastern powers. He was very clever at anticipating the weakest of those powers in a given year, and he'd stage one great upset for his tunnel-walkers every season. Once it was Army or Navy; once he edged Penn State. He'd always lose to those schools when he took his team on the road, of course, and in the Eastern championships he had to struggle to have place winners in a couple of the weight classes.

He'd pick out his best wrestler each year and take him on the lonely and humiliating trip to the national tournament. The boy would get knocked off in the early rounds, but Winter never expected better, and he was kind to these boys and never misled them. He took only one wrestler each year—there was always one who qualified—just so he could write off a trip to the nationals as a school expense. "He has a dark-horse chance," Winter would tell the Athletic Department. It was an inoffensive lie.

Winter knew that he could not bring the old, dark cage and his long tunnel out to Stillwater, Oklahoma, or Ames, Iowa. "Out there," he said, "they have their own tunnels." And he'd tap his shaggy skull. "Very private tunnels, very tough to crack."

I used to wonder about *his* tunnel—how circuitous was it, and how long?

But it was Edith who invited us to dinner that first time. Her reasons were straightforward: she wanted to talk to me about writing. At thirty, she had still not engaged the novel, but her stories—mostly of small, closely observed relationships—had been published, most of them in little magazines, but one of them in either *Harper's* or *The Atlantic*. She was in the habit of taking a creative writing course every year, though she was not interested in completing a degree, or she would work independently with the university's writer-in-residence. That was not me; I was hired by the History Department, and I told her that I'd never taught a creative writing course and never wanted to. She talked so well about her work, though, that I agreed to look at it. For the last two years, the writer-in-residence had been the famous Helmbart, and Edith confessed that she neither liked his work nor him. I was, I admit, pleased to hear this; Helmbart's sort of haughty kingship over what was called "the new novel" was nauseating to me. Edith and I agreed that when the subject of fiction became how to write fiction, we lost interest; we were interested in prose, surely, but not when the subject of the prose became prose itself.

We had a good talk. I was flattered to know that she had read at least one of my books—the third one, about Andreas Hofer. She questioned my insistence on the term "historical novel," which for her had bad associations. But I insisted on the history, I said, because I felt that novels which did not convey real time conveyed nothing. We kicked that one around; I didn't convince her of anything. Severin, she said, had read all my books. I was surprised. I looked at him, awaiting his comment, but he was speaking German with Utch. "Of course, Severin reads everything," Edith said. I didn't know quite how to take that; she could have meant he was not a discriminating reader, a kind of book glutton, or that she admired his reading very much. Edith fixed her eyes on you when she talked to you, and she was animated with her hands—perhaps a habit acquired from Severin.

Helmbart, she said, had spent his time analyzing her "hang-ups"; he'd never talk about her writing or characters at all. She said he told her once that she couldn't begin to write until she could "describe a table and show its soul and its sex." It's this kind of shit that makes him king of "the new novel," I guess.

In discussing my Andreas Hofer book, Edith was wise and, well—kind. I told her that occasionally it angered me that my work was so disregarded. Even the university, when it listed faculty publications, failed to list my books. There would be Helmbart's fiction, and a raft of the usual scholarly articles—a piece, for example, on "the furniture symbols of Henry James." I'd always felt that there was a greater similarity between these articles and Helmbart's tiny fictions than the respective authors would admit.

Edith said she admired the energy of someone like myself—virtually unrecognized, but prolific.

"Yes," Severin said suddenly; I hadn't known he was paying attention. "You really crank them out." I wondered about that, and he said, "It's very hard to find your books, you know. They're all out of print." Sadly, this was true.

"How did you find them?" I asked him. I had never met anyone other than my mother and my editor who had read all my books. (I suspected Utch of having my father's habit with endings.)

"The library here buys everything," Severin said. "You just have to know how to dig them out." And suddenly I pictured my books as some archeological discovery. Severin Winter gave me the feeling that he considered the feat of finding them more significant than that of writing them. He didn't say anything further to me about them then, but I learned later that he liked to categorize books by wrestling weight classes. Such as: "That's a pretty fair 134-pound novel."

He came by our house the next day on his bicycle. Utch was out with the children, and though I suspected he might have come to see her, since he found me alone, I thought that he might mention my novels. He didn't. He'd brought me some of Edith's stories. "She's really very excited to be working with you," he told me. "Helmbart didn't work out."

"Yes, she told me," I said. "I'm really very happy to know another writer here. She'll certainly be a relief from students and colleagues."

"She's very serious about her work," Severin said. "Helmbart gave her a hard time. He told her he felt he could get closer to what was wrong with her writing if she slept with him." Edith hadn't told me that. "I think he thought she was just another faculty wife out to get laid by a new mentor," Severin said.

I suspected his reasons for telling me this, but I laughed. "I thought, right away," I said, "that she was interested in *writing*." He laughed too.

He rode that ten-speed bicycle every day in good weather, pumping up and down for miles in a tank-top style of wrestling uniform—what they call a singlet. He was sweating; he was tanned. "When Helmbart got to the point when he couldn't see Edith without pinching her, she gave it up," he said. We laughed again.

"That was a fine evening we had with you," I told him. "You're an excellent cook."

"Well, I love to eat," he said. "And I enjoyed talking with your wife."

"You have a lot in common," I told him, but he looked puzzled.

"No, not much," he said seriously, but then he laughed again—nervously, I thought—and back-pedaled his bicycle, jamming something in his complicated gears, so that he had to get off to tinker with it. We both agreed to see each other again soon.

It was later that I learned the rest of the story about Helmbart's pinching. From the start, Edith had told Severin about the man's advances. "Next time knee him in the balls," Severin had told her. But that was hardly Edith's style. She kept thinking she must be able to get something valuable from Helmbart. She asked

Severin if he would speak to Helmbart for her, but he told her that this would make the fool so self-conscious that everything he'd say to her would be a lie. I think this was wise. So Edith went on trying, fending off the pinches and squeezes.

Then there was a large party, mainly of English and Art Department people. Because of her writing, Edith was usually invited to such things, and Severin always went along; he enjoyed teasing those people. At this party Helmbart again pinched Edith. She gave him a look, she told me, which was "truly annoyed," then went over and told Severin that she was really fed up. "It's the only time I've really wanted Severin to do anything physically to anyone for me," she said. "I was ashamed at how angry I was, because Severin is rarely that way with people. I don't remember what I told him, but I wanted him to make an ass out of Helmbart. I suppose I expected him to *wrestle* the bastard. It was very unfair of me. Severin had always given me a great deal of confidence in myself by letting me know that he believed I could take care of myself—and here I wasn't able to."

Severin patted her hand and went bobbing off into the party crowd looking for Helmbart. Edith followed him, fascinated. Severin moved up behind Helmbart, who was telling a story to four or five other people. He is a tall man; Severin comes up to about his shoulder. Standing behind him on tiptoe, Severin must have looked like a dangerous elf. He quickly pinched Helmbart hard on the ass and *kissed* him loudly and wetly on the ear. Helmbart dropped an hors d'oeuvre in his drink, gave a little leap, blushed rosy. When he saw it was Severin, he handed the drink to the man standing next to him; the drink got dropped. Helmbart got pale; he thought he was in a fight with the wrestling coach.

And Severin, winking lewdly, said, "How's the writing coming, Helmbart?" Edith was there, hanging on Severin's arm, trying to restrain her laughter. But when he saw the man's face, Severin burst out laughing himself, and Edith let herself go before they were out the door together—laughing, actually baying like hounds. "It gave me such enormous confidence," Edith told me, "that I tossed my head back and took one last look at poor horny Helmbart. He wasn't laughing; he looked absolutely *gelded!* Severin and I kept laughing. It was late afternoon; the children were home with a baby-sitter, getting ready for supper. We drove around. I put my head in Severin's lap; I unzipped him and took him in my mouth. He talked nonstop, driving very fast, all the way home. I don't know what he said, but it was hilarious; even with him in my mouth, I couldn't stop laughing. We ran in the back door, through the kitchen where the children and the sitter were, upstairs and into the bedroom. I locked the door; he turned on the shower in the bathroom, so that the sound would drown out *our* sound—also, I guess, so that the children would think we had rushed home to *wash*. We knew we wouldn't fool the baby-sitter. My God, we went at each other like leopards. I remember lying on the bed, after God knows how many times I'd come, and I saw the steam from the shower rolling out the bathroom door. We took a shower together and soaped each other until we were slick, and then Severin pulled the bathmat into the shower and laid it down on the floor of the tub, and we had it all over again with the soap in a great lather and water beating down like a storm and the soggy bathmat soaking up all of it and *sucking* underneath me like a giant sponge.

"When we finally went downstairs, the children told us the sitter had run home. I think it was Fiordiligi who said, 'What a long shower you had!' And Severin said, 'Well, your mother and I were very dirty.' And we started laughing all over again; even Fiordiligi, who never laughs, started laughing with us, and Dorabella, who laughs at everything. We all laughed until we ached.

"I remember that next morning I hurt all over, everywhere; I couldn't even move. Severin said, 'That's how it feels after a match.' I realized that I was about to start laughing again, and that if I did, we would be doing it *again*. I felt so sore that I tried to hold it back, but Severin saw that, and he got fantastically gentle; he came into me very slowly and we did it again. That was nice, too, but it was completely *different*."

Poor Helmbart, I thought. He never knew what he was up against.

So Severin was clearly not the usual paranoid about his wife, was he? She gave him no cause to be. She married him and lived with him for eight years without having even a quick lover; she was faithful, and only rare fools like Helmbart couldn't tell this when they met her. But I can appreciate why he tried.

Severin Winter was too vain to be jealous. He struck me as very much a man's man; aggressive and egocentric, he took you on his terms. But neither Utch nor Edith really agreed with me. Utch claimed he was the only man she'd ever known who actually treated women as if they were equal to men; I agree that he was equally aggressive and egocentric with both sexes. Edith said that Severin's kind of equality could be very insulting to a woman. He seemed to make no distinctions between men and women—treating both with a kind of maleness which made women feel they were just one of the boys. For the sake of equality, few women really care to have men go that far. Even with his physicality—his hands all over you when he talked —women felt relaxed at once by his touch, but also a little put out. There was no mistaking his touch for a cheap feel; his touches had such an absence of sexuality that women felt he didn't notice them as women at all.

Severin had been married nearly eight years before he'd had time or cause to consider that there might be pleasanter mornings to wake up to, livelier beds to lie in, other lives to lead. The thought upset him. You can see how naïve he was. And when he first had the courage to mention his new thinking to his wife, he was all the more upset to hear that his dangerous day-dream was already familiar to her.

"You mean there have been other men?"

"Oh, no. Not yet."

"Not yet? But you mean you've thought about other men?"

"Well, of course—other situations, yes."

"Oh."

"I don't mean that I think of it very *much*, Sevi."

"Oh."

It was not the first time he found actual equality difficult to bear. He was someone who was always embarrassed to discover his own innocence. I think that a feeling of superiority came naturally to him. With all their chatter about equality, Edith and Utch miss one point about Severin: he thought of himself as protecting Edith from his own complicated feelings. What a shock for him to learn that *she* was compli-cated too.

But if he wasn't essentially a jealous man, he was demanding in other ways. He needed to make himself the source of the important feelings in Edith's life. If he had no need to make her more *his* than she already demonstrably was, he needed her *work* to be his too—and I know this troubled her. Though he was fond of saying that it was sex, when things were bad—or when things were good, for that matter—I'm sure that much of his uneasiness about Edith's and my relation-ship was the intimacy we shared through our writing.

He was not a writer, though Edith claimed that he was her best reader. I doubt it; his categories—his notion of weight classes—were irritating. I never knew when it was our sex that was troubling him, or when it was his notion that I had replaced him as a source of Edith's ideas. I always thought it important to know, but I doubt that he usually knew the difference. "It's the whole thing," he would say—his heavyweight aesthetics crushing us all.

"I'll indulge you all the writers, colleagues and mentors that you want," he told Edith once in a rage, "but presumably you won't need to *sleep* with all of them!" Obviously he was obsessed with his bizarre sensitivity to a kind of double infidelity. That Edith and I could talk together was more painful to him than our sleeping together. But what did he expect? Everything can't be equal! Would he have felt better if Utch had been a wrestling coach?

At least she was a fan. It grieved Winter that Edith wasn't. He'd beg her to come to the matches, he'd bore her with stories of his boys until finally she'd have to tell him that she just didn't care for it. She could see why he liked it, and that was fine, but it had nothing to do with her. "Everything that has to do with you has to do with me," he told her. She didn't think it ought to be that way. "I read everything you write, I read lots of stuff you don't write—and lots of stuff you don't read. We always talk about it!" he'd say.

"But you *like* to read," Edith pointed out.

"So much of that has to do with you," he told her. "What makes you think that I like it so much?"

I understood perfectly what Edith didn't like about the wrestling. She was attracted by an aspect of Severin that could also weary her; she liked his cocky sureness, his explosiveness; she wasn't that way, but she liked it in him, except when it seemed too strong, threatening to suck her up in it. And that aspect was strongest when he was involved with his wrestlers. How crazily committed all Severin's wrestlers looked to her! They seemed hypnotized by themselves, drugged in ego, which unleashed the moment their physical frenzy was peaking. It was too loud, too serious, too intense. It was also more struggle than grace; though Severin insisted it was more like a dance than a fight, to her it was a fight. To me, too. Also, more to the point, it was boring. So few of the matches were really close; often you just watched someone maul someone else—the only issue in doubt being whether or not the obvious winner would finally pin his victim or have to be content with just rubbing him all over the mat. Of course, I was never an athlete; I don't care for sports. I don't mind a walk now and then, but I do it to help me think. Edith was no jock either. She liked wrestlers' *bodies,* she said, "from the lightweights through the middleweights," but big men were repulsive to her. Though she was tall, she liked Severin's shortness. She liked wrestlers' thickness, the queer proportions of their weight that was mostly in their upper bodies. She liked men "with no asses, with small legs." Severin was like that.

"Why do you like me?" I asked her once. I am tall and thin; even my beard is narrow.

"Well, you're such a change," she said. "You're so different that it's nice. Maybe it's your beard; you have an older look that I like."

"Well, I *am* older," I told her. Four years older than Utch and Severin; eight years older than Edith.

Utch's tastes were mysterious to me. She claimed she liked most bodies. She said she liked the older part of me, too, but mainly she liked how much I obviously liked women. "Thought I knew it would be troublesome, I never met anyone who was so attentive to women," Utch told me. She implied that I was a woman's man; in fact, she often used the word "womanize." Well, I am more of a womanizer than Severin Winter, but so is the Pope.

"Don't you think I'm *nice* to women, though?" I asked Utch.

"Oh *ja,* I guess so. You encourage a woman to indulge herself in being a woman," she said; then she frowned. "In being a *kind* of woman," she added. Then she said, "Maybe women are your friends easily because they see that you're not so nice to men. Because they see that you don't have men for friends, perhaps they trust you."

"And Severin?" I asked her. "How is he nice to women?" I was just teasing; I didn't feel I had to know.

"Well, he's different," she would say and look away. She did not like to talk about him.

She would talk about his wrestlers, though. She knew them by their weight classes, by their styles, by everything Winter had told her about them—and he told her everything. Before the home matches, he'd often give her the rundown of the match—picking points, estimating who was going to win or lose. And Utch would sit through the match, taking notes of her impressions for him—how the 142-pound match differed from his prediction, and why. I'd have thought that he would have loved her companionship in this; Edith and I both thought that it would take some of the burden off her. But no, he made us all come to his home matches. Utch would tell us what to watch for in each match. I felt manipulated; it was as if he needed us all there to watch *him*—and he did seem to like looking up in the stands and seeing all three of us.

Utch's favorite wrestler on the team was a 134-pound black from Lock Haven, Pennsylvania, named Tyrone Williams. He was a languid-looking wrestler, sleepy but explosively quick, and it delighted her that he weighed exactly as much as she did. "If he needs someone to work out with," she would kid Severin, "just send him to me." In practice, Tyrone Williams was a good mover, always alert, but he tightened up against outside competition. He had stunning speed, and a slow-motion movement between his bursts that often lulled his opponents out of pace. But he seemed to psych himself out of every match. He was given to trances, sudden lapses in everything which made him appear to have heard a secret final-period bell in his head. He seemed to be already dreaming his way to the showers while still moving stiffly on the mat, groping on his back, gazing up at the high ceiling and the glaring lights. Usually he was pinned, and then he seemed to wake up—jumping to his feet, hollering, holding his ringing ears and staring at his opponent as if he'd been beaten by a ghost.

Patiently Severin would show him the match films later. "Now here it comes, Tyrone. Here's where you go to sleep—you see your head loll back there, your left arm just hanging at your side? Do you see what sort of . . . comes over you?"

"Mother," Tyrone Williams would say reverently. "Incredible, mothering incredible . . ." and he'd go off into a trance right there, in disbelief at his whole performance.

"You see?" Winter would go on. "You let his ankle go and you hooked over his arm; you wanted to hook *under* that arm, Tyrone—you know that. Tyrone? Ty-*rone!*"

Utch loved Tyrone for his lamentable trances. "It's so human," she said.

"Utch could break him of that habit," I said, kidding Severin. "Why don't you let Utch work on his trances."

"Tyrone Williams could have a trance right on top of Utch," Severin Winter said.

I thought this a bit crude, but Utch just laughed. "There's little evidence of anyone suffering trances on top of me," she said, arching her back for Severin and me. Edith laughed; she wasn't at all jealous. We all seemed very close and good-humored in those days.

"Why do you like him?" Edith asked her; she meant Tyrone Williams.

"He's just my size," said Utch, "and I think he's a wonderful color. It's like caramels."

"Yummy," Edith said, but she didn't mean it. She had no favorites among those wrestlers; to her, they were all perfectly nice and boring boys, and as a result they behaved awkwardly around her. Winter had them all to dinner every month; Edith said that they hulked and bumped through the house, knocking paintings askew on the walls. "Somehow they break all the ashtrays—and they don't even smoke. It's as if they need the softness of mats and the space of an arena in order to be agile."

At least once a week, one of them would come to their house to be tutored in German. Reading, listening to music or taking a long bath, Edith would hear Severin crooning to "some bulky boy."

"Wir müssen nur auf Deutsch sprechen," he'd say gently.

"Wir müssen nur auf . . auf what?" the wrestler would ask.

"Deutsch."

"Oh yeah. Oh God, Coach, I feel so stupid."

"Nein, nein, du bist nicht . . ."

Severin liked Williams, but there was a limit to how much he could like a loser, no matter how interestingly they lost. He liked winners better, and the winningest wrestler on his team was a 158-pound stranger from Waterloo, Iowa, named George James Bender. He'd been the state high school champion of Iowa for three consecutive years and had been recruited by the home-state power-house, Iowa State. This was before freshmen were eligible for competition, and Bender had spent a year entering only open tournaments. He'd won them all; he'd never lost. As a sophomore, he was expected to go all the way through the nationals, but he tore up his knee in the Big Eight championships. He'd always been a strange, serious student; he'd won some kind of science prize his junior year in high school. He was a straight-A student at Iowa State; his major was pre-med, but he really wanted to be a geneticist.

On crutches at the national tournament he couldn't wrestle in, Bender introduced himself to Severin. "Professor Winter?" he said; Severin was a professor, of course, but he wasn't used to being called one. "I understand you have one of the few undergraduate majors in genetics in the country, and you have the top geneticist in the world in your department."

"In *my* department?" Winter said. He was thinking of German or wrestling, I guess. He looked at George James Bender on his crutches and suddenly realized that the boy was talking about transferring and wrestling for *him*. Winter had heard of Bender, of course; every coach and wrestler in the country had.

But Bender's knee was slow to heal. He couldn't wrestle for the university the first year following his transfer, anyway, and Severin was shaken in the middle of the boy's ineligible year when Bender had to have a second operation on his knee. He'd been working out lightly with the team—whipping them all, though Winter refused to let him play with the heavyweights. Bender could have whipped them too, but anyone can make a mistake, and Severin didn't want "one of those clumsy football players" to fall on the boy and hurt the precious knee. He didn't re-injure the knee wrestling; he hurt it leg-lifting too much weight on the weight machine.

Winter also wondered if Bender hadn't become too much of "a goddamn geneticist, of all things," to be a real wrestler anymore. He awaited Bender's senior year with more expectations than he'd ever allowed himself to have for any of his other wrestlers. Bender spent the summer at home in Iowa working out every day with a few of those zealots from his Iowa State team. But when he came back East in August to work privately with our geneticist, the great Showalter, Winter fretted because there was no one on our summer campus for Bender to wrestle with.

Bender walked around campus in his long white lab coat. He was nearly as pale as the coat—a short-haired reddish blond with a beard that grew six or seven scattered hairs like corn silk on his face; he shaved them once a week and always managed to cut himself while removing one of those six or seven hairs. He had faded blue eyes and wore black heavy-framed glasses with thick lenses. He looked like a powerful farm boy from decades ago, and he may have been a superior genetics student—the great Showalter certainly liked him as a disciple—but he was the dullest young man I've ever met.

Severin decided he'd have to wrestle with George James Bender himself. He still worked out with his wrestlers, and he'd kept himself in good shape, but he never wrestled a full workout with any of them. Still, he had been good enough so that even now he was in a class slightly above most of them. He'd have had to cut off his head to make weight in his old 158-pound class, but he ran or rode his racing bicycle every day, and he lifted weights. Nevertheless, he was no match for Bender; he knew that he wouldn't ever have been a match for Bender—even as a trim competitor more than ten years ago. But in August no one else was around, and even when his other wrestlers came back to school in September, they wouldn't be up to Bender's conditioning, much less his class.

The only time the wrestling room was tolerable in August was in the early morning before the sun through the skylights had broiled the mats and turned the room into a sauna. But Bender's lab experiments in genetics required his early-morning attention, and he wasn't through with Showalter until almost noon.

Severin Winter was insane. By late morning, the wrestling room was over 100 degrees, even though they left the door open. The mat was hot to the touch. "But they're liquid," Winter said. "A kind of liquid plastic. When it's hot, they're very soft."

Every day he would meet Bender and try to last long enough to give the boy a workout. When Severin needed to rest, Bender would run laps, furiously fast, on the old board track, while Winter lay on the soft, warm mats, staring at the sun, listening to his own heart pounding in unison with Bender pounding his way around the wood. Then they'd go at it again until Severin had to stop. He'd move out of the cage and sit in the shade, cooling off, while Bender returned to his mad running. The heat blew out of the big open cage doors in those waves like mirror distortions you can see rising off a summer highway. A constant sprinkler system kept the mud and cinder floor from turning to dust.

"In this weather," I asked Severin, "why doesn't that fool Bender run outdoors?" It was a shady campus; the footpaths were empty of students; there was always a cool breeze along the river.

"He likes to sweat," Winter said. "You'll never understand."

I'd been walking with my children down to the playing fields beyond the old cage when I saw Severin sitting outside the cage door, collapsed against a survivor elm. "Listen to him," Severin gasped at me; he could hardly talk; his normal breath was still a few minutes away. "Take a peek."

I forced myself to step inside that steaming, dank place. The air choked you. A pounding as rhythmic as a machine's crude function was echoing steadily around the track. George James Bender would be visible for a half-moon turn; then he'd disappear over my head. He was wearing a sweatsuit over one of those rubber costumes, elasticized at the neck, ankles and wrists; the sweat had soaked him and made his shoes squeak like a sailor's.

Winter tapped his dripping head. *"There's* a tunnel," he said admiringly. "You know what you have to have on your mind to do that?"

I watched Bender for a while. He ran cloddishly, but he looked as determined as the tide—like the ancient messenger who would die on arrival, but never before. "I can't imagine that you could have *anything* on your mind," I said.

"Yes, that's exactly it," Winter said. "But try it sometime. Try to have pure nothing on your mind. That's what people don't understand. It takes considerable mental energy *not* to think about what you're doing."

On those hot days in August, I used to go watch Severin get mauled by Bender. Sometimes he'd get so tired that it would be Bender who'd tell him when to stop. "I'm going to run a few," he would say, getting up off Winter, who would lie just as Bender had left him, recovering his arms and legs, rediscovering breathing. When he saw me, he'd wave a finger, and in a few minutes, he'd try speech. "Come to watch me . . . get slammed . . . around?"

He grinned. There was a fine froth of blood against his teeth; some hard part of Bender had split his lip. He flopped on his back. Through my socks, the mat felt like a warm, wet sponge. Winter made all visitors leave their shoes at the door.

"Severin," I said while he was still too limp to complete a sentence, "it's a strange way for a thirty-five-year-old man to have fun."

"He's going to be a national champion," Severin managed to say.

"And you'll be runner-up," I told him. But though he joked about his runner-up history, he didn't like me to talk about it, so I changed the subject. No, I told him a bad allegory which I thought he'd think funny.

I told him about the World War I French ace, Jean Marie Navarre, who swore he hated to kill. Navarre claimed he was an entertainer; when he couldn't locate any German planes, he put on air shows of his acrobatics for the troops in the trenches. He had more than two hundred and fifty dogfights over Verdun, and by May of 1916 he had shot down twelve German planes. But he was wounded shortly after that and spent the rest of the war in and out of hospitals. His temper was bad; his brother died; he took frequent "convalescent leaves"—a dashing dandy, he wore a lady's silk stocking as a cap. In Paris, he is reported to have chased a gendarme along a sidewalk in his car. Somehow he survived the war, but he was killed in a peacetime stunt, less than a year later, attempting to fly a plane through the Arc de Triomphe.

When I saw how the story touched him, I was embarrassed for Severin. "I don't think there's anything funny about that story," he said. Of course he wouldn't; even humor had to be on his terms.

Like the subject of trances: no one agreed. Utch was fond of speculating on how Tyrone Williams might gain control of his famous lapses, but her suggestions were not really coaching methods which Severin Winter could employ. And Edith liked to tease

Severin about George James Bender, to whom she felt he gave too much of his time.

"George James Bender is in the greatest trance of all," Edith said. "I think his *mind* constantly takes showers."

"Don't be a snob," Severin answered. "That's a kind of concentration. It's different from the concentration you need to write, but it's similar in the energy it takes." (You can see how seriously he took wrestling.) "Sure, Bender is an unsophisticated kid, and very naïve. He's shy, and not very attractive—at least, not to women. Of course, he must be a virgin—"

"A virgin?" Edith said. "Sevi, I don't believe that boy has ever had a *hard-on!*"

But she seemed to regret her joke as soon as she said it, though Severin laughed a little. Severin didn't appear bothered, but Utch and I noticed how anxious Edith was with him the rest of the evening, as if she was making up to him; she touched and rubbed him even more than usual, and *she* was the one who said she was tired and would really prefer to make it an early evening. Utch and I went home together, and she stayed with Severin. No one felt really disappointed; we got to see a lot of each other, and everyone had to be generous.

But in the car I said to Utch, "What do you make of that?" I had the feeling that lately there might have been a lot of talk about hard-ons.

"Hm," said Utch, a woman fond of single syllables.

We went to bed; she, too, said she was tired. I lay awake on my side of our bed, not really wanting to pursue the subject, but when I thought Utch might be asleep I asked, "Severin doesn't have any trouble, does he? I mean, you know, with you?"

No answer. I assumed she was asleep.

I was almost asleep myself when Utch said, "No."

I thought about it; I was awake again, and I could

96

feel her awake, too. I thought of some things I really didn't want to ask, but it was as if she heard me asking them to myself. "Of course," she said, "it's my impression that Severin *always* has a hard-on."

That broke a slight tension which occupied, like an electrical field, that small area of the bed between us. I laughed. "Well, I suspect that between times it really does go down, Utch, or get a little soft, and you just haven't noticed."

I'd meant to be funny, but she said, "No."

Then I was awake. I said, "If it never goes down, then he doesn't come, for Christ's sake. Utch? He must not *come*."

"And you say Severin asks too much," Utch said. "You say he asks Edith too much." True, I knew, you shouldn't ask too much.

But I persisted. "Utch, does he come?"

She was quiet a long time. Finally she said, "Yes."

For some reason I had to add, "With *you*, anyway."

Utch reached over and held me in her hand. In the context of this conversation, I felt embarrassed about not being particularly hard myself at that moment. She held me awhile, then let go; it was the way she said goodnight. And together we achieved that practical silence, a kind of wisdom, which you can learn only after a number of years of a good marriage. We both pretended to be asleep until we were.

5

Preliminary Positions

At first, the thought of Severin with Utch was exciting. It rekindled an old lust which had not been entirely absent but which had been perhaps too occasional. Edith said she responded very much the same; that is, the thought of him with Utch re-excited her feelings too. Well, you whet one appetite, you whet them all. Maybe. Utch said she felt that way toward me sometimes; at other times she admitted the effect was not so good. What effect it had on *him* is typically baffling.

Severin was too short to make love to Edith standing up. Not that she particularly liked making love standing up, Edith was quick to add, but I confess I took an interest in learning that he had any physical shortcomings. Edith and I liked to make love in the shower standing up; this would be before we went to bed, where we often made love again. It was an innocent enough beginning; the next thing we knew, we had a ritual. ("The first, next and last thing we always know," said Severin, "is a ritual.")

Edith put her arms over my shoulders and let me soap her breasts. She worked up a thick lather on the back of my neck and ran gobs of it down my back, all over my body. I worked up a lather as stiff as egg whites and dabbed her with it. Then we would wet ourselves under the shower and let ourselves foam together; we had the ideal height-proportions for it (Severin, I suppose, just couldn't reach). She slipped under my arms and hugged herself tight to my chest, and I pushed her against the cool, wet tiles until I could feel her reaching behind me for the towel rod, which was something hard for her to hold on to and yank herself against me.

We went to bed clean and soap-smelling and whispering, touching and looking at each other in the candlelight, smoking cigarettes, sipping a little chilled white wine until we felt like it again. But I never quite felt the same about it in bed with her. She'd told me that, "prone," Severin was just the right size for her ("top or bottom or side by side"). In the shower, I knew I was nice and new.

I never heard him knock; it always Edith who woke me. He would give one sharp rap, and Edith would say, "Just a minute, love," and wake me up. I loved that sleepy, slept-in smell—as if sex were cellular and our aroma of spice and fermentation was the old sloughed-off cells. Sometimes I wanted to make love to her quickly then, before I dressed and left, but she never let me. She said Severin didn't like waiting for me to leave; it was a hard time for him, apparently. I often offered to be the one to leave first. I told him I wouldn't mind waking up him and Utch; I said I wouldn't mind waiting. But he had to be the one. Only once, when he agreed to let me come to them, did he and Utch stay together until I arrived home. And then I was late—as if it mattered! I'd said three or four o'clock, but Edith and I had overslept; I came home closer to five and found him pacing the sidewalk in front of our house, not even staying with Utch, fuming and shivering in the cold. He got into his car and drove home before I had a chance to speak with him.

When you get out of bed at three or four in the

morning, it's always cold. I stumbled downstairs after kissing Edith goodbye—her breath a little sour from the cigarettes and wine and sleep, but it had a ripe smell, like the bed, and it always aroused me. Downstairs, Severin emptied ashtrays, rinsed glasses and loaded the dishwasher. He never wanted to talk; he'd nod goodnight. Once, when I could tell by his restless bustle around the dishwasher that I'd taken too long getting dressed, he offered me a cold can of beer to drive home with. "It helps to cut the phlegm," he said.

And I went home to Utch, whose breath was fruity and sweetly sickish; our bed lay strewn with her clothing, the mattress half sliding to the floor. And then *I* would trot about the house—not emptying ashtrays but disposing of the apple cores and spines of pears, cheese rinds, salami skins, grape stems and empty beer bottles. He knew how food in the bedroom revolted me! "And you know how he hates Edith's smoking," Utch said. "He says you leave ashtrays smoldering like fireplaces all over the house." A slight exaggeration. He was a maniac for the care of his phonograph records, too, and apparently raved at how I treated them. He would always use those inner envelopes; he turned them sideways so that you had to take a record out and put it back twice. "He thinks you abuse his record collection intentionally," Utch said.

"It's like the damn ice trays," I told her. "He bawls out Edith for not refilling the ice trays, for Christ's sake. We're filling a bucket to chill the wine, and he wants all the ice trays refilled the second they're empty."

"And you're in too much of a hurry?" Utch asked.

"Jesus!" I cried.

When I saw Utch in those pre-dawn hours, sprawled out, randy and ravished, I was attracted to her and to the passion I imagined he had evoked in her. I always went to her, amazed that my desire was up again for the third or fourth time that evening. And sometimes she'd respond, as if her appetite were endless too—as if Edith's smell on me drew her out again and made the foreignness of our familiar bodies especially alluring. But often Utch groaned and said, "Oh, God, I couldn't, please, I can't do it *again*. Would you get me a glass of water?" And she'd lie still, as if wounded internally and fearful of silent hemorrhage, and sometimes her eyes were frightened and she squeezed my hand against her breast until she fell asleep.

Edith said that, like me, she felt the same aroused responsiveness when Severin would finally come to bed; she'd keep warm the spot I'd left in their bed for him, and her imagination of him with Utch excited her and kept her awake—though he often fussed and puttered around the downstairs of the house for a long time after I'd gone. When he came to bed, she'd hum and whisper at him; she liked to smell him. We were all in that rich phase where sweet scents turn to decay. "Sex sniffers," Severin called us once.

But Severin Winter would climb into bed like a soldier seeking comfort in a wet foxhole; it was necessary for him to first rid the room of wine glasses, ice bucket, another ashtray, the burnt candle—all of which, Edith said, he touched as if they were tainted. Then he would lie chastely on his far edge of the bed; when she touched him, he seemed to cringe. She'd rub against him, but it was as if he were choking down a gag at her smell. Self-conscious, hurt, she'd roll away from him and ask, "Did you have a bad evening?"

"Did you have a good one?"

"I want to know how it was for you."

"No you don't. That doesn't matter to you."

Whew. Of course, he wasn't always so obviously dark, but he could pervert the most frankly innocent, erotic things. ("You smell rich," Edith told him once, nibbling his ear. "You *reek*," he said to her.)

I know there must have been times for him when the pure sensuousness of our belonging to each other must have excited him and stopped his adolescent brooding, but these times were so rare that I remember them most vividly. For example, once we spent a weekend on the Cape at Edith's mother's place. There were just the four of us—no children; we'd successfully farmed them out. It was late September, and the great Cape house was sunny and cool. Like Edith's mother, most of the summer people had already migrated back to Boston and New York.

We started out in Severin's car so early that we were there before lunch. Edith and Severin were familiar with the place, of course, but it was Utch who first acknowledged our isolation and privacy; she was the first to undress down on the blowy and abandoned beach. I noticed how Edith looked at her. Back in the house, both women looked at each other naked, while Severin prepared an enormous paella and I opened raw oysters for a first course. There was a lot of liberal touching, and everyone was very loud. Severin went for Utch's ass with a lobster claw. In his white cook's apron, with nothing on underneath or behind, he stood with one hand on Edith's long thigh and the other on Utch's round one. As his hands moved up he said to me, "The New York loin is a leaner cut than the Central European variety, but a good cook can bring out the flavor of both."

"Different flavors, surely," I said.

"Long live the difference!" said Edith, who reached under Severin's apron for something and touched hands with Utch there.

I fed Edith an oyster; I fed Utch an oyster. I was wearing my shorts and Edith unzipped them; Utch pulled them down and said to her, "Why are these men hiding themselves?"

"I'm the cook," Severin said. "Don't want to burn anything."

"I'm opening oysters," I said. "One slip of the hand . . ."

Edith hugged Utch, suddenly, around her hips. "You're so solid, Utch, I can't get over it!" she cried, and Utch hugged her back. "It must seem like quite a handful after *me,*" Edith said to Severin.

He spattered and hissed at the stove; he flipped up his apron and fanned himself. Utch ran her square, broad hand down Edith's sloped stomach. "You're so *long,*" she said admiringly; Edith laughed and drew Utch to her; the top of her head fitted against Edith's throat. Utch picked Edith up quickly, with astonishing strength. "And you don't weigh anything at all!" she cried.

"Utch can pick me up, too," I said. Edith looked suddenly alarmed as Utch picked me up with a low grunt.

"Heavens, Utch," Edith said. Severin had taken off his apron and had wrapped himself in sausage links. He pressed himself against Edith, who squealed and jumped away from him, feeling the cool, slick sausage against her. "My God, Severin—"

"Got a whole string of pricks for you, my dear," he said as his paella fumed and conspired behind him.

When Severin and Utch went for another swim, Edith and I made love on the long corduroy L-shaped couch in the living room. We were lying there drowsily, after the act, when Severin and Utch came back cold-skinned and salt-tasting from the ocean; they were shivering. They made me feel like swimming too, but Edith wasn't interested. I leaped up from the couch and ran naked across the pale-green lawn just as it was getting dark and onto the sand which was still warm from the sun. The water stung; I hollered as loud as I could, but there were only gulls and sandpipers to hear me. I sprinted back to the house where so much flesh awaited me.

When I came in through the French doors to the sunroom, I could hear that no one had actually missed me while I was gone. I could not see them in the living room, and I discreetly went into the kitchen and warmed myself over Severin's steaming paella until the three of them were finished. The three of them! Utch told me later that she and Severin, chilly and shaking, had curled up with Edith on the couch because she had opened her arms to their shivering, or they were attracted to how warm and sticky she was. She covered Utch and kissed her, and Severin touched and rubbed them both, and suddenly Utch was pinned under them, with Severin kissing her mouth and Edith kissing her deeply, until Utch felt herself coming and wanted Severin inside her. Edith didn't mind and Severin came in her; Edith held Utch's head against Severin's shoulder; she was mouth-to-mouth with Edith, their tongues exchanging recipes, when Severin made her come. Utch said that Edith almost came then too. Then it was Edith's turn, because Severin had been holding out, and she held Edith's head while Severin came inside her; he came quickly and rolled away. But Edith had still not come, Utch knew, so Utch helped her. Edith was so light that Utch could easily manipulate her; she picked up Edith at the hips and drove her shoulders against Edith's slim buttocks and very lightly touched her tongue to Edith where she was wetter and saltier than the sea. When Edith screamed, Severin covered her mouth with his own. I heard just a short cry before the orchestra of the paella captured my attention again.

Then Severin was beside me in the kitchen, smelling more distinctly than shellfish. He shoved me in the direction of the living room. "Go on," he said, "you don't know anything about paella. Let me. Go keep the ladies . . . happy," he said, and gave me a bewildered roll of his eyes (the most honest, worried and intimate confession I believe he ever made to me). "Go on, man," he said, shoving me again. He dug a wooden spoon deep into the paella, brought up that unlikely and delicious mixture—chicken, pork, sausage, lobster, mussels and clams—and slid the steaming spoon into his mouth. A bright red tongue of pimento hung down his chin, and I found my way to the couch where Utch and Edith were drawn tight together, curled against each other; they were touching each other's breasts and hair, but when I came up they parted and let me fit snugly between them. I did not object to how they used me.

Then we felt like a swim and ran, all three, across the lawn, green-black now, and saw the lights on the channel buoys blinking out in the water. And we all three entered the sea and saw that startling figure alone against the lights from the sunroom's open doors. He sprinted down the lawn toward us and cleared the first long dune like a broad-jumper. At a glance you would have picked him for a winner in a rare pentathlon—cooking, eating, drinking, wrestling and fucking. "Here I come, you lovers!" he shouted. A wave rocked us and tilted the horizon, so that Severin momentarily disappeared, and then he burst through it and hugged the three of us; we were chest-deep in the ocean. "The paella's ready, team," he said, "if we can stop screwing long enough to eat it." A vulgar man.

But we stopped until after dinner, when I think we'd all had a long enough time to engage in the normal, relatively civilized process of eating, which we'd done together many times before, so that our awareness of how we'd behaved that afternoon had sunk in and left us all happy but shy.

Severin reviewed his paella, suspected the tenderness of the pork, cast aspersions on the age of the chicken, suggested shortcuts in the making of the Italian sweet sausage, allowed that clams were, usually, clams, that mussels were better than clams anyway, and that the lobster was the undefeated George James Bender of the sea.

"Don't make me lose my appetite," Edith said. "Show some restraint in your images."

"This is a vacation from restraint," Severin said. "I don't see anyone else showing any restraint." He flipped a lobster claw in my lap; I flipped it back; he laughed.

"This is no vacation," I said. "This is a beginning." It was a toast. Edith stood up and drank down her wine the way I was used to seeing Utch drink hers.

But Severin said, "No, it's just a holiday. It's like calling time out."

Utch wasn't saying anything; I could tell she was a little drunk. Edith announced that she wanted to change her brand of cigarettes. "I want non-filters," she said, crumpling a full pack of mine; she'd been out of her own for hours. "If this is just a time out," she said, "I'm going to enjoy myself."

Severin said he'd go get her cigarettes. "What's the worst cigarette? What's the strongest, vilest, most throat rending, lung-gunking cigarette on sale? Because I'll get you a carton of them," he told Edith, "and we'll force-feed them to you all weekend. You can chain-smoke until they're all gone. Maybe that will cure you."

"Go with him," Edith said to me. "He'll probably buy me a box of cigars."

"You shouldn't smoke," Utch said to Edith. "You know it upsets him." She had a fixed smile on her face, and I knew she wouldn't remember anything she said tomorrow. Her left hand lay in the salad as if it were comfortable there. Edith smiled at her and took her hand out of the salad. Utch winked at her and blew her a kiss.

In the car Severin said, "Christ, we better hurry back or those women will go to bed without us."

"Does it bother you?" I asked. "It seems natural to me that they should have those feelings for each other. I don't know why, but it doesn't bother me."

"I don't know what's natural," Severin said, "but, no, it doesn't bother me, either. I just don't want to get back and find us locked out of the bedrooms. I mean, I didn't come all this way to spend a weekend with *you*." But he was joking; he wasn't really angry.

We had an argument about whether to buy Edith Lucky Strikes, Camels or Pall Malls. Severin insisted on the Pall Malls because they were longer and he thought they would burn her throat more. Riding back, I wanted to tell him how good I felt—how I couldn't believe that he'd suddenly relaxed here, and how optimistic I was about all of us. I wanted to say that I thought our future looked fine, but he said suddenly, "We should be careful no one gets too excited." It was like his saying that we were all on a holiday, and I didn't know what to make of it. "Why does Utch drink so much?" he asked me. "Why do you let her get so plastered?"

I said, "You know, one kind of excitement leads to another."

"I've noticed that in four-year-olds," he said.

"Come on," I said. "I mean, it really excites me when I know Utch has been with you. And being with Edith—well, that also makes Utch very arousing to me."

"Polymorphous perverse," said Severin. "Something like that. It's normally a phase of childhood sexuality."

"Come on," I said. "Doesn't it excite you? Don't you find that generally you're more sexually aroused?"

"There have always been certain moments in the

day when I think I could fuck a she-goat," Severin
said.

I was angry at him. "I hope you don't mean Utch."

"I hope I didn't mean *Edith*," he said.

"You know, Severin, I'm just trying to get to know
you."

"That's a little difficult," he said. "It's a little late. I
mean, it's not as if we were friends first, and things
just naturally led to this. Things began with this, and
now you're Edith's friend, first and last."

"I've never had too many men friends, anyway," I
told him. "I know you have. We're just different."

"I have a few old friends," he said, "but no one
around me now. I don't really have any more friends
than you. I just used to have them."

"And women friends?" I asked. "I mean, since
Edith and before Utch?"

"Not as many as you, " he said. But he was assum-
ing; he didn't know anything.

"How many is 'not so many'?"

"Counting she-goats?" he asked, but there was that
slashed tooth, that mischief-making tooth, that storytelling tooth. "If you want to know, ask Edith," he
said.

"You mean she knows?" I asked.

"Everything. We don't have any secrets."

"Some people would rather not know everything,"
I said. "Utch and I agree—not that we're that frequently unfaithful, or whatever you want to call it—
that if one of us has someone, some light occasion only,
we don't want to know. Just so it doesn't show, just so
it doesn't affect us together. And if it's a little nothing,
why *should* we know? We might get upset when there's
no reason to."

"I couldn't have 'a little nothing,'" Severin said.
"What's the point of having nothing? If I were having
a relationship with someone and it *didn't* show—and

Edith couldn't see it and feel it—then I couldn't be having much of a relationship. I mean, if you have one good relationship, why would you be interested in having a little nothing of a relationship? If you have a good relationship, that's all the more reason to want to have *another* good one. Which is what the trouble is," he added.

I asked Edith once, "Do you tell him everything about us?"

"If he asks," she said. "That's how he wants it." Then she smiled. *"Almost* everything," she said. "But if he always knew what to ask, I'd always tell."

In the car, I asked him, "Don't you think that's an invasion of privacy? Don't you think it violates some-one else's independence?"

"What independence?" he asked me. "I honestly admit the degree of independence that I *don't* have if I live with someone," he said, "and I expect whoever's living with me to do the same." (Later I remember him yelling: "There's a precious amount of having-one's-cake-and-eating-it-too shit going on around here.")

The Cape house was darker than we'd left it. "I'll bet they're in there lapping each other right up, so to speak," Severin said. But I knew how drunk Utch had been when we left, and I wasn't surprised to see her flopped on the couch—passed out from the wine, I was sure, not love-drugged by a bout with Edith. Edith sat braiding Utch's hair while she snored. Braids were not flattering to Utch.

"Brunhilde's been felled by the mead, or the lords of the hall, or both," said Edith. She'd washed her hair; it was done up in a big mint-green towel that came from the bathroom adjoining the Green Room. Like some grand English country home, the house had named bedrooms: the Green Room, the Cove Room, the Master Red, the Lady Yellow. I had never met Edith's mother, but Severin mimicked her perfectly, Edith said, and he had renamed all the rooms for us when he'd shown us the house on arrival. There was the Wet Dream Room—it had a single bed—and the Hot & Cold Flashes Room (Edith's mother's room; she complained of such symptoms) and the Come If You Can Room, so named for being next to Edith's mother's room (and a trial in the early days of their marriage, Severin claimed; Edith laughed), and the Great Green Wrenching Orgasm Room—the most private of the upstairs rooms, most separate from the others and, when the house was full, most coveted. "It has the best orgasm record," Severin claimed. "Daughters have trouble having orgasms in their mother's houses." It had a brass bed which was notorious for falling apart. From the gleaming foot-rail, tied on a satin cord, hung a wrench for emergency repairs.

By her choice of the mint-green towel, Edith had indicated that the Great Green Wrenching Orgasm Room was to be ours. "Love?" she said, touching Severin nicely, "you take Come If You Can, okay? I mean, when Mother's not here, the room doesn't deserve its name, does it?"

But Edith told me later that when I went off to pee, Severin said to her, with a nasty jerk of his head toward the snoring Utch, "You mean Come If *She* Can, don't you? What's the going price for baby-sitting? Why should he get it free?"

I could tell there was something between them when I came back, so I offered to put Utch to bed; Severin waved me off. "She usually just sleeps it off," I told him.

"Any special instructions?" he asked. I thought he was kidding; I saw his tooth. But Edith, left us and went to bed. *Whose* bed, I wondered? "She's in the Green Room," Severin told me. "I'll look after Utch; don't worry about a thing."

I went up to the Great Green Wrenching Orgasm Room, where Edith was sitting up, smoking in bed and fuming about Severin. "He's not going to spoil this weekend for me," she said. "Or for any of us, though he's certainly trying." I reminded her of what had happened between us all in the afternoon; we had enjoyed ourselves, after all, and it had been surprising. She smiled; I suspected that she sulked with him when he upset her, but she had never done that with me.

"Go on," she said tiredly. "Just talk to me." But then she wanted to tiptoe down the hall and say goodnight to Severin. I didn't know what her motive was but I let her go. I surveyed the green walls, the green drapes, the notorious brass bed, the wrench dangling from the foot-rail. I listened to Edith in the hall as she knocked on the door of the Come If You Can Room. "Sleep tight!" she cried out to Severin brightly. "Come if you can!"

When she came back, I got angry with her; I told her that the quickest way to end our relationship was to use our being together as a kind of provocation of Severin. Then she sulked with me. I very much wanted to make love to Edith at that moment because I knew that Utch and Severin *couldn't*, but I saw that her anger with him had made her angry with everything, and that making love to her was unlikely.

When I thought she was asleep, she whispered, "It's got nothing to do with you sometimes. It's just between us. Don't worry. You see, he doesn't know what he wants; it's himself he's upset with most of the time." A few minutes later she mumbled, "He only thinks of himself."

We were both asleep when Severin woke us with his knocking on the door. "Goodnight!" he called. "Be careful what you use that wrench for! It's only meant to fix the *bed!* Goodnight, goodnight . . ."

But Edith started to huff and moan and pant and

111

thrash around, gripping the head-rails of the old brass bed and thumping up and down—sounding like she never sounded when she was actually doing what she pretended to be doing now for his benefit. "Ooooh!" she cried out; the bed heaved. "Uuuuh!" she grunted, and the casters moved us across the green room like some boat on choppy water. "God!" she cried out, her long thin arms as rigid as those brass rails. When the bed collapsed under us, Severin was probably on his way back to Utch, but he heard it. Edith sat laughing on the floor; at least I think she was laughing—it was strange laughter. The bed, detached entirely from the head-rails and clinging still to the right foot-post, had pitched the mattress and us across the scatter rug and sent the night table spinning into the chaise longue.

"Are you all right?" Severin asked at the door. Edith laughed.

"Yes, thank you," I said. Then I wondered how to fix it. I had no idea what one was supposed to do with the damn wrench.

Edith curled up on the chaise with a wild look at me and said, "If you can fix it, I really will fuck you." I'd never heard her talk so crudely. But the bed was hopeless; mechanically, I have never known what goes where. I was going to suggest that we move to another room when we heard Utch being sick down the hall.

"It's okay," Severin was saying soothingly. "Let it all come and you'll feel better." We listened to Utch's terrible retching. I had to go to her, of course; Edith kissed me hurriedly and I went down the hall.

Severin was holding her head over the toilet in the bathroom adjacent to the Come If You Can Room. "I'm sorry," Utch said weakly to him, then threw up again.

"I'm here, Utch," I said.

"I don't care," she said. She heaved some more, and then Severin left us alone together. We inherited the Come If You Can Room and I heard him move with

Edith into the Hot & Cold Flashes Room. Evidently Severin didn't feel like fixing the brass bed at such a late hour, though he had fixed it many times before, I knew.

Utch and I hugged each other in the Come If You Can Room while Severin and Edith had no apparent difficulty coming next door. Hot & Cold Flashes, indeed. I listened to Edith sound the way I knew she really sounded. Utch's strong hand bore down on the base of my spine. We each knew what the other was thinking: we'd all spoken of this weekend as being an opportunity to break the 3 A.M. arrival-and-departure schedule. We'd thought it would be nice to be real lovers, who occasionally got to wake up in the morning together.

But I woke up with Utch, her breath echoing vomit. Edith made jokes about it at breakfast, but Severin said, "Oh, I don't know, it was still a novelty for *us,* Edith. I've always wanted to nail you in your mother's room."

"Poor Mommy," Edith said.

The day cheered up; Utch took off her jersey at noon. Severin, making sandwiches, put a dab of his homemade mayonnaise on one of her available nipples, but no one offered to lick it off and Utch had to use a napkin. Edith kept her blouse on. Severin announced he was taking a swim, and Utch went with him. Edith and I talked about Djuna Barnes. We agreed there was a kind of bloodless immorality to *Nightwood;* it was art, but wasn't it clinical? Edith said suddenly, "I suppose they're doing it down on the beach. I wonder if they ever *talk* about anything."

"Why do you mind if they're doing it?" I asked.

"I don't, really," she said. "It's just that it's Severin's idea that we all keep the times even, or something, and the thought's contaminating. And he knows that you and I didn't, last night."

113

"I think Utch thinks we *did*," I said. "I think she feels she missed out."

"You didn't tell her what happened?"

"No," I said. She thought it over, then shrugged.

When they came back, Edith asked lightly, "Well, what have you two been doing?" She thrust her hand down Severin's bathing suit and squeezed. Utch had put her jersey back on.

Severin winced; his eyes watered; Edith let him go. "Well," he said, "we've been enjoying our holiday." That word again!

"What's it a holiday *from?*" Edith asked.

"Children and reality," he said. "But mostly children." At that time I didn't know how much he implied by "children." Over his head, above the knife rack, was a wretched painting of decapitated fish with scales resembling Gustav Klimt's little squares of color-forms. It was an original Kurt Winter, of course; the Museum of Modern Art hadn't wanted it. Edith's mother had been stuck with a lot of minor paintings over the years. She felt no sense of responsibility for the estate of Van Gogh, but when they rejected a Haringa, a Bodler or a Kurt Winter, *then* she was touched. She ended up buying a lot of paintings the Modern turned down.

"She's such a sweet person," Edith said. "She's especially moved by bad paintings because she feels such embarrassment for the painter, even if he's dead." It's true. There wasn't a decent painting in the bunch of Kurt Winters; she had bought his very worst.

Edith hardly did better. In Vienna, she had met Severin on the twentieth-century floor of the Belvedere, as planned. Though he wore his letter-jacket, confirming her worst fears, they still made a kind of art history together. Pausing by the great square canvas by Gustav Klimt—"Avenue Leading Up to Castle Kammer on the Attersee," c. 1912—Severin said, "See that green? My father just didn't have it. With my father, trees were trees and green was green."

"I want you to know that I'm not officially employed—" Edith started to say.

"This is Klimt's 'Judith with the Head of Holofernes,' 1901," Severin said. "His brother, Georg, made the frame with the inscription."

"The Museum of Modern Art has not committed itself to a price," Edith went on doggedly. "In fact, they might only want one painting. But how much money do you need? Will you go straight to America? Would you consider traveling about first?"

"Schiele's 'Sunflowers,' 1911," Severin said. "Not what you'd expect of Schiele."

"My mother and I might be able to buy one or two paintings ourselves, but what will you do with the money, exactly? I mean, will you work at some job? You're getting a doctorate? In what?"

"Do you like 'The Kiss'?" Severin asked.

"What?"

"'The Kiss,' 1908. It's one of my favorite Klimts."

"Oh, mine too," Edith said. They looked at it for a while, but it was "Judith with the Head of Holofernes" which prompted Edith to ask, "Do you think Klimt liked women?"

"No," said Severin. "But I think he desired women, was tantalized by them, intrigued by them, attracted to them." They regarded Judith's strong jaw, her open mouth, her wet teeth, her startling dark hair. Her flesh was gauzy, perhaps in decay, and her long fingers were in Holofernes' hair; she held his severed head matter-of-factly against her stomach, her shadowy navel almost in line with his shut eye. Her breasts were high, upstanding, girlish but soft. One was naked, the other covered by a filmy blouse; the gold gilt was carefully placed so as not to obscure the nipple. Fruits, vegetation, a possible forest and garden, grew over Judith's shoulder and framed her cold, elegant face. But the dead head of Holofernes was casually cropped out of the painting; his one shut eye and part of a cheek was all of him that was in the picture.

"Tell me what it means to you," Edith said to Severin.

"She's a woman by whom you would not mind being beheaded. She wouldn't mind doing it, either."

" 'Doing it'? You mean the beheading?"

"Both."

They laughed. Edith felt astonishingly wicked. "She had him make love to her before she beheaded him," Edith said. "You can tell by her smile." But there was something lewd about the painting which suggested more, or worse, and she felt like shocking Severin Winter. "Or maybe she tried to after she beheaded him," she said. Severin just stared at the painting, and she asked him, "Which do you think she preferred?"

But it was Severin who shocked her when he said, "During."

He took her next to the Museum of the Twentieth Century. They did not discuss Kurt Winter's paintings there, either.

"Is Frau Reiner going to America with you?" Edith asked.

"What are old friends for?" said Severin. "Old friends don't travel with you. Old friends stay when you leave."

"So you're traveling alone?"

"Well, I might have to take sixty or seventy Kurt Winters along."

"My mother's position isn't very official," Edith said. (She had never realized how sneakers make a man appear to bounce.) "Does Frau Reiner live with you?" she asked.

They were looking at Gerstl's "The Schoenberg Family," c. 1908. "A minor painter who made it,"

Severin said. "Of course he had to die first. Not one of his paintings was exhibited during his lifetime. My father, of course, didn't get the chance to develop very much after 1938 . . ."

"Will you hold on to your mother's apartment, perhaps for vacations?" Edith asked.

"Vacations?" echoed Severin, "If you're living the way you want to, the concept of holidays becomes obsolete. Once Mother and I took a trip to Greece. We were packing up when Zivan or Vaso asked her if she was going to do any modeling there. 'Of course,' Mother said. 'If someone wants to paint, I want to pose.' We were just going to Greece, you see, but my mother liked what she did; she wasn't taking a vacation *from* anything."

"And what do you like?" Edith asked.

"Languages," he said. "I wish everyone spoke two or three languages and used them—all together. There are only so many ways to say things in one language. If we could only talk even more, make more description, add more confusion—but it wouldn't be confusion, finally; it would just be wonderfully complicated. I love complexity," he said. "Take food, for example. I'd like to be a great cook. I want to learn how to cook things better and better—subtle things, overpowering things, delicate and rich things, *all* things! I love to eat."

"Would you like to run your own restaurant?"

"What?" he said. "God, no. I want to cook for myself, and, of course, close friends."

"But how do you want to make a living?" Edith asked.

"The easiest way possible. I can teach German. I'd rather teach cooking, but there's not much money in it. And I'd love to coach wrestling, but I don't have a doctorate in wrestling. Anyway," he said, "how I live matters more than what I do. I have ambitions for the *quality* of how I live; I have no ambitions for making money. Ideally I'd marry a rich woman and cook for her! I'd exercise every day—for the benefit of us both, of course—and I'd have time to read enough to be a constant source of information, ideas and language. Ah, *Sprache!* I'd be free to devote myself to the basics. I would pefer to have my income provided, and in turn I would provide quality talk, quality food and quality sex! Oh, forgive me . . ."

"Go on," Eith said. She wanted to be a writer, and what she did mattered more to her than how she lived, she thought. She never wanted to cook anything, but she loved to eat. This man was saying to her that his ambition was to be a *wife!* "Please go on," she told him.

"I'm afraid you've seen all of my father that's here," Severin said. "The rest is all privately owned. We could have lunch first."

"I love to eat," Edith said.

"We could have lunch at my place," Severin said. "I just happen to have cooked up a *Gulaschsuppe,* and I'm trying a new vinaigrette for asparagus."

"And there's more Kurt Winter to see at your place," Edith said helpfully.

"But some of those are not for sale," Severin said.

"I thought everything was for sale."

"Just the art," said Severin. "All the art is for sale."

The pornographic drawings and paintings of Katrina Marek were not art, of course; they were his mother and his history; they were his *basics*—which perhaps Edith understood about him from the first. The ones of Katrina Marek were in the bedroom; art was in the living room.

"Look around," Severin said as he heated the *Gulaschsuppe.* She found the real thing in his bedroom, of course: a circus of positions and erotic poses surrounded his neatly made bed. She might have been

118

troubled if she hadn't known the model was his mother. But when she thought about it, she wondered if this shouldn't be more troubling. I think that Edith must have seen Katrina Marek as competition. She sat down on the bed. At its foot was a set of barbells which appeared as immovable as her memory of Frau Reiner's use of her tongue.

When he came into the bedroom to tell her the *Gulaschsuppe* was hot, he'd finally taken off his letter-jacket, and Edith knew, with alarm, that if he touched her, she would let him. He opened a window on the far side of the bed. Very enhancing, Edith thought. And now he'll—

"Perfect," he said; from the window box outside he picked up a wooden salad bowl containing the aspara-gus. "Keeps it cool," he explained; "I never have enough room in the refrigerator." He dangled a limp asparagus spear in front of her; it glistened with vinegar and oil. "Taste?" he asked. She opened her mouth and shut her eyes; he cupped her chin, tipped back her head and fed her the asparagus spear. It was delicious. When she opened her eyes, he was banging around back in the kitchen, calling, "Wine or beer?"

Edith did not want to get up. In some of the poses Katrina Marek appeared to be masturbating; Edith realized she had never touched herself in some of the ways suggested by Severin's mother.

"Wine or beer?" Severin called again. She lay back on the bed, and when she heard him coming, she shut her eyes.

"Are you all right?" he asked.

"I've lied to you," she told him. She waited for his weight on the bed beside her, but he remained stand-ing. She kept her eyes shut. "I have no official author-ity to buy any of your father's paintings, and even my mother is just about the most unofficial person at the Museum of Modern Art. I really don't know a single thing about the museum, except that no one there actually likes your father's painting. And *these*," she said, her eyes still closed, waving her arm at the bedroom walls, "my God, these are *appalling*."

She felt him sit down beside her on the bed, but she kept her eyes closed. "These aren't for sale," he said quietly.

"They should never leave your bedroom," she said.

"They never *will* leave my bedroom," Severin said.

Edith opened her eyes. "Aren't you angry with me?" she asked him. "I'm sorry about the Modern."

"I never believed it anyway," he said, which made her a little angry. He just sat there, in profile to her, very properly not looking down at a woman lying on her back. "But there's you and your mother," he said. "You said you might buy some."

Edith sat up. She was convinced he would never touch her, even if she undressed. "What would you do if you got a lot of money, anyway?" she asked.

"I don't want a lot," he said. "I just want enough to be able to take the paintings I can't sell with me." He looked around and smiled; she loved his smile. "That's a lot," he said. "And I want enough money to look around for a job in America without having to take a bad one. And," he grinned, "I'd like enough to be able to go to Greece before I do any of that. I'd like to leave right now," he said, and he lay back on the bed and shut his eyes. "I want to stay in clean little hotels; I want to be on the ocean. It's warm there now, but it's not the tourist season. Nothing lavish, but deny nothing! Eat well, drink well, take some good books along, read in the sun, swim. And when the tourists started coming, I'd come back here, pack up and go to America . . ."

"Say goodbye to Frau Reiner?" Edith asked.

"And to Vaso and Zivan," Severin said. "Tell them I'll be back soon, which will mean," he said, opening his eyes, "that I'll be back before they die. But I probably won't." He shut his eyes again. "Greece is the first thing," he said. "That's where I want to go."

"And how many paintings does someone have to buy so that you can go to Greece?" Edith asked. He opened his eyes. Edith liked his eyes when they were open, but she liked being able to stare at his mouth when his eyes were closed. "Close your eyes and answer me," said Edith. "How many paintings?" He appeared to be thinking, and she slipped off the edge of the bed, went into the kitchen and turned off the flame under the *Gulaschsuppe*. She brought the wine and two glasses back to the bedroom with her. His eyes were still closed, and she slipped off her shoes; she poured them both some wine and edged back on the bed beside him. She wanted to smoke, but he seemed too white in the teeth and too broad in the chest to possibly approve. He was so narrow in the hips, so small in the thighs.

"Maybe five of the big canvases," he said. "But of the five I'm thinking of, you haven't seen two."

"I'll take your word for it," she said, "but I want my pick, for my mother and me." He opened his eyes and she handed him some wine; he sipped; she took the glass from him and motioned him to lie back and shut his eyes again. He did as he was told. "Two conditions," she said when he was lying very still; he opened one eye but she brushed it shut with her hand. She almost kept her hand over his eyes but she thought better of it and rested her hand on the bed close to his face. She knew he could smell the perfume at her wrist; she could feel his slow breathing against her fingers. "First condition," she said, and paused, "is that one of the five paintings be one of *these*—you don't need to look, you know what I mean. I promise it will never be a public painting; I will never sell it or loan it to any museum. Frankly, I want it for my bedroom."

"Which one?" he asked.

Edith looked at the one she wanted. "She's on her back, with one leg lying flat and the other bent at the knee. She's touching herself very lightly, I think, but her face is turned toward us and she's touching the fingertips of her other hand to her lips—as if she's kissing her fingers goodbye to us, or maybe just hushing herself so she won't cry out."

"She's *tasting* herself," said Severin. Suddenly Edith saw the painting. "She's got one orange stocking on?" he asked. "The stocking's half off her right foot? Her eyes are closed? You mean that one?"

"Yes," said Edith, almost whispering. "That's my favorite one."

"Well, you can't have it," he told her. "It's my favorite, too." He didn't open his eyes to negotiate. Edith was surprised, but she charged ahead as if her feelings were unshaken. I am completely lost, she thought; I don't know myself.

"Second condition," she said, "is that you must answer one question, either yes or no. Either one satisfies the condition. You mustn't feel obliged—just be honest: say yes or no."

"Yes," Severin said. When she looked at him, his eyes were open. She tried to put her hand over them, but he caught it and held it lightly against his chest. "Yes," he said again.

"But I haven't asked the question," she said, looking away from him. He would not close his eyes or let go of her hand.

"Yes, anyway," he said. He already knows the question, she thought, and felt humiliated. She pulled her hand away and decided to ask him nothing more. He was cruel; he didn't know when to stop teasing.

But he said, "Now I have one condition." She looked at him. "You have to come to Greece with me." That had been her question: Did he want her to come with him?

She shrugged. "Why would I want to do that?" she said. "I don't have the time anyway." She got up from the bed, found her purse and lit a cigarette. "Is the *Gulaschsuppe* hot?" she asked.

"If you didn't turn the heat off," he said, and rolled away and lay on the bed face-down.

Edith went to the kitchen, turned the heat on under the *Gulaschsuppe* and banged a few pots around, but Severin didn't appear. She looked at a photograph of his mother with Frau Reiner and the two Yugoslav wrestlers. They were clowning for the photographer, who, Edith dimly thought, might have been Severin. The three survivors were all much younger. She could tell that Frau Reiner had at least once had a body, for everyone in the photograph was naked. They stood in front of an elegantly prepared dinner spread out on a table in several courses; they all had knives and forks in their hands. Vaso or Zivan wore a napkin on his head, and between Frau Reiner's ample breasts, a full glass of wine tilted dangerously. Looking older and more dignified than the rest, Severin's mother stood smiling shyly at the camera, her hands folded demurely over her crotch. She was nothing like the Katrina Marek in the bedroom; though naked, she looked fully clothed.

"Did you take this photograph?" Edith called into the bedroom. And he was supposed to say "What photograph?" and she would say, "This one," and he would have to get up off that dangerous bed and come out. But he didn't answer. "Soup's hot!" she called. When she heard nothing, she went back; he hadn't moved since she'd left the room.

"You don't have to buy any of the paintings if you don't really want to," he said, talking into the mattress.

123

"And if you really want that one"—his hand waved at the wall—"you can have it."

"I want to come with you to Greece," Edith admitted. He still didn't move.

"I want *you*," he said. Edith decided, All right, he's said enough. She dropped her skirt at her feet and stepped out of it, then pulled her blouse off over her head so that her hair crackled. She wore a bra in those days, and she unhooked it and looped it over the back of a chair. Then she tossed her panties at Severin, who still lay across the bed like a felled steer. ("The panties fluttered over one of his ears and rested there like a downed parachute," she wrote in one of her more forced pieces.) She was preparing to look at him directly when he sat up and stared at her; he came up off the bed very suddenly, awkwardly handing the panties back to her and dashing from the room. She thought that her shame would kill her, but he called, "Jesus Christ, the *Gulaschsuppe*—don't you smell it?" Boiled over and burnt, she supposed. "My God, what have I gotten myself into?" she whispered to herself. When she got under the covers, she recognized her perfume—that is, Frau Reiner's perfume—already on his pillows. He didn't even look at me, she thought.

But he didn't leave her alone long; he returned shedding clothes. She had not known enough men to know that athletes, like women, are used to changing clothes and therefore are smooth and careless undressers. He stood naked beside the bed and let her look at him; she had thought that only women did that, and she pulled back the covers for him so that he would look at her. He looked her over a little too quickly for her feelings, but he touched her just perfectly and was under the covers with her very gracefully. Well, she thought, nakedness is almost a family tradition with him; maybe he will look longer later.

Before he kissed her and didn't stop, she barely had time to say, "I think I'm going to like you." She was right, of course.

They left for Greece five days later; they'd have gone earlier, but it took that long for Edith to make and send slides of Kurt Winter's best work to her mother. "Mother," she wrote, "I hope the Modern will buy one or two of these. You and I have already bought numbers one through four, and a fifth not enclosed. I am going to Greece; I must get back to my writing."

The morning they were to leave, Frau Reiner and the Yugoslav wrestlers gave them a ritual good-bye. Edith and Severin were in bed, which was where they could have been found regularly in those five days, when Edith heard Frau Reiner and the Chetniks whispering and tromping about in the living room just as she and Severin were waking up. "Frau Reiner still has an apartment key," Severin told Edith, who scowled. "Mother gave it to her," Severin whispered. "And anyway, over the years Vaso and Zivan probably have collected about four keys apiece." What were they up to out there, Edith asked. Severin listened. The sounds they were making were apparently familiar to him; he rolled his eyes. "It's a kind of family joke," he told her.

"What is?" she whispered.

"You'll see," he said; he looked worried. "It's really almost a tradition. You must take it as a sign of great respect." Outside the bedroom door she heard thumping and giggles. "It goes way back," he said nervously; he put his arm around her and smiled toward the bedroom door. It opened, and into the room blew Frau Reiner, as flushed and beefy and naked as a Rubens. Vaso and Zivan were carrying her, with some difficulty, and they were naked, too. At the foot of the bed they quickly assembled in a group pose which Edith recognized as the one from the old photograph. Only Severin's mother was missing; a space for her separated Vaso from Zivan. They all held knives and forks in their hands, and Vaso or Zivan had a napkin on his head. But Frau Reiner was missing the wine glass; her breasts could no longer have clamped it tight in her cleavage. It must have been sad for Severin to see so much sagging flesh. *"Gute Reise!"* Frau Reiner croaked, and the old wrestlers burst into tears.

"They wish us a good trip," Severin told Edith. Later she learned that the photograph had also been taken at a goodbye party for Severin, when he was leaving for Iowa and a future perhaps bright in wrestling.

Then they were all standing around the bed, weeping and patting and kissing everyone. Edith realized that the covers were peeled back and that she was as naked as they. The old wrestlers seemed hardly to notice her—a professional numbness, perhaps—but she saw that Frau Reiner's close survey of her young body reflected both the sincerity of her affection and the agony of her envy. Suddenly Frau Reiner hugged her with a frightening passion; for a grip on her real life, Edith held onto Severin's thigh while he was being buffeted and cuffed by the bawling old Olympians.

Crushed against Frau Reiner's bosom, a playground of history, Edith remembered her mother's letter, which said, "He has no surviving family." Frau Reiner pinned her to the bed; her tears—her sweat? —wet Edith's face; she was at least two weight classes superior to Severin. Edith tightened her grip on Severin's thigh, which, for all the confusion around the bed, might have been Vaso's or Zivan's, and hoped Frau Reiner would not suffocate her. He has no family? Her mother was quite wrong. Edith knew that

Severin Winter's sense of family was more ferocious than most. We should all have been warned.

I admit that my own sense of family suffered from our foursome. I remember the children least of all, and this bothers me. Of course, we all had other friends, too, and our own lives with our children. But I forget where the children were. Once when I was with Edith, Dorabella knocked weakly on the bedroom door. I flinched; I thought it was Severin coming home early, though I couldn't imagine him knocking so softly. There was a hasty confusion of knees and other limbs, and I know Edith was worrying that Severin had heard her.

"Mommy?" Dorabella said. I got down under the covers and Edith let her into the room.

There had been a dream; the child described it in flat, unbroken tones, her hand nervously plucking and patting the lump beside her mother which was me. "Ssshhh," said Edith gently, "don't wake up Daddy."

The child poked me. "Why is Daddy sleeping like that?" she started to lift the covers but Edith stopped her.

"Because he's cold," Edith said.

In the child's dream there were howling dogs and a pig squealing under a car whose wheels "had folded under itself," she said, "like the wheels on an airplane." The pig was crushed, but not dead; the dogs were howling because the pig's squeals hurt their ears. Dorabella ran around and around the car, but there was nothing she could do for the pig. "And then it was *me* who was under the car," the child said, her voice trembling with the injustice of it. "And it was *my* sound that I heard and was making the dogs howl." She was punching my rump like dough, her little fists rolling her knuckles over me.

"Poor Fiordiligi," Edith said.

127

"It's Dorabella, Mommy!" the child cried.

Edith turned on the light. "Oh, Dorabella," she said. "What a terrible dream."

"That's not Daddy's shirt, is it?" Dorabella asked, and I knew whose clothes she was staring at.

"Well, Daddy traded something for it," Edith said. She was very quick; there wasn't a pause.

"What did he trade?" Dorabella asked, and I remember the silence.

Fiordiligi and Dorabella were the Winters' children, of course. My own children I hardly remember at all, and I used to know them quite well.

"What did he trade?" Dorabella asked again. I forget the children, but I remember that silence.

6

Who's on Top?
Where's the Bottom?

Once, when all of us were together, I looked at my boys and announced, "Look at that Jack" (my older one, lean and lithe, with a face even prettier than Edith's). "Look at his back; see the graceful bend to it? That isn't what they call 'sway-backed,' is it? He looks like a Renaissance print I once saw of an archer; he was bent like his bow. Jack is the delicate one. He likes music. I hope he'll be a painter."

And Severin answered, "If he ever develops any strength in his arms, he might be a 142-pounder." Severin liked Bart, my younger boy. He was brick-shaped, and all he inherited from Utch was her breadth of cheek and her shortness. In fact, if we had known the Winters back then, I might have suspected Severin of engendering Bart because the boy's body was nearer to Severin's than to mine. And as to the source of Bart's genes which gave him a turtle's pain threshold, I could only guess. "From Utch, of course," said Severin. "She had a pain threshold like planarian's." How did he know? What did he mean?

Jack was the older but the last one in the water; he was bigger, but in close combat Bart would sink his teeth into him and hold on. When Bart ran at a door, he ran at it as if the door would open for him. I winced to see the child move; a potential collision seemed to precede him like a prow. Neat, graceful Jack was curious, careful and shy. He woke up slowly. He said to me, "Sometimes are you ever sad and feel like crying even when nothing bad has happened to you?" Yes, of course! He was my son; I knew him well. He could spend an hour brushing his teeth because of the mirror—looking at himself as if it would help him figure out a way to be.

But Bart was born a bludgeon, with the ankles and wrists and insensitive cheerfulness of the good peasants in the orchards of Eichbüchl. He woke up breathing deeply, bleating for his breakfast.

When we took the children to the city, Jack looked up, scanned rooftops, hunted for gargoyles, girls waving out windows, spirits in the sky. Bart scuffed along, looked in the gutters for what got dropped there.

Severin's girls dressed up for Jack, wrote him bawdy notes and said, "Sit down, Jack, and let's play 'What Can We Get You?'" They wrestled with Bart, playing with him as they would with a pet. Dorabella told Edith that she was going to marry Jack; Fiordiligi laughed and said, "Then I'll be his mistress!"

"His mistress?" Edith said. "You don't know what a mistress is."

"Yes, I do," said Fiordiligi. "You get the presents."

Severin said, "That Bart, he's my boy. He's going to be a great cook; he'll eat anything."

"He's built like a bookend," I said, "but not like a writer."

"He's going to be at least a 177-pounder," said Severin. "Would you look at the chest on that kid!"

"He's got the sweetest temper," Utch said. Bart was a boy only a mother and a wrestler could love.

"That Jack," said Edith. "He's going to kill more women than the plague." I hoped he would be a good son and show some of them to me. His eyelashes were longer than Utch's and Edith's together.

"Why did you give your children such American names?" Edith asked Utch.

"They're simpler," said Utch, "and the boys like them. What kid in America wants a name like Helmut or Florian?"

"I love Italian names," said Edith. "After I called my first one Fiordiligi I *had* to call the second one Dorabella."

"It was going to be Dante if it was a boy," said Severin. "But I'm glad they're girls. Boys are such selfish shits." He was always trying to make the girls read. "You've got to be smart," he'd tell them, "and you've got to be kind. But if you're kind without being smart, other people are going to make you miserable."

"I love everything Italian," said Edith.

"You've never been there," Severin reminded her. And to us, "Edith is most attracted to things that are unfamiliar to her."

"Not true!" Edith said. "And when I'm familiar with something, do I throw it away?"

"Wait and see," said Severin. Of course, he was looking at me, but I kept my eyes on Jack and Bart. I was impressed that two people I loved so much could be so different.

"That's not surprising," Edith said.

"No," Utch disagreed. "There is one that you always love more."

"Here we all are again," said Severin Winter, "stumbling toward profundity."

Well, he could be funny. But at whose expense?

"He is *not* cruel," Edith said once; she was angry. "You should just stop trying to understand him. I stopped trying, and now I enjoy him much more. I hate it that men feel they have to understand everything." She was depressed, she said, that Severin and I would never be friends.

Also, her writing was taking a turn. An *off*-turn, I thought, but she defended herself with surprising calm. In the beginning she had responded to my criticism; now she seemed to be going off on her own, and I felt it was due to his brainwashing—his 118-pound theorizing, his disparaging remarks about so-called historical novels.

I often heard Severin tell his wrestlers, "If you can't get off the bottom, you can't win." But that's another story.

I remember once when the four of us stayed overnight at the Winters'—all the children, too. We hauled mattresses into the TV room and parked the children there to be mesmerized by various *Late Show* horrors; they ate potato chips all night. In the morning, we couldn't find Severin. I was alone in one of the children's rooms; I'd crawled off from someone's bed to sleep by myself.

We looked and looked. Finally Edith discovered Severin in the TV room, all four children sleeping huddled round him, wedged against him, sprawled on top of him. He had appeared there in the early dawn hours when some *Late Show* ghoul had convinced my youngest son of another reality, and his howls had convinced the other children. Severin had staggered away from one of the warm women, grabbing the nearest garment handy, and had fallen among them and promised not to leave until daylight. The garment was Edith's mauve dressing gown, a sheer, flowered, ankle-length thing. Edith called us all to come see. The groggy children were slowly waking; they curled and snuggled against him as if he were a large pillow or friendly dog—and Severin Winter lay among them in Edith's gown, looking like a transvestite weight lifter dropped through the roof of an elementary school like a benign bomb.

We drove our sons home, Utch wearing Edith's long wrap-around skirt because she'd been unable to find her own.

"I'm sure it'll turn up," I said.

"I remember where I took it off," Utch said, "but it's not there."

I drove with my hand on Utch's leg, or Edith's skirt. Everywhere, comparisons pleased me! But that was another time.

We returned from Cape Cod in a flood of headlights of other weekenders bathing our faces. Edith and I were in the rear seat; under my shirt, her fingers were cool against my stomach. There was a comfortable noise, tire-hum and engine-drone, so that I could speak to her in a normal voice without Utch and Severin hearing. Not that there was anything I wanted to say which wouldn't have been suitable for them to hear: the point is, it was intimate, riding at night that way. The impersonal quality of the flickering headlights illuminating us and leaving us in darkness made me feel isolated, overlooked, special. In the front seat, Utch and Severin sat chastely apart—more due to the design of his car than by choice, I was sure; it had bucket seats. Also, Severin insisted that everyone wear seat belts. In back, Edith and I had slipped ours off so that we could sit closer together; he must have known. I could hear the singsong tones of his voice, occasionally rising above the engine, the tires, and my own voice, but when I strained to listen to him, I realized he was speaking German. A story? Another tale of Old Vienna? What did they talk about?

"Nothing," Utch told me once. I thought she sounded bitter. "Whatever Severin and I have in common is your idea. If you met another American when you were living, say, in Vienna, and the other American was from Cambridge, Massachusetts, would you assume you'd have much more in common than the English language and some regional characteristics?" Whew. Ask a simple question, receive a speech.

But I saw our bedroom after he left it; I saw my wife after he left her. I have seen their communication in the twin apple cores, empty bottles, bitten hunks of cheese and bread, the stems stripped of grapes, the sheets knotted like a great balled fist which I imagine pounding the mattress askew! I have found pillows in distant corners of the room, and once I found the frail chair I usually throw my pants on stuffed upside down in the laundry hamper. On each of the chair legs dangled a shoe (my shoes), so that it resembled a four-legged creature with human feet, perhaps murdered violently and inverted to bleed among our dirty clothes.

"It looks like you two have some rapport," I said to Utch.

She laughed. "I think," she said, giving me a soft poke on the nose, "that you should think what you want to think"—interrupted by a gentle punch on the arm—"because you *will* anyway." She had never indulged in those damn locker-room physicalities, those chin-chucks and rib-pokes and ear-cuffs, until she met him.

Past Boston the traffic thinned out, and we were driving for the most part in darkness. I stopped talking. Severin's German was music. I could tell we were both listening, though Edith never understood the language any better than I did. Utch wasn't answering; he was just going on and on. I couldn't remember when he had turned the radio off (to listen to what I was saying to Edith? to make us listen to him?), but Edith asked him to turn it back on. She had to lean forward to make him hear, and she kissed the back of his neck.

"Put your seat belt on," he told her.

"Can we have some music back here?" Edith asked, ignoring him.

"No," he said. "Not unless you put your seat belt on."

Utch did not turn in her seat.

After a while, Severin turned the radio on; Edith had waited as if she knew he would, but she didn't settle back against me until the music was playing. She didn't put her seat belt on. Severin stopped talking at last. I touched Edith's breasts very softly, I pinched her nipples; I was trying to make her laugh, but she sat stiffly against me as if she were still waiting for the radio. The music was terrible and the station wasn't coming in well. Finally Utch fixed it. She had to take her seat belt off to fiddle with the dials, and when she started to put it back on, Severin spoke a little German to her. She answered and he argued with her; she left her seat belt off, and he took his off, too. Edith squeezed my hand; she was rigid. Severin spoke again to Utch. *"Nein,"* she said.

We were driving faster. I looked between their shoulders at the lengthening red tongue on the speedometer. When he dimmed the dashboard lights, I felt Edith tense against me and heard Utch quietly say something in German. I found myself thinking of Severin's psychological coaching method, his tunnel-walk in the imposed darkness. I felt we were moving at great speed and at any moment would burst into harsh public light and the roar of a crowd. Utch repeated whatever she'd said in German. I felt Edith was about to reach forward—and do what? Tap his shoulder, kiss his neck, fasten Utch's seat belt?

When Severin Winter spoke again, this time Utch didn't say *"Nein."* She lay across the front bucket seats and put her head in his lap. I saw her soft green sweater flow past the space between the seats like water. The dashboard was black. The speed felt the same. Edith pulled away from me, found her seat belt and clamped it shut around her waist; the metallic joining seemed exaggerated. Did Utch have him in her mouth? She wouldn't! Not with Edith and me right there. But did Severin want us to think that she did?

I couldn't let it go on. But I know the value of obliqueness. I said, "How do you think the children are doing?" Edith smiled; I knew I had him. "Does it bother you to leave them overnight, to be so far away from them? It gets easier as they get older, but don't you worry even so?" The questions were for Severin; Edith, of course, didn't answer me. Utch glided back to her bucket seat and sat up. (Later she said, "I should have rolled down the window and *spat* right after I sat up. That would have fixed you. That's what was on your mind, wasn't it? If that's what you were thinking, I should have let you *really* think it."

I yelled, "Then why'd he ask you to do it?"

"He just asked me to put my head in his lap."

"So what did he want us to think?"

"Think what you want to think," she said.)

Jesus! It serves him right—the way he threw up the children so often to Edith, as if they were sacred objects she didn't adequately worship. His idea of love was always tangled with his idea of guilt.

135

In the car, he said stonily, "I think the children are all right. But of course I worry about them, I always worry about them." The dashboard glowed again; the red tongue of the speedometer shrank.

"I just asked because I knew that at first you hadn't wanted to go on this weekend—you didn't want to leave the children," I said. "And I wondered, provided they're okay—and I'm sure they are—if you'd feel better about doing this kind of thing more often now? I mean, I think it's good to get away. It's been a great weekend, don't you think?" Edith and Utch didn't say a word, and Severin must have already known about the new laws—or his new version of the same old laws that he would lay down to Edith as soon as they were alone. He must have been already rehearsing it. That he didn't want her spending time with me unless he was spending equal time with Utch simultaneously. And that we would always arrange ahead of time—so that he could be "prepared" for it (he didn't like surprises). And that being away from the children for such an extended time wasn't an experience he cared to repeat. Without the children we lacked a certain perspective, as he liked to call it. But what was he afraid of? Oh, I know: the children. But what *else*?

He drove Edith from Vienna to Greece in a 1954 Zorn-Witwer, crossing the Yugoslavian border at Jerzersko because, he told her, the name of the place appealed to him and he wanted to see it. No other reason; I've looked at a map, and Jerzersko certainly isn't the best place to cross if you're en route to Greece. The point is, he didn't always need to plan out everything in advance. When they went to Greece, they just went.

I have tried to visualize them as young lovers, and, of course, Edith has told me a lot about their romance, but Winter's car eludes me. A 1954 Zorn-Witwer? Edith said the gearshift slid in and out of the dashboard like a plumber's helper. I've never heard of such a thing. There were places where the floor was rusted away and you could see the road running beneath you. It was some sort of primitive convertible; it had a roll-back canvas roof which leaked. The last year the car was ever made was 1954. Severin had told me that Zorn was a military manufacturing company which turned to farm and road construction machinery after the war. Witwer, he claims, was a failed motorcycle firm. They made unicycles on the side, no doubt. Can anyone believe anyone else? Who the hell ever heard of a Zorn-Witwer? Edith knew nothing about cars. Severin Winter went too far; they drove to Greece in some mythical car.

The weather grew warmer. Winter had a nose for water; he knew where to turn off the main road and find a lake. He found villages the instant they were hungry. When they got to talking about folk art, he would find them a room with an engraved wardrobe and a great feather bed—one with farm animals embroidered on the quilts and pillowcases. In a tiny pension in Thrace, he showed Edith a rare folk toilet: the flush handle was a perfectly carved penis.

They discovered sex in the cradle of democracy. They kept track of the different beds. For a while, Edith favored the bed in Ljubljana, but Severin liked the one in Piraeus—it was so warm there, and they were in sight and sound of the harbor; all night they heard the boats flapping on the water "like thighs slapping together," Severin told Utch. In the morning a fish market opened below their window. Edith lay in bed and heard the fish knives hacking and slitting, the bartering tongues. The suction sound of removing the innards seemed magnified; the garrulous haggle rose and fell. She knew the fishmongers liked to be-

137

head a fish at the exact moment they were making a point about the price. *Thok!* for emphasis. After that, who could argue?

They made love in the morning, sometimes twice, before getting up. They went to bed soon after the evening meal, and if making love made them too wide-awake, which it often did, they would get up, go out again and eat another supper. Then they'd make love again. In the country, they'd often "find some water" in the middle of the day. Apparently that was a euphemism they liked.

Edith's first short story was a thinly disguised version of leaving Piraeus for a drive in the country. (This was before they went island-hopping.)

The story begins with the fish market in Piraeus.

I knew when I first heard them cutting the fish that they'd be sold out and gone by the time I'd see the cobblestones. I made love in the morning and got up late. The fishmongers had packed up, but the hotel's man with the hose hadn't rinsed the cobblestones, which were wet with fish-blood and slime, phosphorescent with scales, flecked blue with intestines. It wouldn't do, our head waiter told us, to leave the mess until evening when potential guests might be alarmed at the gore and think that this slop was the remains of some unfortunate suicide from the fourth floor, or the ritual slaying of a wronged lover caught and ripped apart at the scene of this indiscretion.

I was discreet myself and made him drive me into the country, because though our stone room was cool in the daytime, the hotel maids would listen outside our door. At night and in the morning it was fine to use the room, but by midday we were on the road. It was apparently an under-powered car. We were often stuck behind a slow-moving vehicle—even horse-drawn carts—because it didn't have the necessary kick. The roads were curvy, his arms and the back of his neck were very brown. We were driving toward the ferry crossing at Patras. Where there was a ferry, we knew there was water, and we were looking for water. Though I read somewhere that a girl was rushed to the hospital with severe cramps from making love underwater—an air bubble in one of her Fallopian tubes. Is that even possible? I didn't believe it.

It seemed that wherever we drove in Greece, we drove into the sun. He had his shirt off, I had unbuttoned my blouse and rolled it up under my breasts and tied it in a knot. My breasts were small but they stayed up; my stomach was very brown. It was an old-fashioned, unslanted, glass windshield, which magnified everything a little. In the back, on the floor behind my seat where there was some shade, we kept a watermelon cool in a bucket of water which had been icy cold when we'd filled it; it was turning tepid now. I would slice pieces of watermelon in my lap; the melon was cool and wet and felt lovely against my stomach. I sprinkled water on his shoulders as if I were baptizing him. It was watermelon country; in the villages and on the roadside stands, melons and eggplants competed. He said the watermelons were the winning size, but the eggplants won the color prize.

In an unappealing, dry-looking landscape with short hills spiked with olive trees, we discussed how far away the sea was, and whether we would smell it before we saw it, then we came up on a large, swaying truck full of watermelons. We had to slow down fast. In the back of the truck a teenage Greek boy sat on a mound of melons with a grin on his face which suggested that his mental age was four. From his vantage point, my breasts and bare belly must have looked wonderful to him, and when we pulled out to pass, he didn't want to lose his view. He leaped up and poised an enormous melon over his head; if our wretched car tried to pass, the boy's demented grin implied we would regret it.

For thirty-four kilometers, until the ferry at Patras, that boy on the pile of watermelons sat displaying himself to me. There was nothing we could do. Except for his disturbed face, he was interesting to look at. I sliced more watermelon. We talked about stopping and letting the truck pull ahead, but I confessed that I wanted to see what the boy would do.

Just before the road widened to four lanes to handle the ferry traffic, the boy fell moaning on his back on the watermelon pile and lay writhing among the green globes until he ejaculated into the air. His stuff struck our rigid windshield like bird-dribble, a thick *whap!* against the glass on the passenger side. My head snapped back as if I'd been slapped.

Then the road widened, the road ahead was free, and we pulled out to pass. The boy didn't even try to threaten us; he slumped sulkishly on his pile of melons and didn't even bother to watch us pass. I had expected him at least to spit. I turned my head and saw the truck's driver: an old man with the same shocking face as the boy's, grinning obscenely at me, twisting in the driver's seat, trying to raise his lap to window level to show me *his!*

"Like father, like son," I said, but *my* driver's arms were hard-flexed, his fingers white around the steering wheel, his face withdrawn, as if he'd suddenly seen such an appalling hunger in the world that he felt ashamed to reflect it.

He didn't feel like swimming. For something to do, we took the ferry back and forth across the Gulf of Corinth, standing on deck together, leaning over the rail, imagining history and civilization. I told him it excited me, but he said he felt as alone at that moment as he felt whenever *he* masturbated. I have never understood why men have such trouble with that.

For the first time in my life, I was shocked at myself. I knew I could make love *anywhere*. We glided back and forth across the Gulf of Corinth. My desire was excruciating; I touched him as much as he would let me and whispered that when we got back to the hotel, I would make him come before he was inside me.

Eventually, of course, he snapped out of it. He came around.

I'll bet! He always did. He used to sulk when the four of us were together, trying to make Edith and me feel guilty, trying to provoke Utch into calling a halt to the whole thing. Utch would beg him to tell her what he wanted. All right, she'd tell him sometimes, we'll stop if that's what you want, but you have to *say* something. But he'd be a stone and she knew what she'd have to do to bring him out of it. Of course; that's what he *wanted* her to do! Why didn't she see? I don't know how he managed to make self-pity so alluring.

"When he's in one of his moods," Utch said, "the only thing I can do is fuck him out of it."

I complained to Edith, but she said, "What's wrong with that? You can't worry about what's right until you know what works." But sex is only a temporary cure.

We were an hour from home, both of the women asleep, when Severin stopped because he had to pee. Utch woke up when he got out and dashed into the short dark trees clumped along the roadside like soldiers. We were alone on the road now; it was as if no one else was returning from a weekend, as if around here they didn't take weekends off. I don't know exactly where we were.

When Utch woke up, I asked her to move in back with Edith; I wanted to talk with Severin. I sat quietly beside him until I was sure both Edith and Utch were asleep. Every town had a church, every church a lighted steeple. Finally I said, "I think you're calling all the shots. I think everything's on your terms. But there are four of us."

"Oh is that *you* there?" he said. "I thought Utch's voice had changed."

Ha-ha. "We see each other as if we're registered for courses—same time, same place. That's *your* idea. If that's how you want it, that's fine for you, but a little of it should be on our terms, too, don't you think?"

"I have a recurring dream," he said. "You want to hear it?"

Oh, suffering shit, I thought, but I said, "Sure, Severin, go ahead." I know that in sexual matters it is difficult to say things directly.

"It's about my children," he said. I had heard him talk about them a hundred times, almost always in wrestling terms; he called them his weakness, his imbalance, his blind side, his loophole, the flaw in his footwork, the mistakes he would always repeat and repeat, his one faulty move. Yet he could not imagine not having children. He said they were his substitute for an adventurous, explorative life. With children his life would always be dangerous; he was grateful for that, the perverse bastard! He said his love for Edith was almost rational (a matter of definition, I suppose), but that there was nothing reasonable about the way he loved his children. He said that people who didn't have children were naïve about the control they had over their lives. They always thought they were in control, or that they could be.

I complained about how much "control" meant to him; I argued that people without children simply found other things to lose control over. "In fact," I said, "I think human beings find that control is more often a burden than not. If you can give up your control to someone or something, you're better off."

I have seen how his wrestlers look at their opponents with a cold, analytical scrutiny, a dead eye. Severin Winter gave me such a look. Though he couldn't have been oblivious to the ridiculousness of his controlled behavior, he cherished the ideal.

"God save us from idealists, from all true believers," Edith said once.

God save us from Severin Winter! I thought.

His dream, as he called it, was not entirely fiction. Over and over again, he was stuck behind the watermelon truck, unable to pass, his life controlled and manipulated by the willful, masturbating Greek on the melon pile—threatening him, forever holding him at bay, squirting his vile seed and more and more of his kind into the air, on his windshield, everywhere—until the mindless depravity of it forced Severin in his dream to pull out to pass. But the watermelons the boy held over the passing car would suddenly become Severin's children, and—too late to meekly fall back in the lane behind the truck—Severin Winter would see his children hurled down on him and splattered against the windshield.

"How's that for a dream?" he asked.

How's that for a loophole? I thought. How's that for a flaw in the footwork? How's that for a faulty move?

"God save us all," I muttered. He had turned off the dashboard lights again, but I knew he was laughing. What I wanted to say was, Spare me the allegory, just stick to the facts. Who's controlling *this*? All of us or just you?

The car stopped; we were home.

"I'd give you your choice of whom you'd like to remove from the back seat," Severin said, "but there's the awkwardness with the baby-sitter, and I'm anxious to see the children."

"We've really got to sit down and talk sometime," I said.

"Sure, anytime," he told me.

I crawled in back to shake Utch, but she was awake. I saw at once that she'd been awake for all our talk; she looked frightened. I nudged Edith gently as I backed out of the seat and kissed her hair above her ear, but she slept soundly.

When Utch went up to Severin, he shook her hand —his idea of understatement? Utch wanted to be kissed. He said, "Get a good night's sleep. We can sort out all the stuff later."

I knew that our belongings intermingling—Edith's clothes in my suitcase, Utch leaving her gloves at their house—really pissed him off. One morning, Edith told me he opened his drawer and pulled out a pair of my underpants. "These aren't mine," he said indignantly.

"I just pick up what I find lying around," Edith said cheerfully.

"They're *his!*" he roared. "Can't he keep track of his own fucking underpants? Does he have to leave his goddamn laundry around?"

He stretched my underpants, snapping the waistband out wide enough to contain us both, then wadded them into a ball and kicked them into a corner. "They like to leave their things behind so that they'll have an excuse to come back. She does it too," he muttered.

To Edith, he simply wasn't making any sense. She brought back the underpants—to Utch—that morning. She and Utch thought it was very funny.

It wasn't long afterward that I pulled on what must have been the same pair. Something was wrong; the crotch had been slit through with a razor, so that it was like wearing an absurdly short skirt. One was left free to flap, so to speak.

"Utch?" I said. "What happened to my pants?" She told me that they were the ones Edith had brought

144

back. Later, I asked Edith if she had cut them—perhaps as a joke? But she hadn't, of course. It was no joke; it was *him*. He was not one to be subtle with his symbols.

"Damn him!" I yelled to Utch. "What's he want? If he wants to stop it, why doesn't he say so? If he's suffering so goddamn much, why does he go on with it? Does he like being a martyr?"

"Please," Utch said softly. "If anyone's going to stop it, we know it's going to be him."

"He's teasing us," I said. "And he's testing Edith and me—that's it. He's so jealous that he assumes that we *can't* stop it, so he's trying to see how much we'll take. Maybe if Edith and I call it off, he'll see that nobody's going to hurt anybody else. Then he'll feel better about it and want it again."

But Utch shook her head. "No, please don't do anything," she said. "Just leave him alone, just let him have things his way."

"His way!" I screamed. "You don't like his way either—I know you don't."

"That's true," she said. "But it's better than no way at all."

"I wonder," I said. "I think Edith and I should say that we'll stop it right now, and maybe that will convince him."

"Please," Utch said. She was about to cry. "Then he *might* stop it," she said and burst into tears.

I was frightened for her. I hugged her and stroked her hair, but she went on sobbing. "Utch?" I asked. I didn't recognize my own voice. "Utch, don't you think you could stop it, if you had to? Don't you?"

She squeezed me; she pressed her face against my stomach and wriggled in my lap. "No," she whispered. "I don't think I can. I don't think I could stand it if it were over."

"Well, if we *had* to," I said, "of course you could,

145

Utch." But she said nothing and went on crying; I held her until she fell asleep. All along I'd thought that it was Edith and I who had the relationship which threatened Severin, though not Utch. All along I'd felt that Severin was disgruntled because he felt everything was unequal, that Edith and I shared too much —the implication being that he and Utch had too little. So what was this?

Weeks before, at a large and public party, I could sense that Severin was angered by the attention Utch was giving him, and by the attention Edith and I were giving each other—though we were always far more discreet than they were. Utch, a little drunk, was hanging on Severin, asking him to dance and making him uncomfortable. Much later that evening, when he came home and woke up Edith and me, he said as I was leaving, "Take care of your wife." I was irritated by the imperious tone in his voice and went home without saying a word. I thought he meant that I shouldn't let her drink so much, or that she'd confided in him about some act of neglect. But when I confronted Utch with it, she shook her head and said, "I can't imagine what he's talking about."

Now I wondered. Was he warning me of the depth of Utch's feelings for him? His vanity knew no bounds!

It was late at night when I carried Utch to bed and left her to sleep in her clothes; I knew I'd wake her if I undressed her. I called Edith. I didn't do it often, but we had a signal. I dialed, then hung up after only half a ring, waited and dialed again. If she was awake and heard the first ring, she'd be waiting to snatch the phone up immediately the next time. If the ringing persisted even for a whole tone, I'd know she was asleep or couldn't talk, and would hang up. Severin always slept through it.

When she answered now, she said, "What is it?" She sounded cross.

"I was just thinking of you."

"Well, I'm tired," she said. Had they been arguing?

"I'm worried," I confessed.

"We'll talk later," Edith said.

"Is he awake?"

"No. What is it?"

"If he wants to stop the whole thing," I said, "why doesn't he?"

There was no answer. "Edith?" I said.

"Yes?" she said, but she wasn't going to answer my question.

"Does he want to stop?" I asked. "And if he does—and, Jesus, he *acts* as if he does—then why doesn't he?"

"I've offered to stop," she told me. I knew this was true, but it always hurt me a little to hear it.

"But he doesn't take you up on the offer," I said.

"No."

"Why?"

"He must like it," she said, but even without her face in front of me, I knew when she was lying.

"He has a strange way of liking things," I said.

"He thinks I have leverage on him," she said.

"Leverage?"

"He thinks he owes me something."

"You never told me," I said. I didn't like the sound of leverage, of debts owed, at all. It seemed an important omission, and I had always believed Edith told me everything important for lovers to know.

"No, I never have told you," she admitted. By her tone, she wasn't about to begin, either.

"Don't you think I should know about this?" I asked.

"There are lots of things you believe in not telling," she said, "and I've always thought that an attractive philosophy. Severin believes you tell wives and lovers

147

everything, but you don't believe that, so why should I?"

"I tell important things," I said.

"Do you?"

"Edith—"

"Ask Utch," Edith said.

"Utch?" I said. "What does Utch know about it?"

"Severin tells everything," Edith said.

"I love you."

"Don't worry," she said. "Whatever happens, everything will be all right."

This wasn't what I wanted to hear. She seemed resigned to something I didn't know anything about.

"Goodnight," I said. She hung up.

I tried to wake Utch, but she lay in bed as hard and round and heavy as a watermelon. I felt like biting her. I kissed her all over, but she just smiled. Leverage? Another wrestling term. I didn't like its application to couples.

In the morning I asked Utch what Edith had on Severin, or what he *thought* she had on him.

"If Edith felt good about it," Utch said, "she'd have told you herself."

"But you know. I want to know too."

"It hasn't been any help to me," Utch said. "Severin wanted me to know; if he'd wanted you to know, he'd have told you. And if Edith wanted you to know, she'd tell you."

"If she didn't want me to know," I argued, "she wouldn't have told me I could find out from you."

"Well, you *can't*," Utch said. "I promised Severin I'd never tell. Go work on Edith for her version." She rolled away; I knew her position—knees drawn up, elbows in, hair hiding her face. "Look," she said; I knew what was coming. "We're playing by your rules. You're the one who says, 'If you see someone else, I

148

don't want to know. If I see someone else, you don't have to know.' Right?"

"Right," I said. I pushed my face into her hair. "And I think I know that in all these years there hasn't been anyone else for you, right?"

"Don't ask," she said. She was bluffing, I was sure. "And I think I know that there have been a few for you," she added.

"Right," I said.

"I wasn't asking."

"Well, I *am* asking, Utch."

"You're changing the rules," she said. "I think you ought to give a little advance notice when you change the rules." She backed her hips into me and drew my hand between her thighs. "One rule is, Take it when it's offered."

She was already wet; she rubbed herself against my hand. "Which one of us are you thinking of?" I asked her. Was that cruel?

But she said, "All of you," and laughed. "Two and three and four at a time," she said. I was in her mouth very quickly and she covered my ears with her thighs. Utch tasted like nutmeg, like vanilla, like an avocado; she was careful with her teeth. Was it only with me that Edith lacked control in this position? Did Severin really say to her, "You've both got quite the setup. Utch and I are supposed to keep each other occupied while you have a perfect guiltless affair. It wouldn't do to have Utch and me feeling useless and pathetic, would it?" How could he regard Utch that way? She tasted sweeter than roast lamb, like the pan juices; she had a mouth large enough for illusions.

I asked her, "Do you feel manipulated? Is *that* what Severin feels? And I *know* you never had another lover before Severin, right?"

She pushed herself firmer against me. "I never asked you about Sally Frotsch," she said, "though you never changed your mind overnight about a baby-sitter before." I was in and out of her mouth so her sentences were short. I was amazed at what she knew. "Or that Gretchen What's-her-name? An independent study in *what?*" I couldn't believe it. "And that poor divorced Mrs. Stewart. I never knew you were so talented fixing hot-water heaters." She put me neatly back in her mouth and kept me there.

Did she know about the others? Not that there were many, and they were never serious. I couldn't think of a time when it seemed likely that she'd had a lover; there'd never been a man I was suspicious of. But who could be sure? At least I knew that until me, Edith had never been involved. I reached into Utch's mouth to ask her, but she rang my ears with her thighs. What her thighs said was, "Better go ask Edith again." I resisted, but her rhythm made it hard to hold back. And Severin? Surely that moral absolutist could never have had a dalliance before he and Utch went to the mat together.

"Ask Utch," Edith had said. I was trying. When I came, her mouth turned as soft as a flower with the petals pushed back. But though I'd felt her on the edge at least twice, I knew that she hadn't come herself. "It's all right," she whispered. "I'll get mine later." From him or me? I wondered. I went to the bathroom and drank three glasses of water.

When I came back to the bedroom, she was helping herself to get there. Occasionally she got overstimulated and could only finish by herself. It was delicate because sometimes I could help her, but other times I got in the way. It was a matter of not getting too involved. I lay down beside her but didn't touch her. I watched her touching herself, her eyes shut tightly, her concentration a marvel. Sometimes if I touched her then, it would be just what she needed; other times, it would destroy it. I recognized her rhythm; I knew she was close. Her breathing skipped, then picked up; her lips made a familiar circular motion. Sometimes a word would push her over; any word would do; it was the sound of my voice which mattered. But when I looked at her squint-shut eyes and her clenched face, I suddenly knew that I had no idea which one of us she was seeing—or if it was either of us! I wanted to shout at her, "Is it him or me?" but I knew that would distract her. And then she was coming, her voice starting in her throat and reaching deeper, her whole diaphragm moving like a lion's way of roaring. She slowed her rhythm, as if drawing out each note of a groan. She was coming and nothing would stop it; I could do anything—scream, bite, even slide into her. It was downhill now, but I did nothing. I watched her face for some clue. I listened for his name—or mine, or someone else's.

But what she said wasn't even in English. *"Noch eins!"* she cried. Twisting, grinding into the bed. *"Noch eins!"*

Even I could understand it; I'd been in enough bars to know it. It's what you say when your beer's finished and you want another. *"Noch eins!"* you holler, and the waiter brings you "one more."

Utch lay relaxed with one hand still touching herself and the other to her lips. She was tasting herself, I knew; she liked herself, she had told me. In that pose she looked like Kurt Winter's drawing of Katrina Marek.

We historical novelists are frequently struck by meaningless coincidences, but I wondered if I knew Utch at all—and whether the four of us were wise to want to find out more about each other than we already knew.

I lay beside my wife who wanted one more. She looked content to me.

7

Carnival's Quarrel
with Lent

Then one night Severin took Utch to the wrestling room. Throughout dinner we had all noticed that he was not as morose as usual—not as caustic, not as consciously trying to make us feel guilty for his great unnamed *Schmerz*. When he helped Utch into her coat, he winked at Edith. I could see she was surprised. She was used to getting a martyred look from him— that son-of-a-bitch, as if he were saying, "Well, here I go, off to do my duty." He made it appear that sex with Utch was just another good husband's task, as if he were doing us all a favor.

But on this night he touched Utch a lot at dinner and spoke German quietly to her. Both Edith and I were struck by how attentive he was; I noticed Edith watched them more than usual. Was he trying to make her jealous? She'd told him repeatedly that she wasn't in the least jealous. "Of course you're not," he said. "It's a perfect setup. You've got yourself a lover of your choice, and you've placated me with a poor cow- like creature whom you've no need to be jealous of— and you know it." But Utch wasn't a "poor cow- like creature." That swinish, snobbish, self-important *cuntsman!* I've seen my bedroom after he left it; there was little evidence of condescension there.

So—one night—he was cordial, devilish, comically

lewd. He goosed Edith goodnight, and when he was helping her into her coat, he cupped Utch's breasts.

"I think he's coming around," I told Edith after they'd left. She watched their headlights run across the ceiling of the living room, but said nothing. "Don't you see what he's doing?" I persisted. "He's trying to make you jealous. He's trying to induce *his* reaction in you."

She shook her head. "He's not acting naturally," she said. "He hasn't been like himself since the whole thing began."

I tried to reassure her. "I think he's adjusting to it. He's letting himself relax more with Utch." Edith shut her eyes; she didn't believe me, but she wouldn't elaborate. "Well, anything's better than having him mooning around," I said, "waiting for one of us to ask him 'What's wrong?' so that he can say 'Nothing.'" Edith did not look convinced.

We took our love shower and went to bed, but she was restless. She wanted to call my house and ask Severin something, but she wouldn't tell me what. I argued against it. We might catch them in the middle of something, and he might think the phone call was intentionally timed—

"Bunk," Edith said; she was cross with me.

Severin came back later than usual. I'd gotten out of bed to pee and when I came back I found that he'd taken my place. He was giggling, lying in bed next to Edith with all his clothes on. I had the feeling he'd been waiting outside the door for me to get up, just so he could pull this stunt. He undressed under the covers, churning up the bed, disturbing Edith, who woke up, startled, stared at us both, shook her head and rolled over.

"Well, you're in high spirits," I said; it was awkward getting dressed in front of him, but he obviously enjoyed it.

153

"Take the old ashtray when you go, okay?" he asked.

I decided to keep his game going; I said, "I've been meaning to speak to you about the apple cores, Severin. I don't mind the crumbs in bed, really, but the apple cores and cheese rinds are a bit much."

He laughed. "Well, you won't find a mess tonight," he said. "We've been as neat as a pin." His teeth, I swear, glowed in the dark. I wanted to kiss Edith goodnight. Was she asleep? Was she angry? I blew out the candle on the dresser.

"Blah-*urf!*" Edith said, as if he'd touched her suddenly.

"Goodnight, Edith," I said in the dark. His hand reached out and caught my wrist as I passed their bed. His grip frightened me; it didn't hurt, but I knew that it could hold on all day. Maybe it was just an affectionate goodnight grasp. "Goodnight, Severin," I said. He laughed and let me go.

I was chilled in the car. I had a momentary vision, terrible and clear, of coming home and finding Utch murdered in our bed, her limbs twisted and tied into some elaborate wrestler's knot; the rest of the house would be "neat as a pin."

I shouldered open the door and found her sitting at the kitchen table, fully dressed, drinking tea and picking at the remains of an impressive-looking breakfast. It was almost dawn. She smiled when I came in; she looked sleepy but happy. "What's the matter?" she asked.

"I thought something might be the matter with *you*."

She laughed. They certainly had a bounty of giggles and chuckles tonight, I thought.

"What have you been doing?" I asked, surprised to see her dressed. When I opened the bedroom door, the bed was cleanly made, as tucked-in as at noontime, the pillows undented.

"We went to the wrestling room," Utch said. She burst out laughing and blushed. Then she told me.

Severin had parked the car at the rear of the new gym and blinked the headlights on and off, on and off. When a watchman came out of the maintenance entrance, Severin called out, "It's me, Harvey. I'm going up to the room tonight."

"Okay, Coach," the watchman said. Utch realized that this was not the first time he'd done this.

It was midnight when he led her through the dark corridors; he knew every turn. They undressed in the locker room. Only Utch shivered. They dressed in clean wrestling robes, the crimson and white ones with the ominous hood. Like monks engaged in some midnight rite, they walked through the fabulous tunnel; he kissed her; he felt her under her robe.

In the blackness of the tunnel, Severin never even brushed a wall. Utch felt his arm reach out for the door just as they reached it. Moonlight glazed the mud and cinder floor of the old cage and the skylight dome was etched with dark vines of ivy. The old board track shrieked when they walked around it. The pigeons under the eaves were disturbed and fretted like grandmothers. Somewhere a highjump bar clanged; she froze, but he kept walking smoothly, in rhythm. Severin Winter was familiar with that place at night.

Inside the wrestling room, the moonlight made the mats ripple like a blood-colored pond. Utch said she was excited, but a little frightened. He took off her robe; the mats were a perfect body temperature against her skin. They "rolled around," she said; they "loosened up." She tried some yoga positions; he showed her some stretching exercises. The thermostat kept the room warm constantly, and soon they were both sweating. Utch said she never felt so limber. Then Severin moved to the ghostly white rim of the starting circle on the center mat, his bare toes lined up behind the line.

He waited for her; he was not smiling. Utch said she felt uncertain, but she trusted him. She stood across the circle from him and breathed deeply; she let her head loll, stretching her neck. His hands were restless against his moonlit thighs. She shimmied her fingers the way Tyrone Williams did before the whistle.

"Wie gehts?" asked Severin in his tunnel voice.

"Gut," Utch said—huskily but loudly.

Now Severin heard some whistle in his head, and he started across the circle toward her—not rushing, not coming at her directly. Again she felt a little fear, but when his hand shot out and cupped the back of her neck, she came alive; she dove in under his chest and hit him at the knees, driving hard. He glided away, then floated toward her again; she swiped at his head —a mistake, she knew—and he had her. He dropped in so deeply under her that she was surprised; he hit her hard but cleanly; nothing hurt. He had her so snugly that nothing moved. The round weight of his shoulder was in her crotch, his arm snaked through her legs, the palm of his hand lay flat against her spine. She reached back to break her fall and discovered she was already down on the mat; she squirmed off her back (he let her) and bucked back into him, got up to her knees and tried to stand. He rode her closer than a coat. He was the opposite of rough; he made her feel that she had two bodies which moved in time with each other. There was no strain, but his weight wore her down. Her arms grew heavy lifting his arms; her back dipped under the weight of his chest. She let her head droop and felt his mouth on her neck. She sank back onto the mat. Their bodies glistened—even seemed phosphorescent—in the moonlight. The mat gave off heat. Their bodies slid. Bending was never easier. Slickness was everywhere, but her heels found a way to grip the mat. Over his snug shoulder she saw the moon sailing through a maze of vines. Either the pigcons were talking excitedly or she was failing to recognize her own voice; she swore she felt their wingbeat lifting her lightly off the mat. She was coming, she came, she was waiting for him; when he came, she expected the hand of an invisible referee to smack the mat hard and flat, indicating a fall. Instead there was a crushing weight, a foreign silence; the great fans for the blow-heaters whirred on, a sound too constant to be called a noise. They rolled apart, but their fingers touched. She doesn't remember who started laughing first when he got a towel and wiped up what they'd spilled on the mat. He flipped the towel back into the corner, where Utch said she imagined it reproducing towels all night. The next day, a great stack of towels would be towering there to greet the shocked wrestlers.

Their laughter caromed around the old board track; it echoed in the caverns under the swimming pool. They swam; they took a sauna; they swam again. I imagined them conquering new territory, leaving prints and spores behind like dogs.

"Christ, did you *talk?*" I asked. Utch smiled. I couldn't imagine how many eggs they'd eaten; the sink seemed full of shells.

"*Ja,* we talked a little."

"What about?"

"He kept asking me how I was: '*Wie gehts? Wie ghets?*' And I kept telling him: '*Gut! Gut!*' "

How good? I wanted to ask, as sarcastic as a stone, but Utch's placidity among the toast crusts and yolk stains made me mute.

Over our kitchen table is a print of Pieter Bruegel's *The Fight Between Carnival and Lent;* I lost myself in an image from years before. I imposed myself on Bruegel's painting. I walked into his cosmos; I shrank, put on wooden clogs, browsed through the old Netherlandish town.

"Are you all right?" Utch asked, but it was 1559; I

smelled the waffles baking (it was almost Ash Wednesday; Shrovetide customs were everywhere). I wriggled in my leggings. My codpiece itched.

In the great painting, I nudge against droves of the subservient masses, dark and cloaked. They are milling about the church, but their devotion is dull. Women are selling fish. Lent and her followers prepare for a joust—a gaunt woman drawn into battle by a nun and a monk. Astraddle a barrel, probably sour from ale, a fat representative of Carnival thrusts forward a suckling pig on a skewer; his masked revelers surround him, comic and lewd with their instruments. Everywhere, children tease or ignore them; everywhere, cripples are ignored. The inn is busier than the church. I watch a performance of the comedy, "The Dirty Bride." I imagine I am touched—tweaked under my breechclout —but nearly every woman's smile is randy. I push on, I am beseeched, I have difficulty not stepping on the maimed and deformed—the beggars, the blind, the dwarfed, humped, bent and bizarre. Bodies take up every available space. A woman with a pilgrim's emblem on her hat pleads to me: "Kind sir, regard this legless, stump-armed thing before me." Its upturned mouth is a hole.

From the twentieth century, Utch calls to me: "Are you coming to bed?"

How should I know? I'm just playing my life by ear. But in the painting fantasy I always recognize myself: I am the well-dressed one. A well-to-do burgher? Possibly a patrician? I have never identified my station exactly. I am in a black tunic, fur-lined, expensive; my hair is cut like a scholar's; a rich purse hangs at my chest, a richly bound prayer book protrudes from my pocket; my cap is soft leather. I pass a blind man, but he is more than blind; appallingly, he is without eyes! His face is unfinished—the cruel intention of the painter: where the sockets should be, pale, translucent scar tissue stretches over slight indentations. Without looking at him, I give him a coin. A numbing smile, by nuns in unison, follows me. Am I a big tipper? Do they desire something from me? I am pursued, or perhaps simply followed, by a boy or a dwarf carrying what appears to be either an easel or a piano stool. For *me*? Am I a painter? Will I sit down somewhere to play? Actually, I'm the only one in the painting who clearly isn't a peasant, the only one who has a servant. The item my servant carries looks like one of those golf seats, but it is probably my church stool. Others— peasants lugging crude country furniture—are also bringing their own seats to church; only I have a servant to carry mine. I think I must be a lawyer, or maybe the mayor.

I have never bothered to find out. I am more pleased guessing at my identity and purpose. I am moving from the church toward the inn; this seems wise. Once I made up a story of my day in the old Netherlandish square. It was to be my second historical novel, but I never followed through. I went little further than to approach my father for a loan. That was in 1963. I had finished with my higher education and was a young, available Ph.D. who did not want to be available just yet. I wanted to go to Vienna, see the original Bruegel, discover my main character's role and choose my supporting cast from among that Shrovetide crowd. The book, based on Bruegel's painting, would have been called *Carnival's Quarrel with Lent*. At one point in the novel, my characters would all come together and be doing just what they're doing in the painting. I had already selected the well-to-do man with the prayer book in his pocket to be me, to be the narrator of the book.

"I don't know how you come up with such academic and pretentious ideas," my father said.

"I'll look for a teaching job next year," I said. "I'd

just like this year off, to get a good start on the book."

"Why don't you forget the book? Wasn't the first one enough?" he asked. "I'd rather finance a vacation —something good for you." I maintained silence; I knew what he thought of historical novels. "Why don't you find out everything about the painting *before* you go all the way to Vienna to see it?" he asked. "You might find out that your leading character is the town tax collector or a Flemish fop! There's available iconography of every painting Pieter Bruegel ever made. Why don't you be *professional,* for Christ's sake, and find out what you're doing before you start doing it?"

He didn't understand; he thought that everything was a thesis project to be accepted or rejected. I'd told him a hundred times that I didn't really care about the history behind everything as much as I cared for what it provoked in me. But he was hopeless, a diehard *factualist* to the end.

He gave me the money; in the end, he always did. "Apparently it's all I have to give you that you'll take," he said. "My God, Vienna!" he added with disgust. "Why not Paris or London or Rome? Take my advice and have a good time before you start taking yourself so seriously. Next thing, you'll get married. Oh God, I can see it: some countess, in name only. Penniless, but used to the finer things. Her entire family of raving hemophiliacs wants to move from Vienna to New York but can't bear to leave the horses behind.

"Take my advice," my father said from his easy chair. "If you have to knock up anybody, knock up a peasant. They make good wives; they're the cream of womanhood." Books, magazines, notecards slid about in his lap; my mother stood surprised beside him. I thought of Bruegel's painting and of my father as he might appear in it: scrolls in both hands, sitting legless, as amputated as a beggar, his goblet of bad wine pinched between his stumps.

"You want to make a novel from a sixteenth-century painting!" my father cried. "An education clearly wasted—at least, run amok. Why don't you try the Orient? They make excellent wives."

Shellshocked, I left for Europe. I said goodbye to my mother at the airport (my father refused to drive). "Thank God you have enough money to do what you want to do," she said to me.

"Yes, I do."

"I pray you'll remember your father in happier moods."

"Yes, yes." I tried to remember some.

"Thank God for your education, despite what your father says."

"I do."

"He's not himself lately," my mother said.

"God?" I said, but I knew she meant my father.

"Be serious."

"Yes, yes."

"He reads too much. It depresses him."

"I'll send you pictures of Vienna," I promised. "The prettiest postcards I can find."

"Just tell us the good news," my mother said. "And don't try to write anything on the backs of the postcards. There's never enough room."

"Yes, yes," I said, remembering another thing that depressed my father: people who write on the backs of postcards. "Do they think they're saying anything?" he used to yell.

He gave me a note when I shook hands goodbye with him. I didn't look at it until the plane was descending on Schwechart Airport. Suddenly, in the midst of our downward pitch and roll, the stewardesses played an old recording of Strauss's "Blue Danube." The eerie, gooey music blaring from nowhere startled nearly everyone, and the stewardesses smiled at their little trick. A man beside me went into a rage.

"Aaach!" he cried to me; he knew I was an American. "I am Viennese," he told me, "and I love Vienna, but I get so *embarrassed* when they play that wretched Strauss. Why don't you break that awful record?" he hollered at the stewardesses, who went on smiling.

The man reminded me of my father, and I remembered the note. As the plane touched down, I read it.

Say hello to Schmaltz for me.
Give my regards to Kitsch City.
Love, Dear Old Dad

And the rest is history. Edith Fuller and I came to Vienna and fell in love with our tour guides. In her case, Severin elected to be her guide, but in mine Utch was more literally employed.

I met her when I went to see the Bruegels in the Kunsthistorisches Museum. I asked for the standard tour in English. I said I was especially interested in the Bruegel rooms, and that I wouldn't mind skipping the Rubens and all that. It was November, stone-gray and Baroque-cold. The tourist season was over; Vienna was turning indoors. A tour guide would be available in a moment; I was told I could have a special Bruegel tour. ("He's one of the favorites.") I felt as if I were waiting in a delicatessen for one of the more popular meats. Everything felt cheap. I remembered what my father had said and wished I had come prepared and could stride through the Bruegel rooms as an authority on the Northern Renaissance. I wondered if I had conceived of an historical novel from the point of view of a tourist. When my guide was introduced, I was struck by her Russian name—and also by the tilt of her nametag perched on her high breast.

"Fräulein Kudashvili?" I said. "Isn't that Russian?"

"Georgian," she said, "but I am an Austrian. I was adopted after the war."

"What's your first name?"

"My name is Utchka," she said. "I am not familiar with Americans.'"

"Utchka?"

"Ja, it's slang. You won't find it in the dictionary."

Nor are there words, I'm sure, for all the things Utch and I did in Vienna those first few weeks of November 1963. Are there words, for example, for the faces of Utch's exroommates in her *Studentenheim* on Krügerstrasse? Over a line-up of gleaming sinks, we three shaved each morning in the *Herrenzimmer.* Willy had a goatee which he avoided like his jugular; Heinrich had a mustache no thicker than the artery at his wrist. I watched their razors and whistled. After the third night I spent with Utch, Willy shaved off his goatee, tears in his eyes. After the fourth night, Heinrich emasculated his mustache. Then Willy emptied a can of shaving cream into his curly blond hair and leered over my shoulder, as my own razor shakily skimmed my throat. After the first week with Utch, I asked, "These fellows down the hall, the ones I meet in the men's room each morning—you know them?"

"Ja."

"Uh, what were they to you?" I asked.

And Utch would go on and on about her guardian Captain Kudashvili, about Frau Drexa Neff's steam room, about attending the memorial service for Stalin. And every morning while I shaved, Willy and Heinrich took off more hair. It was my second week in the *Studentenheim* when Willy shaved the furry ridge off his stomach and made strong strokes through the blond clump hiding his navel.

"Their demonstrations are getting worse," I told Utch. "I don't think they like me."

So Utch told me about the Benno Blum Gang—especially the man with the hole in his cheek, her last bodyguard. The next morning Heinrich loomed over my shoulder in my mirror, and shaved a quick swath through the dark forest on his chest, slashing a hidden nipple in the process. His blood turned the shaving lather pink; he dabbed it on his eyebrows and grimaced at me.

"I think I'll grow a beard," I said to Utch. "Do you like beards?"

We went to the opera and the zoo; like the opera fans, the animals kept to themselves. She showed me the little streets, the famous Prater, the parks with their neighborhood orchestras, the gardens, Kudashvili's old apartment house, the Soviet embassy. But it was November; it was more fun indoors. Her room at the *Studentenheim* was almost anti-girlish; she was twenty-five, after all, and had inherited no mementos from her mother. She had grown up with a Soviet Army officer and, more recently, with dictionaries and art history. She had grown up a little with Willy and Heinrich too, though I wouldn't know this until later. She had a narrow single bed, nearly as firm and compact as Utch herself, but she allowed me to rest my head between her breasts.

"Are you comfortable?" I kept asking her. "Are you all right?"

"Of course!" she said. "Aren't Americans ever comfortable?"

In the mornings, I still had to brush my teeth; I could not avoid the *Herrenzimmer* altogether. As my beard grew, Willy and Heinrich grew balder, and I said to Utch, "It's as if they're trying to suggest symbolically that my presence has deprived them of something."

I heard more about the man with the hole in his cheek, another symbol. Utch had compressed him into all her bodyguards, into all her years of growing up in the occupation. The man had become Benno Blum; she dreamed of him; she swore to me that even now she occasionally fantasized him; he would appear in the windows of passing cabs or in the aisles of swaying *Strassenbahns,* no doubt lurking behind a raised newspaper. Once she saw him when she was conducting a tour in the Kunsthistorisches. He appeared like a fallen angel in the bottom corner of a huge Titian, as if he'd dropped out of the painting and, wholly out of grace, was waiting to be discovered.

For two weeks Utch kept her job and I had to trail behind her tours. But it was November; the tourists were going south or home; guides were being laid off. She said she liked the job because it was nonpolitical. In winter, she was often in the service of the Soviet embassy's M. Maisky. She had been the interpreter for a ballet troop, a string ensemble, a mystic, a colonel out of uniform and several "diplomats" with an undisclosed rank and purpose. Most of them had made Russian propositions to her. She had always thought of her future as narrow. "I can either be a Communist in Vienna," she told me, "or I can be a Communist in the Soviet Union."

"Or you can come to America with me," I said.

"I don't think America's a very good place to be a Communist," Utch said.

"But why are you a Communist?"

"Why not?" she said. "Who else took care of me?"

"I'll take care of you."

"But I don't know any other Americans," she said.

Her room was full of plants; she liked the color green. We could talk and breathe hard in there all day and night and always have fresh oxygen. But it was November; some of the plants were slowly dying, too.

In the *Herrenzimmer* one morning Heinrich shaved his head. My beard had grown almost a half-inch. Heinrich's skull glinted at me. "I think Utchka and I are going to live in America," I told him. He didn't appear to understand English; he stared at me, filled his mouth with shaving cream and spat in the sink. His opinion was pretty clear. I turned back to my sink; I'd been getting ready to brush my teeth when Heinrich's shining dome distracted me. When I picked up my toothbrush, all the bristles were shaved off; Willy had done the deed while I'd been talking to Heinrich. I looked at Willy, standing at the sink next to mine; he was grinning at me, changing razor blades. He didn't appear to understand English either.

"That's funny," Utch said. "Willy and Heinrich have had about seven years of English in school. Sometimes they speak it to me."

"Fancy that," I said.

"Was ist 'fancy'?"

So we went to the gold-edged, red-brocaded office of M. Maisky in the Soviet embassy. M. Maisky looked loose-skinned and old; he gazed at Utch the way a sickly uncle lavishes fondness and bitterness on a robust niece.

"Oh Utchka, Utchka," he said. He went on and on in Russian, but she asked him to speak English so that I could understand him, too. He regarded me sadly. "You want to take her away from us, dear boy?" he asked. "Oh Utchka, Utchka, what would poor Kudashvili say? America! Unashamedly he weep would!" Maisky cried.

"He would weep unashamedly," Utch corrected.

"Yes," Maisky said, his old gray eyes aswim. "Oh Utchka, Utchka, to think of all the years you grow that I have watched! And now this . . ."

"I'm in love," Utch said.

"Yes," I said stupidly. "So am I."

"How could this happen?" Maisky wondered. His suit was a loud gray, if that's even possible; his tie, a shiny sort of cardboard, was gray too, and so were his hair, his once-white shirt, the tinted lenses of his glasses and even the color in his cheeks.

"Sir," I said, "I think it will be necessary for Utchka to say she's not a Communist anymore—or even that she never really was—so that my country won't delay her immigration. But we hope you know that this isn't personal. She has told me how you've helped her."

"Renounce us, you mean?" Maisky cried. "Oh Utchka, Utchka . . ."

"I hoped you'd understand." Utch said, unmoved by poor old Maisky. I was quite touched by him, actually.

"Utchka!" Maisky shouted. "If you go to America, there can be no God!"

"There is no God anyway," Utch said, but Maisky gazed heavenward as if he were going to summon Him. Perhaps he will call upon the Workers of the World, I thought, but he just shook his head.

Outside it was all November; Maisky regarded the weather. "I am by everything so discouraged," he said. "This weather, the price of things, East-West relations —and now this." He sighed. "By the deteriorating quality of life everywhere I am discouraged, though perhaps where you're going it will be exciting because everything deteriorates a little faster over there." He arched his stiff back and gave out a gray groan. "By the values I see young people abandoning I am discouraged. The sexual liberties taken, the terrible self-righteousness of children, the probability of more wars, the extravagance of having so many babies. I suppose you want to have babies too?"

I felt guilty for all the things discouraging Maisky, but Utch said, "Of course we'll have babies. You've just gotten old." I winced. Who was this callous young woman I wanted to take home with me? She was not sentimental; I saw her inspiring blank shock in my mother. But perhaps she would flatter my father's pessimism.

Later Utch said, "Some things about America *do* bother me."

"What?"

"The terrible poverty, the automobile accidents, the racial violence, the sexual crimes . . ."

"What?"

"Does everyone cook in—what you call it?—a barbecue pit?" she asked. I tried to imagine her vision of America: a country of one vast smoldering cookout—with rapes and police skirmishes, car crashes and starving black children on the side.

We acquired the necessary papers for Utch at the American consulate. The man we talked to was discouraged by many of the same things which were discouraging to M. Maisky, but Utch and I remained cheerful. We returned to the *Studentenheim* on Krugerstrasse, where Utch practiced her renunciation speech. When I went to the *Herrenzimmer,* Willy was shaving his eyebrows. "At this moment," I told him, "Utchka is practicing her entry into the United States."

"Go practice your own entry," he said.

Heinrich came into the *Herrenzimmer* bare-chested, stood at the mirror and aimed the shaving-cream can at himself as if it were an underarm deodorant; he filled both armpits with a lathery foam, turned away from the mirror and flapped his arms against his sides like some violent, awkward bird. Lather squirted on the walls, oozed over his ribs, dappled his shoes. "I think you better marry her before you take her anywhere," Heinrich said.

"*Ja,*" said Willy, eyebrowless, as startling as a newborn owl. "That's the only decent thing to do."

I went back to Utch's room to ask her if she agreed. We compared our philosophies on marriage. We spoke of fidelity as the only way. We considered conventional "affairs" as double deceptions, degrading to everyone involved. We regarded "arrangements" as callous—the kind of premeditation that is the opposite of genuine passion. How people could conceive of

168

such things was beyond us. We speculated on the wisdom of couples "swapping"; it hardly seemed wise. In fact, it seemed an admission of an unforgivable boredom, utterly decadent and grossly wasteful of the erotic impulse. (Philosophy is a pretty simple-minded subject when you've just fallen in love with someone.)

There were further permissions needed from and granted by the American consulate before we could get married. Since Austria is a Catholic country and I wasn't Catholic and Utch was long lapsed, the easiest thing was to be married in a nondenominational church. The American consul told us that this church was preferred by most Americans who got married in Vienna. It was called the American Church of Christ and was in a modern building; the minister was an American from Sandusky, Ohio, who said he'd been raised a Unitarian. "But it doesn't matter," he told us; he smiled a lot. He said to Utch, "They're going to love your accent in the States, honey."

The church itself was on the fourth floor and we took an elevator to it. "Some young people like to use the stairs," the minister told us. "It gives them more time to think about it. Last year one couple changed their minds on the stairs, but no one's ever changed his mind in the elevator."

"What's 'change your mind' mean?" Utch asked.

"Isn't she charming?" the minister said. "She's going to knock them over back home, you know."

The form for the American consulate required the signature of a witness—in our case, the church janitor, a Greek named Golfo who had not yet learned to write his last name. He signed the form "Golfo X."

"You should tip him," the minister told me; I gave Golfo twenty schillings. "He wants to give you a present," the minister said. "Golfo witnesses lots of our weddings and he always gives a present." Golfo gave us a spoon. It was not a silver spoon, but it had a tiny

169

colored picture of St. Stephen's Cathedral engraved on the handle. Perhaps we were to pretend that we had been married there.

The minister walked us around the block. "You should expect that you'll have your little differences," he told us. "You can even expect some pretty good unhappiness," he said. We nodded. "But I'm married myself and it's just great. She's a Viennese girl, too," he whispered to me. "I think they make the best wives in the world." I nodded. We all came to a halt suddenly because the minister stopped walking. "I can't walk around that corner," he told us. "You'll have to go on by yourselves. You're on your own now!"

"What's around the corner?" I asked him. I assumed he'd been speaking metaphorically, but he meant the actual corner of Rennweg and Metternichgasse.

"There's a pastry shop there," he said. "I'm on a diet, but I can't resist the *Haselnusstorte* if I see it in the window."

"I want a *Mokkacremetorte,*" Utch decided; she tugged me along.

"There's too much *Torte* in this city," the minister confessed, "but do you know what I miss the most?"

"What's that?"

"Hamburger," he said. "It's just not the same as back home."

"Hamburger is cooked in the barbecue pits, right?" Utch asked.

"Oh, listen to her!" our minister cried. "Oh, you have a winner there!" he told me.

On our way back to the *Studentenheim* Utch drew her breath in, dug her nails into my wrist and screamed —but the vision she thought she'd seen had disappeared down the escalator that underpasses the Opernring. She thought she'd seen the man with the hole in his cheek. We historical novelists know that the past can be vivid; it can even seem real. "But it is *so* real," Utch told me. "He actually seems to age between the times I see him; I mean, he now appears like I think he would look if he were ten years older than when the Russians left. He's grayer, he's bent a little bit over—you know."

"And the hole itself?" I asked. "Does it ever change?"

"The hole's a hole," Utch said. "It's an awful thing. You think at first it's a shadow, but it doesn't move. You think it's some kind of dirt, but it goes *in*—like a door that's open. And the eye is pulled a little toward the hole, and the cheekbone is funny on that side of his face."

"A nightmare," I said.

We discussed the frequency and occasions of the vision. Did he appear at times, such as now, when she was breaking away from her past—when, say she was freeing herself from her history—as if the vision were the psychological part of herself that was reluctant to abandon her past?

No, not necessarily; she didn't believe there was any pattern to it. She shrugged; she did not try hard to figure such things out. I suggested the man was a father-replacement. After all, he had been provided by Kudashvili for her protection; since she couldn't ignore that Kudashvili was dead, she had replaced him with the most vivid protection-symbol in her life. For years she had followed the arrests of the Blum Gang in the papers, and I told her that if she had ever seen a photograph of the man with the hole in his cheek—captured at last, or killed—she would probably have felt a great loss.

"Not me," Utch said. (Years later, she would say, "Psychology is better suited for plants.")

She did exercises like a man—sit-ups and push-ups and others. Captain Kudashvili had done them, of course. I certainly liked watching her do them.

171

"How do you say, 'We're married' in German?" I asked.

"Wir sind verheiratet," she said.

I went down the hall to the *Herrenzimmer,* but Heinrich and Willy weren't at their sinks; it was not the shaving hour. One of them had left a can of shaving cream on the glass ledge. I shook up the contents, imagining writing with lather the full length of the mirror: *WIR SIND VERHEIRATET!,* but there didn't seem to be enough left. When the man with the hole in his cheek stepped out of the crapper stall behind me, the shaving cream can went off in my hand.

He was quite old, and the hole was just as Utch had described it. I couldn't tell if it was black because it was bottomless, or because his flesh had somehow stayed scorched. That terrible raw hole drew your eyes, but you couldn't stand looking at it.

"Wir sind verheiratet," I told him, because that's what I'd been prepared to say.

"Yes, yes, I know," he said tiredly, impatient with me. He moved slowly to the row of sinks and leaned on one, staring at himself in the mirror. "So," he said after a pause, "she tells you about me—I know by how you stare."

"Yes," I said, "but she thinks you're a fantasy. So did I."

"Good, good," he said. "Just as well. The job is over. You are going to take her away, and I am too old and too poor to follow her anymore. America!" he cried out suddenly, as if something hurt him. "I wish someone is taking *me* to America!"

He looked at me. He didn't look like a gangster or hired killer or bodyguard or spy anymore; he looked like a seedy jeweler who spent nothing on his health or clothes, but only on expensive rings and necklaces for women who always left him. He would better have spent his money on an elaborate brooch to hide the hole; what he needed was a kind of cheek pin. Of course, it would be complicated to attach. I did not think he wore a gun.

"What do you think of my English?" he asked.

"Pretty good," I said.

"*Ja,* it is," he said. "She learns it, so I learn it. She walk around that old museum, I walk around it too. She go out for *Strassenbahn* rides at the worst times, I try to go after her. Most of the time she never sees me, but a few times I am careless. I get old," he said. "That is what happens."

"Why do you follow her?" I asked him. "Are you still working for the Russians?"

He spat in the sink and shook his head. "Russians and Americans are the same," he said. "I promise Kudashvili. I tell him I look after her until she goes to live with him. How do I know Kudashvili is going to be killed? I made a promise: I look after his Utchka. But no more. Who is thinking she takes twenty-five years to get married?"

"My God," I said. "You should have told her."

"She hates me," he said. "It's unfair, of course. So once I work for Benno Blum, so what? So then I work for Kudashvili. Does she think *him* an angel?"

"Come tell her now," I said. "Come let her see that you're real. But you better let me say something first, or—"

"Is you crazy?" he asked me. "It's all finished. She never see me again, why let her see me now? She thinks I'm a dream. You tell her she's not going to dream me anymore. That is the truth. You marry her, now you look after her."

"Oh, I will, I will," I told him. He seemed even more sincere than our minister. My pledge to him seemed more charged than my marriage vows. But suddenly he sagged against the sink, took a short, sick look at himself in the mirror, turned away sobbing and slumped against the row of crapper stalls, weeping softly.

"I am lying to you," he said. "All these years I hope she sees me just once without screaming and shaking like she see a monster. When she is younger, she look at my face as if it doesn't really bother her—just that she is sorry for me, that such a thing happen to me. She is a sweet little girl, I must tell you."

"What did you lie about?"

"I watch her get into that mess with those two boys. I think one time I am going to kill them both! I think another time I am going to kill *you*," he said, "but you are so *hit* by her—I can see. I am hit by her like that, too."

"You're in love with her?"

"*Ja!*" he choked, "but it's over, finished! And you better not ever say a word to her about this or I am hunting you down wherever you go to live. Even if it's Oklahoma," he said, "I am finding you and cutting your eyeballs out."

"Oklahoma?"

"Never mind!" he wept. "I take care of her. Kudash-vili himself never do it any better! He say to me once that he is going to watch her every minute until she marries the right sort of man, and I say, 'What are you going to do if she falls in love with the *wrong* sort of man?' And he say, 'Kill him, of course.' Now there is a love that is pretty strong, I must tell you."

"Love?" I said.

"*Ja!*" he shouted furiously. "What do you know about it? All you care about is fucking!"

He pulled himself together, smoothed his suit and tucked his shirt in tight. I had been wrong; I saw the gun when he straightened his tie. It had a horn handgrip, bluntly protruding from a high chest-and-shoulder holster of green leather.

"If you ever tell her about me," he said, "I am hearing it across the world. If you do not take care of her good, I am feeling my pistol cock, I am feeling it in my lungs. The way I feel," he said, "I can dream that you die and make it so."

I believed him; I think I still believe him. As he walked past me to the door, the long overhead light tried vainly to penetrate his ghastly hole.

"Goodbye," I said. "And thank you for looking after her."

I must have looked untrustworthy, because suddenly he seemed to need to convince me. He walked down the row of sinks, turning all the faucets on full, then up the row of stalls, flushing all the toilets. He flushed the long urinal too, and the *Herrenzimmer* roared with the rush of water. When he drew his gun, I thought I was about to join Benno Blum's awesome statistics.

"Put down that shaving-cream can," he ordered. I set it on the sink beside me; he took quick aim and blew it, spinning, down the line of sinks; it landed in the last one, bobbing in the filling bowl, a hole drilled neatly in its middle. What was left of the shaving cream spurted and then flowed and then dribbled from the hole. One by one, the toilets stopped flushing; one by one, he shut off the faucets in the sinks while the shaving-cream can bled on.

"Auf Wiedersehen," he said. He shut the door behind him. When I peeked out in the long hall, he was gone. No Heinrich, no Willy, no Utch to see him go.

Back in Utch's room, I hugged her, told her I would never hurt her, told her she would always be safe with me. "I'm going to live with you, yes," she said. "But I'm not going to be guarded by you." I didn't elaborate.

There remained only one last thing to do. We rented a car and I drove Utch to Eichbüchl, the town she'd been born in—twice, so to speak. She had not been there since Kudashvili had taken her away.

On the outskirts of Wiener Neustadt, where Utch's

father had been caught sabotaging Messerschmitts, we drove past the vast, untouched ruin of the Messerschmitt factory. Barbed wire circled it. Messing around in that debris was *verboten* because so many bombs had been dropped there, and not all of them had gone off. Two or three times a year one of them exploded; probably cats and squirrels and prowling dogs set them off. It was feared that if the place was not enclosed, children would play there and blow themselves up. Leveling the ruins was slow and risky work; it was not a job for bulldozers. The great shell sat by the roadside as lifeless as a gutted ship. On the far side of town the long, pocked runway lay unused—the largest landing area in Europe even now, bigger than Orly or Heathrow. It would be a simple matter to repair the runway surface, but the people of Wiener Neustadt were against it; they had heard enough planes overhead.

We found the village of Eichbüchl past the monastery at Katzelsdorf where Utch's mother had borrowed books. There were lots of new houses in Eichbüchl—weekend places, belonging to doctors and lawyers from Vienna. The peasants were still there, but like peasants everywhere throughout history, they were a part of the landscape—the background of the place. You had to look carefully to see what it was that they actually did. In Eichbüchl they grew apples, raised bees, butchered a frequent pig, an occasional calf. They made their own sausage; they grew their own vegetables; they hunted pheasant, rabbit, deer and wild boar. Everyone had a potato cellar with apples in it, and potatoes and cabbages and beets; everyone had a vineyard plot and made his own wine; everyone kept a few chickens and ate his own eggs; two people had their own cows and everyone got milk and cream from them. There was just one *Gasthof,* one place to drink, one place to eat the one dish a day on the menu. The day we stopped there, it was Serbian bean soup, black bread and wine or beer. It was midafternoon. There was what looked like a barn a little way up the one-street village road, but Utch did not want to look at it; nor did she want to ask anyone about Frau Thalhammer's little girl who'd impressed a Russian officer.

The old lady who ran the *Gasthof* did not appear to recognize her or her resemblance to her mother. She was only mildly interested that I was an American; another American had been there about eight years ago; I was not her first. In the *Gasthof,* some old men were playing cards and drinking wine. Utch looked at them quietly; I knew she was thinking about the stalwart village menfolk who had raped her mother, and I said, "Go on, introduce yourself. See what they say. Isn't that why you wanted to come?" But she said she simply didn't have any feelings anymore. The men were so old that they were not the men in her mind. Everyone who looked like the men in her mind was her own age now, and innocent then; everyone who would have been the right age then was too old and innocent now.

She picked at her soup and added, "Everyone except *that* one." She fixed her eyes on one of the cardplayers —old like all of them, yes, but rougher and stronger-looking. He was not a pitiable old man; his arms were thick and muscled, his shoulders and neck were not stringy. He had a tough, aggressive jaw and his eyes moved quickly, like a young man's. Also, from time to time, he looked with interest at Utch. I wanted to leave but Utch had to watch the man; she thought she might work up the nerve to speak to him.

The man seemed to be discomforted by the way Utch looked at him; he fidgeted in his chair as if Utch made him itchy or his legs were cramped. When he stood up I realized that the crutches hooked on the back of the long bench were his; he had no legs. When he lurched out from behind the table of cardplayers. I understood why his arms and neck and shoulders were so young. He swung his way toward our table, a stumped puppet, an amputated acrobat. He balanced on his crutches in front of us, swaying slightly, sometimes inching the tip of one crutch forward or backward to keep himself steady. The handgrips of the crutches were worn smooth, the armpit pads sewn from old bed quilts. Initials, names, etchings of faces and animals were engraved on the dark, oiled crutches —as complex and historical as the archways of some cathedrals. He smiled down at Utch.

She told me later that he asked her if he was supposed to know her; was she back for a visit? "Everyone grows up so fast," was the way he put it. She told him no, she was visiting for the first time. Oh, he had misunderstood, he said. When he left, Utch asked the lady who ran the place how he had lost his legs. The war; that was all the old lady would say. The Russians? Utch asked. The old lady admitted that it might have been on the Russian front; that was a popular place to have lost limbs.

But when we were outside the *Gasthof,* one of the old cardplayers came up to us. "Don't listen to her," he told Utch. "He lost his legs right here in the village. The Russians did it. They tortured him because he wouldn't tell them where his wife and daughters were hidden. They did it to him on a cider press. He never told them, but they found them anyway, of course."

Why such an old man would want to tell strangers such a story is beyond me, but Utch claims her translation of the dialect was accurate. We drove out of Eichbüchl before it was dark, Utch crying softly in the seat beside me. I stopped the car near the river, just to hold her and try to comfort her. The river was called the Leitha, a clear, shallow stream with a pebbled bottom—very beautiful. Utch cried for a while, until,

178

of all things, we found ourselves staring at a cow. It had lazed away from the herd down by the river, and grazed up to the roadside. It looked at us curiously. "Oh my God," Utch sobbed.

"It's okay," I said. "It's just a cow."

The cow stared at us blandly, stupidly; all history looks pretty much the same to cows.

Finally Utch laughed out loud—I suppose because she *had* to. "Goodbye, Mother," she said to the cow. Then I drove us across the wooden-plank bridge, over the Leitha, where all the other cows looked up at us as we rattled the bridge. "Goodbye, Mother!" Utch yelled as I drove faster. November was everywhere. The vineyards were plucked clean; the root vegetables were stacked inside the cellars; the cider was surely pressed.

Utch cried most of the night in her room full of plants at the *Studentenheim* and I made love to her whenever she wanted me to. For a couple of hours she was out of the room, and for a while I thought that she was taking a hot bath down the hall. But when she came back about dawn, she told me she'd been saying goodbye to Heinrich and Willy. Well, goodbyes were clearly in the wind; we were leaving the next day.

In the *Herrenzimmer* I said goodbye to Willy and Heinrich. They were polite, quiet, up to no mischief. I said I was sorry about what had happened to their shaving-cream can, but they refused to accept apologies of any kind. "You've got a good beard going," Willy told me. "Why do you want to shave?"

Then we were in the cab, heading for Schwechart Airport. A cold gray day for flying, a poor ceiling. At the airport I bought an international *Herald Tribune,* but it was a day old. It was November 22, 1963. We were waiting for an evening plane. The loudspeaker at the airport made announcements in German, French, Italian, Russian and English, but I didn't listen. In the

179

airport bar I recognized lots of other Americans. Many of them were crying. I had seen strange things in the last two days, and I had no reason to expect that the strange things would cease. Like everyone else, I watched the television. It was a video-tape replay. The reception was lousy, the narration in German. I watched a big American convertible with a woman climbing out of the back seat and onto the truck behind to help a man hop up over the rear bumper and climb into the car. It didn't make much sense.

"Where is Dallas?" Utch asked me.

"Texas," I said. "What happened in Dallas?"

"The President is dead," Utch said.

"What president?" I asked. I thought she meant the president of Dallas.

"Your President," Utch said. "You know, Herr Kennedy?"

"*John* Kennedy?"

"*Ja,* him," Utch said. "Herr Kennedy is dead. He got shot."

"In Dallas?" I asked. Somehow I couldn't believe that my President would ever even go to Dallas. I stared at Utch, who wasn't even familiar with Kennedy's name. What must she think of this place she is going to? I wondered. In Europe, of course, they kill their aristocracy all the time, but not in America.

In front of me a large, befurred woman bawled her head off. She said she was a Republican from Colorado but she had always liked Kennedy, even so. I asked her husband who had done it, and he said it was probably some dirty little bastard who didn't have a decent job. I saw that Utch was bewildered and tried to tell her how extraordinary this was, but she seemed more concerned for me.

When we changed planes later that night in Frankfurt, we found out that whoever they thought had shot Kennedy had himself just been shot by someone else

—in a police station! We saw that on television too. Utch never blinked, but most of the Americans went on crying, outraged and scared. For Utch, I suppose, it was not at all unusual; it was the way they would settle scores in Eichbüchl. Nobody had taught her to expect any other part of the world to behave differently.

When we landed in New York, some magazine had already printed the picture of Mrs. Kennedy which was to be around for months. It was a big color photograph —it was better in color because the blood really looked like blood; it showed her stunned and grieving and oblivious of her own appearance. She had always been so concerned about her looks that I think the public liked seeing her this way. It was the closest thing to seeing her naked; we were voyeurs. She wore that blood-spattered suit; her stockings were matted with the blood of the President; her face was vacant. Utch thought the photograph disgusting; it made her cry all the way to Boston. The people around us probably thought she was crying for Kennedy and the country, but she wasn't; she was reacting to the face in the photograph, that grief, that look of being so totally had that you just don't care anymore. I think that Utch was crying for Kudashvili, and for her mother, and for that terrible village she came from, which was just like any other village. I think she empathized with the vacancy on the face of the President's widow.

We took the subway to Cambridge. "It's sort of like an underground *Strassenbahn*," I explained, but Utch wasn't interested in the subway. She sat tensely, the wrinkled picture of Mrs. Kennedy in her lap. She had thrown away the magazine.

In Harvard Square we walked past a lot of Kennedy mourners. Utch stared at everything but she saw nothing. I talked about my mother and father. If the suitcases hadn't been so heavy, we would have walked the long way home to Brown Street; as it was, we took a cab. I talked on and on, but Utch said, "You shouldn't make jokes about your mother."

Mother was at the door, holding the same damn picture of Mrs. Kennedy that Utch had. It may have been one of those false sororities of identifying yourself with another person; it works out all right because you never find out that you meant wholly different things by whatever it was that united you.

"Oh, you've really gone and done it!" my mother cried to me and opened her arms to Utch.

Utch ran right to her and cried against her. My mother was surprised; it had been years since anyone had cried all over her like that. "Go see your father," Mother told me. Utch's crying appeared inconsolable. "What's her name?" Mother whispered, rocking Utch in her arms.

"Utchka," I said.

"Oh, thats a nice name," Mother crooned, rolling her eyes. "Utchka?" she said, as if she were humoring a baby. "Utchka, Utchka."

I didn't see my wife again for hours; my mother kept her hidden from my father and me. Occasionally she would appear to offer pronouncements, such as, "When I think of what happened to that poor child's mother . . ." or, "She's a remarkable young woman and I don't know what you've done to deserve her."

I sat with my father, who explained to me everything that would happen to the country in the next ten years because of Kennedy's assassination, and everything that was going to happen regardless of the assassination. The distinction confused me.

Utch was restored to me at dinner; whatever had accumulated to unbalance her appeared to be in control. She was relaxed, alluring and mischievous with my father, who said to me, "I think you got a good one. Jesus, when your mother was running in and out earlier I had the impression that you'd brought home some war waif, some woman of catastrophe." When the old bore finally stopped muttering, the house was asleep.

I looked out on the dark sidewalk. I think I must have been looking for the man with the hole in his cheek, to see if he was checking up on me. But history takes time; my marriage was new. I would not see him for a while.

The next morning my father asked, "How's that stupid Bruegel book coming?"

"Well, it never got off the ground," I admitted.

"Good for it," he said.

"I've been thinking of another one," I said. "It's about peasants." Unknown to us both at the time, this idea would become my third historical novel, my book about Andreas Hofer, the hero of the Tyrol.

"Please don't tell me about it," my father said. "I feel like flattering you; your taste in women is admirable. I think it exceeds your literary taste. *The Fight Between Carnival and Lent,* indeed!" he scoffed. "Well, it looks like Lent lost. That girl is Carnival through and through! If I ever saw a less Lenten figure, I do not recall it. Bravo, Carnival!" he cheered. The old lecher.

But he was right. Utch was a Carnival character all the way.

For example, how she slept. She did not curl tight and protect herself; she sprawled. If you wanted to cuddle against her, she didn't mind, but she herself was not one to cuddle. Edith slept like a cat—contained, a fortress, snug against you. Utch spread herself out as if she were trying to dry in the sun. When she lay on her back, she didn't seem to notice where the covers were, and she lay on her stomach like a swimmer frozen at the instant of the breaststroke kick. On her side she lay like the profile of a hurdler. In the middle of the night she would often lash an arm out and swat the bedside lamp off the night table or bash the alarm clock across the room.

I attempted to have humorous conversations with Severin about Utch's flamboyant shapes asleep. "It's obviously a kind of violent reaction," I surmised, "no doubt a rejection of being cramped inside the cow."

"I sleep that way myself," he said seriously, and that was that.

Edith and I were the snugglers; we tucked ourselves up against each other, neat and small. We often joked about Severin's and Utch's loose sprawls, trying to imagine them fitting on a bed.

"That's obviously why they went to the wrestling room," I said to Edith. "It's the biggest bed in town."

Edith sat up suddenly and turned on the light. I blinked. "What did you say?" she asked. Her voice was oddly dead. I had never seen her face look ugly before; perhaps it was the sudden, harsh light.

"He took her to the wrestling room," I said. "Last week, when we thought they were acting so strange? They went to the wrestling room." Edith shivered and hugged herself; she looked as if she was going to be sick. "I thought Severin told you everything," I said. "What's wrong? Doesn't it suit them? Can't you just see them rolling around on the mats?"

Edith swung her legs off the bed, stood up and lit a cigarette. She clutched her fists against her thighs; I had never noticed how thin she was; the veins at her wrists and on the backs of her hands stood out. "Edith?" I said. "What's wrong with them going to the wrestling room?"

"He knows what's wrong!" she wailed awfully; she seemed so unaware of her own body that I felt ashamed to be looking at her. She paced back and forth beside the bed. "How could he *do* that!" she cried. "He must have known how he'd hurt me." I

didn't understand; I got out of bed and went to her, but she made a startled, awkward move back to the bed and drew up the bedcovers to hide herself.

"Go home, please," she whispered. "Just go home. I want to be alone."

"Edith, you have to talk to me," I said. "I don't know what's wrong."

"It's where he used to take Audrey Cannon!" she screamed.

"Who? What?"

"Ask *him!*" she yelled at me. "Go on! Please get out, go home. *Please!*"

I stumbled out in the hall, dressed on the stairs, found my car keys and drove home. I heard her lock the bedroom door behind me. There is nothing so confusing as finding out that you don't know someone you thought you knew.

Severin's car was parked in my driveway. At least they weren't at the wrestling room again. As I crossed the sidewalk, I heard Utch's German song. It was her coming song, but it was going on longer than usual. Through the walls of my house, through the shut windows, I heard my wife coming. What a voyeur's treat our sidewalk was. Something was knocked over, and Severin snorted like a certain hooved species. Utch was a soprano, though I'd never known it; I had not heard her sing quite that way.

I looked down the dark street, imagining the crude conversation I could have with a sudden passer-by. "Boy, someone's really getting it in there," he'd say.

"Sure is," I'd say, and we'd listen.

"Boy! She goes on and on!" he'd say.

"Sure does."

"Some guy sure has a lively one," he'd say, the envy showing on his streetlit face. "That guy must have some wang on him."

And I'd say, "Oh that's a lot of bullshit, an old myth. It's got nothing to do with your *wang*."

And he'd listen to Utch's highest aria and say, "Oh yeah? If its not a wang making that happen, there's somebody who knows something I don't."

Finally Utch came. I heard her broken voice and saw a faint light flicker in our bedroom. No doubt their breathing had blown the candle out. I thought of the children and how scared they'd be if they ever woke up to that sound. I thought of what a long time it had been since I *had* thought of the children. And down the dark street I looked for my accuser, the man with the hole in his cheek. "I am hearing that," he'd say. How had he put it? *I am feeling my pistol cock, I am feeling it in my lungs.* It seemed like a good time for him to come save Utch. I would have hung my head if I'd seen him; I felt I had let her get into trouble though I didn't exactly know what kind.

I closed the door of my house loudly, opened the closet and rattled the coat hangers, though I had no coat to hang up. Severin surprised me; he sprang into the living room naked, ready to maul the house-breaker. "It's just me, for Christ's sake," I said. His wang, I was relieved to see, looked more or less like anyone else's. Utch came up behind him and handed him his pants; she'd already slipped into her robe. I guess they could tell something was wrong by the way I looked.

"Edith's upset," I said. "It's probably my fault. I told her that you two had gone to the wrestling room." Severin shut his eyes; Utch touched his shoulder. "Well, no one told me *not* to tell her," I said. They just stood there, Severin with his eyes shut and Utch looking at him. It was clear that they both knew what Edith was upset about. I was angry that I was the only one in the dark. "Who's Audrey Cannon?" I asked angrily. Utch took her hand from Severin's shoulder and sat down on the couch. "Come on, Severin," I said. "You used to take *her* to the wrestling room, too." I may have sounded bold but when I looked at Utch, I got scared. She was looking at me with the kind of pity which could only be knowledge. She was telling me that I didn't really want to know, but I asked anyway: "Who is Audrey Cannon?"

8

The Wrestling-Room Lover

In September the wrestlers who didn't play football or soccer ran laps at the stadium track or plodded through the leaves on the cross-country course. Later they would have plenty of laps to run on the board track in the old cage; as long as the weather stayed warm, they ran outdoors. They were not all cut in the curious mold of George James Bender.

They played basketball together—funny, stumpy-looking figures bungling the ball, missing the basket cleanly, jarring the backboard. Two of them took up handball until one of them ran into the wall. Other sports appeared to frustrate and bore them, but by October they took on many restless sports, built their wind and lost some weight—and when they'd finished exercising they'd make for the wrestling room, turn up the thermostat and "roll around."

Unless they'd been wrestling through the summer months—and only the Benders of the world did so—

Severin did not allow them to actually wrestle. It was too eary, he said; they weren't in shape. They co-operated, putting each other through moves and holds at half-speed. Occasionally they got playful and brief flurries of real combat would erupt, but for the most part, they just drilled. They also sat on the soft mats with their backs against the padded walls, letting the temperature rise to eighty-five, ninety, ninety-five, moving around just enough to keep loose.

Anyone seeing them in the wrestling room would have thought they were a parody team miming wrestlers, moving with an exaggerated gentleness antithetical to their purpose. They lumbered and rolled and carried each other around in an almost elderly fashion. Some of them, tired from running in the woods or straining against the weightlifting contraptions, actually slept. They came to this hot-house wearing double layers of sweatsuits with towels around their heads, and even as they slept they kept a sweat running. Tight against the wall and in the corners of the room where they would not accidentally be rolled on, they lay in mounds like bears.

Severin Winter, their coach and German professor, came by the wrestling room just to look in on them—like a father observing his children in some incubator phase. He did not really believe that these hibernating metabolisms represented life as he knew it; not yet. He appeared almost embarrassed for his wrestlers, as if, in the shape they were in, there was nothing he could offer them but hope and a few words to enhance their German vocabularies. (At this time of year, he *did* hold occasional German classes in the wrestling room.)

But in the pre-season before Bender was on his team—the same pre-season before he and Edith knew us—Severin was low on hope. "I knew he was low on hope," Edith told me, "because he talked a lot about going back to live in Vienna. That's a low-on-hope sign with him."

"No, no," Severin disagreed. "First it was the insomnia. It all started with the insomnia."

I could have told him that insomnia after eight years of marriage is very little trouble. If I'd known him then, I could have recommended some remedies less drastic than the one he chose. (When my typist, the History Department's secretary, was typing the manuscript of my third historical novel, I couldn't sleep and knew I wouldn't until it was done. I found that the only place I could sleep was in her tiny apartment while listening to her typing new pages. Her name was Miss Ronquist. I told Utch I was using the department's big office typewriter to type the manuscript myself, and that the only time I could use the typewriter was at night, when the office was closed. It was impossible to reach me by phone because the university switchboard shut off all calls after midnight. It took a long time to type that manuscript. Miss Ronquist was tired all the time and could manage only about five pages a night. Slow for a typist, but she found other ways to help me sleep. And when the book was finished, I went home and slept very well with Utch. Nothing was amiss; no one was upset.)

But Severin was inexperienced with insomnia, and his reaction was typically unreasonable. You can tell a lot about someone by how he deals with insomnia. My reaction—to insomnia and to life in general—is to give in. My best-trained senses are passive; my favorite word is *yield*. But Severin Winter would not yield to anything, and when he had insomnia, he fought it.

It began one night when he was lying awake beside Edith after they'd made love. She was drowsy, but he lay there like an overcharging battery. "I have nothing to do," he announced and got out of bed.

"Where are you going?" Edith asked.

"I can't sleep."

"Well, read something," Edith said. "The light doesn't bother me."

"There's nothing I want to read right now."

"Well, write something and then read *that*."

"You're the writer," he said. "One's enough."

"Why don't you wait until I fall asleep," Edith said, "and then very gently see if you can make love to me again without waking me up."

"I tried that last night."

"You *did?*" said Edith. "What happened?"

"You didn't wake up," he said. He put on his running shorts and track shoes, then stood there as if he didn't know what to do next. "I'm going to ride the bicycle around," he decided. "That will make me tired."

"It's after midnight," said Edith, "and you don't have a light on the bike."

"I can see the cars coming. Or I can hear them if they're sneaking around with their lights off."

"Why would they be doing that?" Edith asked.

"I don't know!" he shouted. "Why am I doing *this?*"

"I don't know," Edith confessed. *I'm* the writer, she thought. I should have his energy, I should be as crazy.

But I don't think either of them really understood it. When I told Severin that I sympathized with his insomnia, he told me that I understood nothing. "I'm not like you," he said. "I was simply unable to sleep. I went out to ride my bike. That's how it started."

It was a warm early fall night. He rode through the sleeping suburbs, his racing bicycle going *tzik-tzik* past all the people safely in bed. He passed only a few lighted windows and these he pedaled by slowly, but he was rarely able to see anything. He was glad he didn't have a light; it made this journey more secretive. In town he held to the sidewalks; in the country, he could hear and see the occasional cars coming and simply get off the road. That first night he rode for miles—all around the campus, out of town and back in. It was almost dawn when he unlocked the gym and carried his bike into the locker room. He slipped into a wrestling robe, went up to the wrestling room, lay down on the great warm mat and slept until the sun through the skylight woke him. He took a sauna, swam and rode home in time to bring Edith her breakfast in bed.

"It was marvelous!" he told her. "Just what I needed."

But that didn't take care of it. A few nights later he was up pacing the house again. Outside, lurking near the garden shed, his white racing bicycle glowed in the moonlight like a ghostly thin dog. "It's waiting for me," he told Edith. Soon he was out riding three or four nights a week. At first, like a lot of things with Severin, he turned his habit into an endurance feat. He tested himself for distance, striking out for the farthest towns and making it back before first light. Then he timed himself for forty-mile jaunts. But always, before dawn, he would catch an hour's deep sleep in the wrestling room.

Edith didn't object. He made love to her before setting out and was back in the house before she was awake; fresh from a sauna and a swim, he'd often wake her nicely by making love to her again. One night a week his loss of sleep would crash down on him and he'd fall into a stupor after supper and drowse about the house until the middle of the next day. But that was merely his body knowing what it needed.

To hear him tell it, nothing was wrong until the first night he rode past the old cage, after midnight, and saw the light on in the wrestling room. At first he thought it was the watchman's error, even though he saw an unfamiliar car. Severin Winter was on his way to another county and thought he'd see about the light when he visited the wrestling room later for his dawn nap. But he hadn't ridden much further when the light began to bother him and he turned back. Whoever was in the wrestling room after midnight would certainly be up to something nonathletic. He imagined the fun of catching a judo couple copulating on the mat, their stupid pajamalike costumes wildly abandoned.

He was going to go straight to the room, but then he thought he might have more authority if he dressed for the part he was about to play, so he suited up in full wrestling gear. As he made his stealthy way to the tunnel, he reminded himself to give the watchman a piece of his mind. Not even faculty had permission to be in the gym after 10 P.M., and since Severin was the only person in the Athletic Department who ever used the facilities at such odd hours, he probably felt his monopoly was threatened.

He stalked around the old board track like a predator, and at the closed door to the wrestling room, his suspicions seemed to be confirmed: music was playing in there. Severin was a Viennese with an education; he recognized Schumann's "Papillons." At least the invaders had taste, he thought. He could not conceive what lewd karate act awaited him, what weird rite was in progress within! Silently he slipped the key in the lock. Suddenly anxious, he wondered what anyone could be doing to the accompaniment of Schumann.

All alone, a small, dark woman was dancing in sleek black leotards. She was tiny, sinewy, tense; her movements as graceful and nervous as an antelope's. She did not notice him slip in and slide the door closed behind him. She was working very hard to an insistent, staccato passage. Sweat drenched her elastic body; her breathing was hard but deep. A portable tape recorder was responsible for the Schumann; it sat neatly out of the way on a stack of towels in the corner as she ranged the room in an athletic interpretation that was close to gymnastics. Severin leaned against the padded wall of the wrestling room as if his spine were sensitive to Schumann.

He knew who she was, but something wasn't right; he also knew she was *crippled*. Her name was Audrey Cannon; she was an assistant professor of Dance and Theater Arts, and something of a metaphor for everything that was ironic and unlikely. She was a former dancer who taught dance, but she was a tragically graceless, even awkward person whose career had been ruined by some mysterious accident which was never discussed. She limped—in fact, she *clomped* her way around campus. The way she was used as a metaphor was cruel; of a ridiculous plan, say, someone might joke, "That makes about as much sense as Audrey Cannon teaching me how to dance."

She was a single woman, pretty and small but so shy and self-conscious and seemingly scarred that no one knew much about her. She declined invitations to parties and went to the city every weekend; she was thought to have a lover there. Edith claimed that the best story about Audrey Cannon had been invented by Severin. It was not malicious; it was pure speculation. Severin used to say that the woman's past "shone on her face like a fresh sin"; that her accident was no doubt a wound of love; that in her mid-thirties she had lived more than any of them; that the accident probably happened on stage as she was dancing with her leading lover, and that a jealous woman in the audience (who had been taking rifle lessons for months, for just this occasion) precisely shot off her left foot so that she would never be graceful again. She was still a beautiful woman, Severin claimed, but her awkwardness made her feel ugly. "Dancers are concerned with grace," Severin said. That he thought her beautiful was a surprise to almost everyone; no one else thought she was even very attractive (Edith described her as "neurasthenic"). But Severin claimed that her beauty was in her grace, which was in her past. He claimed that he could love a person's past. We historical novelists are rarely as sentimental.

When Severin Winter saw Audrey Cannon dancing, he must have imagined that some hypnotic power had possessed her. It was no cripple who was dancing on his wrestling mats. But when the tape recording ended, he was treated to another shock: she collapsed into a neat bundle in the center of the mat, breathing hard and deep, and when she'd recovered herself enough to stand, she *limped* toward the recorder in the corner like the crippled woman she'd previously been.

She was a very private woman in the midst of a very private moment, and when she saw Severin frozen, against the padded wall she screamed. But Severin bounced out on the mat, calling, "It's all right, it's all right, it's just *me*—Severin Winter. Miss Cannon? Miss Cannon?" as she huddled, cringing on the mat, wondering, no doubt, what her dance had inspired.

They talked a long time. He'd caught her with all her defenses down and she had to tell him about her whole life; she felt as if he'd *seen* her whole life. He would never tell Edith or me what that "whole life" was. He remained faithful to that intimacy. "I think when a private person tells you everything, you're bound to each other in a way no one really planned," he said. But Edith reminded him bitterly that he'd always thought Audrey Cannon was beautiful; he'd had feelings for her even before their dramatic meeting. I never heard him deny it.

Audrey Cannon could dance on wrestling mats because they were soft; they gave under her slight weight and didn't distort her balance the way a normal surface would. It was an illusion, of course. I think she was able to dance on wrestling mats because of the trance she put herself in; it's my opinion that Severin Winter's wrestling room inspired trances. She said she had relearned dancing there. Harvey, the watchman, had made an exception for her.

"But we just *talked!*" Severin insisted. "That first night she just talked to me. We talked all night." No sauna, no swimming? "No! Just talk—"

"Which is the worst kind of infidelity," Edith said. Of course; it's what bothered Severin the most about Edith's relationship with me.

That first night, then, there was nothing more intimate than storytelling—except that she showed Severin her crippled foot, the muscular, highly arched remnant missing the ball of the foot and the three biggest toes. Jesus, what a sick story! A dancer with a maimed foot!

And he told her the history he'd imagined about her. And did he tell her he'd always thought she was beautiful? "No!" he cried. "It wasn't like that. I was just available . . . to listen." Well, it was no jealous woman who shot off her toes. Audrey Cannon had squared off her left foot years ago when mowing her lawn in a pair of sandals; she pulled a rotary-blade power mower over her own foot. It cut the first three toes off clean, chewed the next-to-last one and took all but a bit of the ball of her foot. There was so much blood she didn't know anything was missing. When they told her in the hospital she was convinced that some over-eager doctor had amputated everything too hastily.

I think I know the part of the story which must have touched Severin to his curious core. When she came home from the hospital, there was her lawnmower out in the yard where she'd left it, with a severed sandal-thong nearby. And when she looked under the lawnmower, there were her toes and the ball of her foot, looking like a halved peach. "Her old toes!" Severin said. "And do you know what? They were covered with ants."

My God, what a love story.

"But if you just talked, that first night," I said, "why didn't you tell Edith when you went home? You never said a word."

It discomforts Severin Winter to believe in his own premeditation. But he must have known that later there would be more than talk. I think he knew back when he knew nothing about her, except that to him she was beautiful.

We always know.

Still, he likes to stress the fact that he went back to riding his bicycle after that first meeting. Knowing she was in his wrestling room, riding by and seeing the light, he would ride on, reaching ever more faraway towns, pedaling furiously and not allowing himself to reach the wrestling room until his customary pre-dawn hour when Audrey Cannon would have long since limped home. No harm, was there, in his habit of looking for traces of her? Small, warm dents in the mat. Her dark hair in the sauna. A ripple not yet vanished from the surface of the swimming pool.

In the morning, bicycling home to Edith, he'd take the route by Audrey Cannon's small apartment. Just to see if her car was legally parked? To see if her window shade was properly down?

What a fool. I am familiar with the ways we talk ourselves into things. One way is by pretending we are talking ourselves out of them. Severin can tell me all day that he's not like me. ("I was falling in love with her!" he has cried. "I wasn't out to grab a quick piece and get my rocks off any old way like *you* do!") But a part of him knew what he was getting into. He can use any euphemism he likes.

The fact remains that one night he rode by the gym and couldn't keep the pedals going. He felt faint of heart at the notion of yet another faraway town. He circled the old cage, he stood in the dark trees, he crouched by the softly blowing rows of tennis nets, he scuffed up dirt on the baseball diamond, but he kept ending up back where he began. Suddenly he was tired of bicycling, of course; also—pure coincidence, of course—he had not made love to Edith before starting out that night.

And did he shower in the locker room before he slipped into a clean robe? I'll bet he did. And was it simply neglect which made him dress lightly under the robe? When he slid the door closed behind him, he saw that Audrey Cannon wasn't dancing. Schumann was playing, but she was resting. Or meditating? Or waiting for Severin Winter to make up his mind? And did he say, "Ah, um, I came to ask you if I could watch you dance?" And did Audrey Cannon stumble up to her foot and a half?

Clearly, there were positions in which her lost toes were no loss.

So much for bicycling; so much for Severin's fabled endurance. When he came home to Edith now, he wasn't up to making love to her. He had pedaled to too-faraway towns, established new time records. When he came home now, he slept until noon. How long did he think Edith would put up with it?

I don't think he saw anything clearly. Outside the wrestling room, out in the real world, he had no vision. He saw and thought and acted clearly under the moon-lit dome, within the clear circles inscribed on the wrestling mats, but he left his mind behind whenever he hung up his clothes in his locker.

Severin's feelings and worries were always as obvious as boils; he could conceal nothing. ("I'm not good at lying, if that's what you mean," he told me. "I don't have your gift.") He must have known that Edith would find out. How long did he think she'd believe that he was bicycling all night in the rain? And after Thanksgiving, it snowed. For a while she thought that Severin was just indulging his masochism—the last struggles of an over-the-hill wrestler, one more feat of foolish stamina.

What else could she have wondered when he bought the Air Force survival suit, the bright orange one-piece zippered sack designed to float in the ocean or withstand subzero weather? The pretty white bike came back bent, rusted, its vital parts scraping. Day-times, Severin would repair and oil it. He put up a map in the kitchen—supposedly of all the roads he'd traveled. That he was too tired to make love when he returned was understandable; that he was often too excited to make love before he left was slightly harder for Edith to bear. And what was that music he whistled around the house?

Though all his wrestlers were supposed to keep their nails cut, some of them were sloppy, so Edith was used to an occasional scratch on his back or shoulders. But not on his ass; those were *her* scratches or they were nobody's. And gradually she was sure that they weren't hers.

Twice she actually said to him tentatively, jokingly, in real but concealed fear: "Sometimes it's as if you have a lover."

I don't know what his reply was, but I can't imagine him responding naturally.

What finally convinced her was the way he was with the children. He took too long putting them to bed, told them extra stories, and often she found him stand-ing in their room after they'd fallen asleep, just staring at them. Once he was crying. "Aren't they beautiful?" he said. She recognized the look in his eyes: he was saying goodbye to them, but at the same time he couldn't.

The night of the great December blizzard, Edith

woke up with the shutters flapping, the storm door slamming, the wind howling under the eaves like mating cats. The trees appeared to be bent double. She doubted that a bicycle could even be held upright in such weather. It was 3 A.M. when she managed to get the car unstuck in the driveway and slithered her way down the snowy streets. She had always believed the part about the wrestling room and gym and sauna and swimming; she could smell the chlorine in his hair while she was sniffing him for other odors. She saw the light on in the wrestling room. She also recognized the parked car; on the dashboard was a pair of ballet slippers. The slippers weren't the same size as each other, but neither were Audrey Cannon's feet.

Edith sat in her car with the windshield icing over and the dark hulk of the new gym squatting over her. Ironically, she thought of how angry Severin would be with her for leaving the children alone at this hour on a night like this. She drove home. She smoked in the living room and played a record; she smoked in the bedroom, where she found Severin's ring of extra keys. There was the extra car key, the extra house key, the extra gym key, the extra wrestling room key . . .

She did not want to go there. At the same time, she imagined confronting them. She did not want to slide open the door to the wrestling room and catch them at it; on the other hand, she imagined various shocks she might give them. They would be walking around the old board track—did she always limp? would they be wearing anything?—and Edith would start toward them around the track, headed for a confrontation.

No. She lit another cigarette.

She imagined catching them in the tunnel. Surely he would lead his maimed dancer through the tunnel; he was always showing off. At mid-tunnel, by the light switch to one of the squash courts, Edith would brace herself and wait for him to walk into her. His startled hands would grope and find her face; she was sure he would recognize her bones. He might scream; then Audrey Cannon would scream, and Edith would scream too. All three of them yelling in that echoing tunnel! Then Edith would flick on the squash court light and show herself to them—blind them with herself.

Somehow her distress had woken Fiordiligi. "Where are you going?" the child asked; Edith had not realized that she looked as if she was going anywhere, but her coat was still on, and when her daughter asked, she realized she *was* going. She told Fiordiligi that she'd be back before breakfast.

All the slithery way back to the gym, Edith thought of the smell of chlorine in Severin's hair. When she saw that the light was still on in the wrestling room, she let herself into the gym and groped her way through it with her cigarette lighter. Once her lighter went out and couldn't be relit and she cried for a few, controlled minutes in what turned out to be the men's showers; they opened into her swimming pool. She found the underwater lights, flicked them on and then off again, climbed the stairs and sat in a corner of the first row of the balcony. She wondered if they swam in the dark or turned on the underwater lights.

It seemed to her that she'd been there for a long time before she heard their voices; they were coming through the showers from the sauna. She saw their silhouettes—a short, thick one and one which limped. They dove separately into the pool; there were moans from each when they surfaced, and they met near the middle of the pool. Edith was surprised that they had turned on the lights; she'd expected that Severin would prefer the dark, but she didn't know *this* Severin. They were as graceful and playful as seals. She thought with particular pain that Severin must love Audrey Cannon's smallness; how strong he must feel with her; he was a strong man anyway, but with her he was also big. For a moment she wished she could hide in the balcony; she felt so ashamed that she wanted to disappear.

Then Audrey Cannon saw her sitting in the first row of the lower balcony, and her voice pierced them all; in the sound-bouncing swimming pool it came at them in stereo. She said, "It's Edith, it must be Edith." Edith was surprised to find that she was already on her feet and coming down the stairs toward them; in a moment she was standing at the side of the pool. Lit up, bobbing in the aqua-green glowing pool, Audrey Cannon and Severin were suddenly as vulerable as creatures in an aquarium. Edith said that she wished she had secretly assembled an audience—that she had filled the entire balcony, perhaps with the wrestling team, certainly the German Department, and of course his children. "Later I wished I'd had the courage to be waiting there for them with just Fiordiligi and Dorabella," she said. "Just the three of us, perhaps with all of us in our pajamas."

"He really *was* thinking of you," Audrey Cannon told her, but Edith roamed the rim of the pool as if she were looking for hands to stamp on, as if she were a cat intent on eating every fish in the bowl. When Severin tried to get out, she shoved him back in. She was crying and shouting at him, though she doesn't remember what she said. He said nothing; he treaded water. While he held Edith's attention, Audrey Cannon slipped out of the far side of the pool and limped toward the showers. It was the last Edith ever saw of her: her narrow, bony back, her lean sprinter's legs, her small pointy breasts, her hair as dark and rich as wet chocolate. Her painful, grotesque limp jarred her sharp hips but failed to even jiggle her high, hard ass, as small as a twelve-year-old boy's.

"I could catch you, you cripple!" Edith screamed

201

after her. "I could run you down and snap your fucking bones!" But Severin hauled himself out of the pool and offered her a larger, unmoving target. She began to beat him with her fists, kick him, scratch him; she bit his shoulder and would have sunk her teeth into his throat had he not pried open her mouth with his strong fingers and held her at arm's length. She bit deeply into his thumbs; he used his thighs to shield himself from her knees, but she remembers the spurts of blood. She was wearing the Tyrolian boots he had given her, and she mashed his toes with them. She kicked and bit and hit as hard as she could until she was too tired to swing her arms anymore. She tasted the blood from his thumbs in her mouth. She looked at the tears streaming down his face—or was it simply water from the pool? She realized that she was doing what he probably most wanted from her, and that if she shoved him back in the pool, he would probably gratefully drown. She could not bear what he had done to her, but his obvious guilt sickened her even more.

On their silent way home, she told him that she would never let him see the children again, that he would have to beg her to even see a photograph of them. He sobbed. She realized how helpless he was, and the terrible power she had over him made her feel ugly; it made her be cruel, but it also made her feel that she needed to love him. "You've confused me terribly," she told him.

"I've confused *myself* terribly," he said, which enraged her. She scratched him slowly and deeply down one cheek; she drew blood; he never moved his face. She was horrified that she could do this, and even more horrified that he would let her. "The whole thing gave me an awful responsibility," she told me.

For weeks she thought of leaving him, reconsidered, tried to hurt him, tried to forgive him—and he took it all. "He was un-Severined," she said. He was completely at her mercy except when she wanted to strike back at Audrey Cannon. Then he said dumbly, "I loved her. I loved you at the same time."

What melodrama.

One night Edith said she was going to call Audrey Cannon. When she picked up the phone, Severin pushed the buttons down; Edith whacked him on the fingers with the receiver over and over, bloodied his nose and wrapped the phone cord around his neck. But you couldn't strangle Severin Winter, not that thick neck. He made no move to protect himself but he wouldn't let her make the call.

"What were you going to do?" I asked him. "If Edith hadn't caught you, where would it have ended?" Edith had saved him and he knew it. He must have wanted her to catch him all along. How strange it must have felt to him to be in a situation where he was completely passive.

Audrey Cannon moved to the city and commuted to school for her classes; she announced that she would keep her position at the university only as long as it took her to find something else. Though I'm told she occasionally appears in town, no one has ever pointed her out to me. Both Edith and Severin say they have never seen her.

A long time after Audrey Cannon last swam naked in the university pool and a short time before they met us, Edith and Severin made love together again. She beat him all over his back and pulled his hair and drummed him with her hard heels, but she loved him again. Afterward she lay crying and told him that she could never forgive him for all the time alone, lying awake, she had suffered, imagining the strength of the passion for this crippled dancer that had driven an honest man to lie.

It was after they made love again that Edith told

him she was going to pay him back. "I'm going to get a lover," she said, "and I'm going to let you know about it. I want you to be embarrassed when you make love to me wondering if I'm bored, if *he* does it better. I want you to imagine what I say that I can't say to you, and what *he* has to say that you don't know."

"Did you just think of this?" he asked.

"No," she said. "I was waiting for you to really want me again. I was waiting to see if you'd ever enjoy making love to me again."

"Of course I do."

"Yes, I could tell," she said. "But now I've got this leverage on you. I can feel it, and you can too. And I don't like having it any better than you do, so I'm going to use it and then it will be gone and I won't have it anymore."

"Everything isn't equal," Severin said.

"Listen to who's talking," she answered. Later in the night she woke up; the bed was empty. Severin Winter was crying in the kitchen. "No, I won't ever do that," she told him gently. "Come back to bed. It's all over." She hugged him. "Don't worry, I love you," she said. But later she whispered, "But I *should* do that. But I won't." Later still she said, *"Maybe* I won't. You always say you like to know what I'm thinking."

She felt they both wore fresh scar tissue which each could see on the other. "It made us self-conscious with each other," Edith told me.

And Severin told me, "So, you see, you and Utch were inevitable. We'd talked about foursomes before, and I think we were each interested in the *idea,* but we each had our doubts. I think we both thought it was better than the clandestine affair, but that it could be terrible if you didn't find the right people. Well, I never felt that you and Utch were the right people

204

for us—not for me, at least. But since there were other motives for Edith . . . do you see?"

"What are you trying to say?" I asked. Utch had gone to bed. He couldn't have said all this to her, I thought. "If you're trying to tell me that Edith is having this relationship just to pay you back, I don't believe it."

He shrugged. "Well, it's not *just* to pay me back. There are always other reasons . . . for everything."

"Edith and I are genuinely attracted to each other," I said.

"You and Edith wouldn't ever have gotten together at all," he said evenly, "if there hadn't been this other thing. I just didn't quite have the right to ask her not to."

"And what about Utch?" I asked.

"I'm fond of Utch," Severin said, "and I would never hurt her." Fond of her! That ass! Such fondness I have rarely seen.

"Do you mean that you don't have any reasons of your own to keep our relationship going?" I asked. "Do you expect me to believe that you're just doing Edith a favor?"

"I don't care what you believe," he said. "I'm simply telling you why the whole thing *began*. Things were not equal between Edith and me, do you see?"

"I see that you're jealous," I said. "Never mind how anything began. I see how you are *now*." But Severin just shook his head and said goodnight. I wondered if Edith would let him in.

He persisted in this line about equality with Edith too. He made us feel as if we had nothing to do with it! He reduced us; he implied that the responsibility was all his.

"It wasn't all *your* decision!" Edith screamed at him.

"It was all my *in*decision," he said. "And I'm never

going to be less than equal to you again. It's all right now," he told us all lightly. "I feel I'm back to being even now."

"*You* do," Edith said scornfully. "It's always *you*. And I suppose you'll never sleep with someone else again?"

"No, never," he said. He was enough of a fanatic so that you could believe him or at least believe that he believed himself.

"I don't want to talk to you about this anymore," Edith said coolly. "I refuse to listen to you."

"Don't treat him like a child," Utch said to her.

"He *is* a child," Edith said.

"Look," I said. "There are four of us, and there are four versions of all of us, and there probably always will be. It's silly for us to try to make each other agree. All of us can't be expected to see what's happened in the same way."

"There are probably five or six versions," said Edith, "or eight or nine." But Severin could not keep quiet.

"No," he said. "I see it better than any of you because I've never really been involved in it." I could have killed him for saying that with Utch right there. He *was* a child. "If I'm a child," he said, "that's okay with me."

"With you, yes!" said Edith harshly. "It's always what's okay with you—*you, you, you!*"

But this was later. That night she *did* let him in. They came by our house the next morning, after all the kids were in school. Edith would not look at me; she held Utch's hand and smiled at her. When I saw that Edith had a bruise on her face, I grabbed Severin's wrist and said, "If you were pissed off last night, you could have hit me before you left. I'm not any match for you either, but I could have offered more resistance than Edith." He looked at me as if he doubted this. A mark the color of a plum stretched

Edith's skin tight over one cheek and tugged one eye half-closed; her bruise was the size of a good novel.

"It was an accident," Edith said. "We were arguing, but I was just trying to get away from him. I twisted loose and ran into something."

"A wall," Severin muttered.

"Coffee?" Utch asked everyone.

"I don't want to stay that long," Edith said to Severin, but she sat down at the kitchen table. "We want to stop it," she told the sugar bowl.

"Well, *I* want to stop it," Severin said. "It's not good for Edith and me." Utch and I said nothing. "I'm sorry," Severin said, "but it just isn't working out. I told you I've felt—well, *pressured* to keep going on with it. It's not a pressure that Edith or either of you has put on me; it's all my own doing. I simply felt compelled to make something work which I never felt quite good about. I felt I owed it to Edith. But she really didn't make me feel that."

"Yes, she did," Utch said. I was surprised. Edith sat, her lips together.

"No, she really didn't," Severin said quietly. "It was just me. I thought it would seem more natural as it went on, but it hasn't. I thought that things between Edith and me would get better, but they haven't."

"What things?" I asked. "What things were wrong before this started?"

"This whole business made things between us worse," Severin said. Edith still said nothing. "It made me feel badly with Edith—it made me feel badly *about* her. I got to thinking that the only times I was behaving well were when I was with Utch. I haven't behaved very well with Edith, and I don't like to behave as I have. I'm very embarrassed about it."

"Nothing's your fault," Utch told him. "Nothing is anybody's fault."

"I *did* hit Edith," Severin said, "and I've never

done that before. I feel terrible about that. Before this whole thing began, I would never have lost that much control."

"That's my fault, too," Edith said. "He *had* to hit me."

"But I shouldn't have."

"Maybe you should have," Utch said. What in hell was she saying, anyway!

"Anyway," Severin said, "it's over. That's the best thing."

"Just like that?" I said.

"Yes, just like that," Edith said, looking directly at me. "That *is* the best thing."

"May I talk to Edith alone?" I asked Severin.

"Ask Edith."

"Later," Edith told me. And again I felt that the more we knew each other, the less we actually knew. "I want to talk to Utch now," Edith said.

"*Ja,* get out," Utch said to us. "Go sit outside, go take a trip around the block."

"Go to a movie," Edith suggested. "A double feature," she added. Severin stared at his hands.

Then Utch screamed some German at Severin; he mumbled, "*Es tut mir leid.*" But Utch went on and on. I took Severin's arm and made him stand up while Edith steered Utch toward our bedroom. After a while, we heard both of them crying in there. The language they were speaking was stranger than English or German.

Severin went and stood outside our bedroom door. "Utch?" he called. "It's better not to see each other for a while. Then it gets a lot easier."

It was Edith who opened the door. "Forget what you're thinking," she snapped at him. "I wish you'd stop trying to make this like the Ullmans. It's not the same." She slammed the door.

"Who are the Ullmans?" I asked Severin, but he pushed past me and went outside.

"I have to go to the wrestling room," he told me. "I don't suppose you want to come along." It didn't sound like an invitation. I was struck that at least Edith and Utch could talk to each other.

"Who were the fucking Ullmans?" I yelled at him.

"The fucking who?" he asked.

"Severin," I said. "Suppose what's wrong between you and Edith doesn't stop; suppose it's not us who are making things bad, but just you or something else. Then what?"

"Nothing's wrong between Edith and me," he said walking away; he was leaving the car for Edith.

"I can't stay here," I said. "They want to be alone. I'll come with you."

"Suit yourself."

For a short-legged, stumplike man, he walked fast. I was winded halfway to the gym; I thought of his lungs sucking up more than his share of air—air that other people could use.

"What did you hit her with?" I asked. The mauve mark on Edith's face was almost a rectangle, too big to be covered by a fist. I didn't think that Severin Winter would slap anyone with his open hand.

"It was just something lying around the bedroom," he said.

"What?"

"A book," he said. Of course; leave it to him to hit a writer with what hurts.

"*What* book?" I asked.

"Any old book," he said. "I just used it. I didn't stop to read it."

We were near the gym; I had no intention of actually going in there. Coming toward us were two of Severin's wrestlers. I recognized their hipless, assless, bowlegged walk, and their shoulders crouched awkwardly alongside their ears like yokes on oxen.

"Did the Ullmans come before or after Audrey Cannon?" I asked.

"You have no right to anything that's not freely offered," he said to me.

"For God's sake, Severin. This is going to upset Edith and Utch terribly!"

"If we keep on with it, it could upset them more," he said.

The wrestlers merged with us. One of them—that dolt Bender—gave Severin Winter an apish blow on the back, a clout with his cat-quick paw. The grinning one with the baboon arms was Iacovelli. He was in my Introduction to European History course, and I'd once had to tell him that the Dordogne was a river in France; Iacovelli had thought it was the name of a king. Dordogne the First, I suppose.

"Hi, Coach," Iacovelli said. "Hello, Doctor." He was one of those who thought a Ph.D. was rarer than admiralty, but it's odd that he didn't seem to know that Severin Winter had one too.

"I'll call you," I told Severin.

"Ja," he said. Watching him heading for the gym, flanked by his wrestlers, I couldn't resist yelling, "I know whose book it was. It was *mine!*" I had just given Edith a copy of my first historical novel, the one about the French village being wiped out by plague; it was long out of print and the only one of mine that Edith hadn't read. We'd spoken of our early styles, and I'd wanted her to see my first effort. What a book to hit someone with! Over four-hundred pages, a heavy weapon. (Later he would say to Edith, "The presumptuousness of that bastard to think that it was *his* book. As if a 118-pound novel could leave any marks on a person at all, not to mention a bruise." But it *was* my book; it *must* have been! No doubt they

210

had been arguing about me when it happened, and what better symbol could he have found for his frustration?)

But Severin ignored me. He never turned or broke his bearish gait. Only Bender looked back at me, as if he thought I might have been calling to him. His machine-steady gaze was as lifeless as the building he was entering: gray, concrete, steel and glass—its insides of chlorinated water, disinfected mats, ice frozen by cooling pipes, ointments and powders which dealt harshly with fungi of the feet and crotch, and countless bouncing balls pumped full of air. That was Severin Winter's world, and I knew I did not belong in it.

So then it was over. Severin retreated to his wrestling room. I went to the library and waited until I thought Edith and Utch had talked all they needed to. But it was hard to imagine them talking at all.

When I went home, the kids were playing in the kitchen and Utch was cooking. She was making a complicated meal, though I doubted she felt like celebrating.

"Get out of here and find something to do," I told the kids. "Don't get in your mother's way." But Utch said she wanted them around; she liked the feeling that she was in a busy place. I sliced radishes, and Jack read to us from an old edition of *Europe on Five Dollars a Day*. He read all the parts about what to do with children in various cities, then told us which city he wanted to visit. Bart ate radishes as fast as I could cut them up; occasionally, he spat one at Jack.

All through dinner, Utch chattered with Jack and Bart pushed his uncaten food in my direction. I remembered that it had been a long time since we'd eaten with the children. After dinner, while Jack was promising to fix Bart a bath without pushing his head under, Utch said, "When the children go to bed, I think I'm going to die. We've got to keep them with us. Can't we all go to a movie?"

I took a bath with Bart and Jack; their small bodies were as sleek as wet puppies. Afterward the first pair of underpants I tried to put on was the pair Severin had redesigned with a razor. As I threw them away I wondered why Utch had kept them. Now she was splashing in the tub with Bart and Jack; it seemed she would never stop talking to them. The second pair of underpants I tried on also had the crotch slit through, and so did the third and the fourth. *All* my underpants were uncrotched with a single slash.

I slipped on my old corduroys without underwear and we went to the movies. It was one of those films without sex and full of simple violence, and therefore all right to take your children to. Someone named Robert is a kind of rookie in the wilderness; he meets various savages, white, Indian and animal, all of whom teach him how to survive. The film is about survival, I guess. Robert learns how to make mittens out of skinned squirrels; he wears rabbits on his feet; he keeps his head warm with an Indian head of hair. He meets lots of weaker people who are crazy or cowardly or about to become one or the other; they haven't learned all of Mother Nature's harsh little tricks as well as he has. Robert enters the wilderness blond, clean-shaven, boyish and wearing clothes that fit him. He emerges bearded, wrinkled and bundled in animal hides, looking like the animal which grew the hides and somehow shrank inside its own skin. He learns not to be afraid and not to feel anything. Apparently a part of survival is getting over things. By the end of the movie, Robert has adapted to the wilderness and is very good at getting over, for example, the rape, mutilation and murder of his wife and children.

The film was absolutely humorless about this crap, which the audience took very seriously—all except

Utch. She knew a little bit about survival, and she started laughing at the very first scene of meaningful slaughter.

Jack whispered, "Why is that funny?"

"Because it's not truthful," Utch told him.

Pretty soon Jack started laughing every time his mother did, and Bart, who was used to cartoons, laughed with them. I felt badly, but I laughed more than any of them. We were at odds with the audience; a certain hostility came through to us, particularly during the films funniest scene. I had to take Bart to the bathroom and so missed some of it but in the part I saw, Robert is about to open a door to an old woodshed. This takes a long time so that the audience can absorb the increasing tension. We know that behind the woodshed door is a crazed mother who's been hiding there for days with her dead children all stashed around her like groceries. There's been an Indian massacre and the mother hides in the woodshed and kills everyone who peeks in the door, then drags the bodies inside with her to wait for more Indians. It's unclear whether she or the Indians have massacred her children. Robert is about to open that terrible door, and we're supposed to hope that by this time he has learned enough from Mother Nature to be smart about it. Of course, it would be smartest not to open the door at all, but it appears he is going to.

Some rows in front of us several young girls in the theater tried to warn Robert. He puts his squirrel-skinned hand on the latch. "No, no," the young girl's moaned. But from some other part of the house, another voice hollered, "Go on! Open it, you simple son-of-a-bitch!" Utch and the kids burst out laughing, and so did I, though I recognized that crazy voice. It was Severin Winter, of course.

When the movie was over, I hurried Utch and the kids to the car. It was not that I felt we had to avoid the Winters at that moment; it was just that it was raining. "Stop pulling me," Utch said. "I like the rain." But we were in our car and driving away when they came out with their children.

"I see Fiordiligi!" Jack said. "And Dorabelle!" Bart shrieked.

"Open it!" Utch shouted, but her laughter chilled me.

When the kids were in bed, Utch said, "I'm not going to break down."

"Damn them, anyway," I said. "They've always called all the shots."

"Oh, now it's 'them,' is it?" Utch asked. Then she took my hand and said, "No, we'll all still be friends, won't we?"

"After a while," I said. "Sure."

"I know it's going to be bad at first," she said, "but it will be comfortable to see each other again without the sex, won't it?"

"I hope so," I said. "We can just go back to being friends."

"You simple son-of-a-bitch," she said; then she shook her head and cried for a while. I held her. "We never *were* friends," she said. "We were just lovers, so there's nothing to go back to being." I thought of shaggy Robert opening doors around the world, tromping around in the bodies of dead creatures, his face gradually simplifying into an expression of stupid endurance. And this pointless, gory journey of always one more unwanted discovery was called survival and thought to be heroic.

"I don't even know if we were lovers," Utch bawled.

"Of course you were," I told her.

"I think we were just *fuckers!*" she cried.

"No, no. Give it time. Time is what matters."

"You think history actually means something,"

Utch said to me bitterly. I wondered who had told her that it didn't. "Don't touch me," she said. Then she softened. "I mean, not for a while."

I undressed. "I need some new underwear," I said, but she was silent. "Why did you do it?" I asked her gently; I wasn't forcing her.

"How could you have let this happen to me?" Utch said; her face was frightened, hurt, accusing. "You weren't looking out for me!" she cried. "You weren't even thinking about me!"

I wondered if Edith and Severin were shouting tonight.

"You're even thinking of her right now," Utch said. (The poor, dangerous woman in the woodshed with her murdered children strewn around her had grinned at Robert and told him, "It's a good thing I'm so smart. I knew just where to hide the children so that no one would hurt them.") Utch grinned at me with an unsettling expression and snatched the razored underpants from my hand. "I did it," she said, and she put them on her head like a hat.

"I know you did," I said; I was trying to be comforting, but she kept shaking her head at me as if I didn't understand. Then I understood that she had done that *first* pair, too—the pair I thought Severin had slashed. She saw the change in my face and nodded vigorously. "Yes, yes," she said brightly. "That's right, it was *me!*" She seemed delighted by this revelation until she started to cry again. "I love him," she sobbed. "Don't you see what terrible trouble we're in?"

"It'll be all right," I said. She laughed for a while, then cried herself to sleep.

Then Jack had a nightmare and woke up whimpering. He was remembering a dirty trick from the movie. A lot of tough old savages are reminiscing about the meanest things they've ever seen, and one of

215

them tells the story of how he saw someone's belly slit open just a little bit—enough to pull out a part of the intestines and wave this offal in front of a dog who tried to bolt it down whole, then ran off with it, unraveling the person's insides in a nasty fashion. But I told my delicate boy that the world wasn't like this at all. He wouldn't have that nightmare again, I said. "It'll be all right," I said. Ah, the lies we fall asleep to.

Bart slept through Jack's dream like a turtle in its shell. Utch was asleep too. I waited for Jack to go back to sleep; I waited until I knew Severin would be asleep too. I was wide-awake and I was sure that Edith was too. I smoked about my quiet house; I could see Edith smoking from room to room. I had to speak to her, to hear her voice. When I thought I had waited long enough, I tried our signal of letting the phone ring half a tone, then hanging up. I waited. I could see her moving to the phone, lighting a fresh cigarette; she would curl a long strand of hair behind her ear. I could feel the way her hand would lie on the receiver, waiting for my second call. Her wrist was so thin, so angular. I dialed again. As usual, the phone didn't even ring once all the way through before the receiver was snatched up.

"Edith is asleep," said Severin Winter.

9

The Runner-Up
Syndrome

When it was over and before all of it had sunk in, feelings were raw in the supermarket, distant in parking lots, awkward whenever the four of us encountered each other. Because, of course, such meetings were out of context with what we'd once been together. And the children still wanted to play with each other. We could manage as much as a week without encounters; then, when we did meet, the shock of how we'd grown apart made the occasion more unsettling.

In a brief exchange with Edith—absurdly, we were in line at different tellers' windows—I said, "Utch and I hope we can see you again soon. I know it's going to be hard at first."

"Not for me," she said brightly.

"Oh."

"Forget it," said Edith. "That's what I'm doing."

But she didn't mean it. She was clearly insulating herself from her real feelings for me; she had to, no doubt, because of Severin's nonstop, needling ways.

Utch's silence bore into me like a wound. She said that when she ran into Severin, he would not look her in the eye. "I disgust him," she said and when I tried to hold her, she pulled away.

At first her insomnia only made her go to bed later

and later. She slept in her underwear. Then she began getting up in the night to take walks.

"Since when were you ever a walker?" I asked, but she just shrugged; she didn't want to tell me where she went. I know insomnia had to be handled delicately.

Months earlier we had planned to make the weekend of the national wrestling championships a lovers' interlude. Edith and I would stay with all the children while Utch followed George James Bender and Severin to his vicarious victory in Stillwater, Oklahoma. We all agreed that Bender would be so far gone in his tunnel trance that he wouldn't notice the strange but familiar woman who was one door down the motel hall from Severin's room. Edith and I were frequently seen together, but with the children around us all day, we would not be, as Severin continually feared, linked together in an overtly public manner. He had finally agreed: Utch would be his fan while he nursed Bender, match by match, through the nationals, and while Bender slept the dead sleep of gladiators, Severin and Utch could shock the motel's bed-vibrator.

Ah, Stillwater, Oklahoma—a Paris looming in Utch's future. But it never came off.

"It was a Paris in your future too," Utch said. "You were looking forward to all that time here with Edith, waking up with her in the morning, sneaking feels all day, resting up for another night. Don't say it was just me who was looking forward to it."

"Of course not," I said. "We were *all* looking forward to it."

"*He* wasn't," Utch said. "I think Severin was dreading it."

I tried to comfort her, but she would just go out walking again. The whole time Severin was with Bender in Stillwater, she walked. And one evening while he was away she walked to the Winters' house to see Edith. I can't imagine why. She found the Winters' house full of the wrestling team and Coke and cheeseburgers and potato chips. Iacovelli and Tyrone Williams and all of Severin's other non-champion wrestlers were baby-sitting; Edith had gone to Stillwater with Severin and George James Bender.

Edith in Stillwater? A swan in the cornfield!

I have never been in Stillwater, Oklahoma, the home of the Oklahoma State Cowboys, a traditional wrestling power. What could it be like? A flat land, trampled by cattle, cowboys and wrestlers, and seeping oil? Even its name sends a shudder through me: *Stillwater*. I see an oasis, a swampish lagoon, a string of air-conditioned motels, thirsty wrestlers on horseback malingering around the one saloon. The big drink of the town is *Tang*. Poor Edith!

"Why did she go, if she didn't want to?" Utch asked.

"Because he didn't dare leave her alone here. He didn't trust her," I said.

"You don't know that," Utch said.

"He's never trusted her," I said. "Throughout this whole thing."

We could only follow what was going on in the papers, and wrestling is not popular with *The New York Times*. On Thursday there was only this:

Iowa State Favored for Team Mat Title

STILLWATER, Okla. (AP)—Host Oklahoma State, third-ranked, hopes to upset defending national champion Iowa State in the national collegiate wrestling tournament beginning here today. Oregon State's second-ranked Beavers and the fourth-ranked University of Oklahoma Sooners are also contenders. Iowa State has three returning individual champions, but one of them—158-pounder Willard Buzzard

(23–0–1)— is not picked to repeat. Though the defending champion, Buzzard is seeded second behind Eastern collegiate champion George James Bender (20–0–0)—the only wrestler east of the Mississippi favored to win a championship title. Bender, voted outstanding wrestler in the Eastern tournament at Annapolis two weeks ago, has pinned eighteen out of his last twenty opponents . . .

No information on what brought Edith to Stillwater. No itinerary of her day. Did she attend the Historical Museum of the City of Stillwater? Did she see the prize portrait of the largest Hereford ever slaughtered in Oklahoma?

On Friday *The New York Times* offered more bare statistics. In the 158-pound class, Willard Buzzard of Iowa State advanced through his preliminary matches with a fall over a Yale boy in 0:55 of the first period and a decision over Colorado State, 15–7. Lehigh's Mike Warnick, runner-up to Bender in the Easterns, advanced by upsetting the Big Ten champion from Minnesota (4–4, 5–4 in overtime) and by pinning the cadet from Army in 1:36 of the second period. Oregon State's Hiroshi Matsumoto flattened Wyoming's Curt Strode in 1:12 of the first and mauled an imported Iranian from UCLA, 11–1. And George James Bender—treading water—advanced with two falls, pinning Portland State's Akira Shinjo in 1:13 of the third, and Les McCurtain, the hope of Oklahoma, in 1:09 of the first. These four also passed untouched through the quarterfinals.

Et cetera. It's a wonder to me that they all weren't *bored* into a pinning position. I could just see Severin whispering over his fruit cup to Bender—the table strewn with match results, brackets of the possible outcomes, notes about what Matsumoto is looking for when he sets up. And Bender, a mat burn raw on his chin and one eye weeping from a poke by Portland State, would gobble his shrimp cocktail, the tiny fork foreign to his stubby fingers, his knuckles swollen and taped. "Watch how much of that crap you eat," Severin would be saying. Between them, Edith would pick at her lobster bisque. "You should know better than to order lobster in Oklahoma, Edith," Severin would tell her.

What could be going on? Utch went to see how the wrestlers were doing with the Winters' children. I knew she was hurt that we had not been asked to look after them.

"The children seem happy," she reported when she returned. "They're certainly eating a lot of hamburg." Probably raw, I thought, but Utch went on. "The team says that if Bender beats the Japanese in the semis, he'll go all the way. They say he used to beat Buzzard every day in practice back at Iowa State."

"Do you think I care?" I asked her. She sulked; I knew she was wishing she was there. "He should have taken you anyway," I said to her. "You could have kept to your separate rooms, after all. But he's so paranoid that he can't believe a thing is over even when he's called it off himself. My God, did he think I'd be sneaking down to his house to rape his wife every night he was gone?"

"If I was there," Utch said, "I'd sneak into his motel room and rape *him*." I was shocked; I couldn't say anything. She took another walk. I pictured Edith out walking in Stillwater—the cowboys drunk, the cattle staring at her, the coyotes ululant.

In Saturday's *New York Times* the 158-pound class had narrowed down predictably. Iowa State's Willard Buzzard had a hard time with Lehigh's Mike Warnick, but survived the semifinal round to beat Warnick by two points, 12–10. (Bender had pinned Warnick in their Eastern final match; by comparative scores, Buz-

221

zard appeared to be in trouble.) Bender, coasting 9–0 in the third period on his semifinal with Oregon State's Hiroshi Matsumoto, separated Matsumoto's shoulder and advanced to the finals by forfeit—as good as a fall. "Well, that's that," Utch said. "The Jap was supposed to be the only one who could give him any trouble. He's got it wrapped up."

" 'Wrapped up!' " I said. I hated that goddamn language. "I hope he gets stuck in an elevator and misses the match. I hope he eats a diseased steer and throws the whole thing. I hope he's seduced by a cowgirl and wilts under pressure. I'm going to set up a shrine to Willard Buzzard and pray to it all night. I hope Bender loses himself in a genetics problem—preferably his own. I hope Severin is so humiliated that he never dares to coach anyone again!"

"Stop it," Utch said. "Please stop it. Do we have to hate them now? Do we?"

On Sunday *The New York Times* said nothing. The finals took place after 8 P.M., Oklahoma time, and the results would be in Monday's paper.

"I could call the boys over at the Winters'," Utch said. "I'm sure they'd know."

"Jesus, 'the boys,' " I said. "Go ahead, if you must."

"Well, I can wait, of course," Utch said, and she did.

I ran out of cigarettes a little after midnight and had to go to Mama Paduzzi's Pizza Parlour. It was the only place in town open after midnight and was always full of students, or worse. I met Edith at the cigarette machine. Severin hated smoking so violently that he now refused to buy them for her if she ran out. Edith disliked the pizza place so much that she actually looked pleased to see me. Two seedy youths were hanging around the machine, eyeing her.

"You're back," I said.

"It's not that far."

"I thought it was another country," I said.

"Oh, it *is*." We laughed, and then she seemed to remember when we had last laughed together and looked away. "I left my headlights on," she said. Outside, she got into the car, turned the lights out and sat staring at the wheel. "I can't see you at all, under any circumstances," she said. "It just doesn't work out very well."

"If Severin would just *talk* to Utch sometime," I said. "She's pretty bad, she is really, well . . . *taken* with him, you know."

"I know that," she said, exasperated. "Didn't *you* know that? Severin *can't* talk to her. I don't think he can stand her. He doesn't want to hurt her any more than he already has."

"He doesn't have any right to hate us," I said.

"It's me he hates," she said. I touched her arm, but she pulled away. "Go look after Utch," she said. "I'm all right, I'm not suffering. I'm not in love with you."

"You didn't have to say that," I said.

She started the car; I saw that she was crying. But for whom?

When I got home, Utch had left a note; she had gone to see Edith. But I knew she hadn't found Edith at home. At 4 A.M. I went to the Winters' house to get her. She was curled up on their living room couch and wouldn't come home with me. Severin had gone to bed.

"He went to bed hours ago," Edith told me, "and I'm about to go to bed myself." She said Utch could stay on the couch if she wanted to, and she did. I left her after about an hour; it was clear she wasn't going to talk to me.

It was the university paper that I saw on Monday; I never did see how *The New York Times* wrote it up. But the school paper had more local information.

Bender Upset in Finals; Winter to Resign

An interesting headline, I thought, and it wouldn't have made *The New York Times*. I couldn't believe it. I doubted that Iowa State's Willard Buzzard could, either. Bender was quoted as saying, "I just didn't get up for it." Willard Buzzard—a former teammate of Bender's at Iowa State—said he sensed that Bender wasn't ready for him from the very first takedown; Bender looked listless. Remembering their old practices together, Buzzard said, "George used to push me around pretty good, and I never forgot it. I owed him this one." Buzzard wrestled a very physical, aggressive match. "I just never rose to the occasion," said George James Bender. Coach Severin Winter agreed. "George wasn't himself. I think he shot his wad the night before." Winter was referring to Bender's semifinal victory over Oregon State's Hiroshi Matsumoto. Coach Winter announced to the reporters in Stillwater his plans to retire. Back on campus, he denied that Bender's loss in the finals had any influence on his decision. "I've been thinking about stepping down for some time. I'd like to spend more time with my wife and children, and continue my studies for the German Department." Asked if he would stay with the team until a new coach could be found, Winter said he would. "I hope to still get up to the wrestling room from time to time," Winter said, "just to roll around." Bender had nothing but praise for Severin Winter's coaching. "He was instrumental in getting me to the finals," Bender said. "He got me there, and it was up to me to take it from there. I'm sorry I let him down." Coach Winter shook his head and smiled when asked if he thought Bender had let him down. "We only let ourselves down," Winter said. "We should try to minimize all this responsibility we feel we owe other people."

A curious remark to find in a sports column.

"Incredible!" I said to Utch. "What was the score? The stupid paper doesn't even give the score."

"Buzzard was leading twelve to five in the last period when he pinned Bender."

"A slaughter," I said. "I don't believe it. Bender must have been sick."

I could see the look of bored superiority that Utch suddenly showed before she turned her face away. She was afraid I had seen it, and I had. "What is it?" I asked her. "What happened out there?"

"Bender didn't get up for it," Utch said, her back still turned to me. "Just what the paper says—he shot his wad the night before."

" 'Shot his wad!' " That disgusting sports talk!

" 'I just never rose to the occasion,' " Utch said, quoting Bender, but suddenly she burst out laughing. I did not like the tone of her laughter; harsh and derisive, it was not her tone.

"You talked with Edith," I said. "What happened?"

"You'd have liked to talk with her, wouldn't you?" Utch said.

"Never mind," I said. "What did she say?"

There's nothing vengeful in Utch, and I was surprised to see her face so suddenly determined to pay me back. For what? "Edith was angry that Severin made her come along," she said.

"See?" I said. "What did I tell you?"

"Shut up," she said; her temper was quicker than I'd ever seen it. "If you want to hear the story, shut up."

"Okay."

"You're going to love this story," Utch said; there was a meannesss in her voice I'd never heard. "It's just your kind of story."

"Just tell it, Utch."

"Edith was angry that he didn't trust her, angry that he wouldn't leave her here for three nights and three

225

days because of you. He said he trusted Edith but not you; that's why he wanted her to go."

"What's the difference?" I said. "If he *really* trusted her, it wouldn't matter whether he trusted me or not, right?"

"Shut up," Utch said. She was wound up and seemed on the verge of hysteria. "Edith resented what Severin had made of her independence—or so she said," Utch went on. " 'I wanted to teach him that he couldn't cram his life down my throat and not leave me free to live mine,' was the way she put it. 'Within reason, of course; I'd always accepted the limits that he set up,' she told me. 'Therefore, when he said the whole thing had to stop, we all stopped.' That's what she went on and on about," Utch said.

"Go on."

"Well, he wouldn't even let her do what she wanted when they got to Stillwater," Utch said. "She wanted to fly to Denver for a day and a night; she'd never been to Denver. But Severin made her stay. Finally, she just wanted to amuse herself in her own way in Stillwater, instead of going to the wrestling every day."

"And he wouldn't let her?"

"Edith says he wouldn't."

"Jesus."

"So, Utch said, "she decided to show him that if he wouldn't trust her, she wouldn't be trustworthy. She hit him close to home."

" 'Close to home!' " I yelled. "Would you stop that language, those horrible sportscaster phrases!"

"Bender was exhausted after Friday's semifinal," Utch said. "Severin told Edith to drive Bender back to the motel; Severin said he'd meet her there after the rest of the semis were over. They had a rented car, and Bender doesn't know how to drive."

"He doesn't know how to drive?"

"He doesn't know how to do a lot, apparently," Utch said.

I stared at her. "Oh, no," I said. "Oh, no you don't. You're lying."

"I haven't told you yet," she said.

"You're lying anyway!"

"Then Edith was lying," Utch said. "She took Bender back to the motel."

"No."

"And she put him to bed."

"No, no . . ."

"Apparently," Utch said, her voice—mocking—imitating Edith's voice, "he couldn't get up for it, he never rose to the occasion."

"I don't believe any of this," I said. "Edith *seduced* Bender? It couldn't have happened!"

"Maybe she told him it was the coach's orders," Utch said. "Maybe she said it would relax him. Anyway, she told me he was unable to."

"She's lying," I said.

"Maybe she is," Utch said. "I don't know."

"Yes, you do," I said. "Go on."

"So Severin came back to the motel and found them together."

"I don't believe—"

"And Bender was very hangdog about the whole thing."

" 'Hangdog!' " I cried. "Good Christ . . ."

"I mean, he'd been unable to do it with Edith, and he'd let his coach down . . . I suppose that's what he thought."

"Bullshit!" I screamed.

"And the next night just before the match, Severin told Bender, 'I hope you get your ass knocked off.' And Severin sat in the coach's chair and watched the match in an absolutely emotionless way. So Bender lost, of course."

"And I suppose Edith sat in the balcony and waved a pennant and cheered her heart out!" I hollered. "Oh, come on!"

"Do you know what Edith said to Severin?" Utch asked. "She said, '*Now* we're even, if you still think being even matters.'"

"And I suppose Severin decided that he'd had enough of wrestling and resigned?"

"Right."

"Wrong," I said. "Edith's a lousy storyteller, or *you* are."

"Edith thinks you're a lousy writer," Utch said. "She doesn't believe you can teach her a thing."

"Did she say that?" I asked. But Utch just put her head down and sighed, and I knew that was all I was going to hear.

"Severin told you that," I said. "Edith wouldn't say that about me." But when Utch lifted her face, she was crying.

"Don't you see?" she asked. "It just gets uglier. We've stopped it, but we *can't* stop it. It just goes on and on. You shouldn't let it."

"Utch, come here," I said. I went toward her but she ran from me.

"You haven't even noticed what's wrong!" she screamed.

"What?"

"I can't come," she cried. I stared at her. "I can't *come!*"

"Well, you don't have to shout about it," I said. She ran out the door into the yard yelling, "I can't come! I can't come! I can't come!" Then she went into our bedroom and sprawled on our bed and cried. I left her alone.

I called Severin and said, "Look, how are you two getting along? Utch told me."

"Told you what?"

"Edith told Utch what happened out there," I said.

"Oh, *ja,*" he said. "Bender really blew it."

"Be honest with me, Severin," I said. Then I told him the story I'd heard. He denied it, but of course he *would* deny it.

A little later Edith called Utch and said that Utch had betrayed her. Apparently Edith had told her not to breathe a word to me—knowing Utch would breathe right away, of course. Utch answered that Edith had betrayed Severin's confidence by telling the story in the first place. Then I called Edith and told her I knew it was a lie.

"Of course it is," she said. But she meant that Utch had lied.

"No, *you* lied," I said.

"Fuck you." Edith said.

We didn't see the Winters for weeks and when they invited us to dinner, we weren't sure what the dinner was for.

"They're going to poison us," I said, but Utch didn't smile. "Severin likes to make everything official," I said. "He needs to hold a banquet to announce that everything is indeed over between us."

"Maybe they want to apologize."

"For what?" I said. "For using us? I'm sure they're not sorry."

"Shut up," Utch said. "Maybe they want to try the whole thing again."

"Fat chance."

"And if they wanted to try it again," Utch said, "you'd jump at the chance."

"Like hell I would."

"Ha!"

"Shut up."

When Severin greeted us at the door, he said, "Edith's given up cigarettes, so we're not going to have a very long cocktail hour. That's when she feels most like smoking." He kissed Utch on the cheek the way I'd seen him kiss his children and shook my hand. For a wrestler, Severin had a very weak handshake, as if he were trying to impress you with how gentle he was.

Edith was eating a carrot stick in the living room; she turned her cheek and let me kiss her while both her hands clutched her carrot. I remembered the first evening we had eaten with them; they were both much freer with themselves.

"We're having squid," Severin said.

"Severin spent the whole day cooking," Edith said.

"Actually, it's cleaning them that's the most time-consuming," he said. "First you have to strip the skin off. It's sort of like a film—a membrane—very slimy. Then you have to take the insides out."

"Squid are like prophylactics," Edith said. "It's like turning a rubber inside out."

"Edith helped me do it," Severin said. "I think she gets her rocks off turning squid inside out." Edith laughed, and Utch snapped a carrot between her teeth like the neckbone of a small animal.

"How's the work coming?" I asked Edith.

"I've just finished something," Edith said. She was eating one carrot after another. I wanted to smoke but there were no ashtrays.

"Have you put on weight since you stopped smoking?" Utch asked.

"I only stopped a week ago," Edith said. I couldn't tell about her weight; she wore a shapeless peasant dress, the kind of thing she never wore. I felt that Severin had dressed her for the occasion, making certain that the outline of her taut body was not visible to me.

"Time to eat!" Severin said.

The squid was on a large platter in white ringlets and grayish clumps of tentacles in a red sauce; it resembled little snippets and chunks of fingers and toes. Upstairs we could hear Fiordiligi and Dorabella taking a bath together; splashes, the tub filling, their girlish voices, Fiordiligi teasing, Dorabella complaining.

"I haven't seen the girls in a long time," Utch said.

"They're taking a bath," Edith said. Stupidly, we all listened to them taking their bath.

I would have been grateful for the interruption of our awkward silence by the great shattering crash, except that I knew exactly what it was. There was a sound like the machine-gunning of several upstairs windows, followed in a split second by the shrieking of both children. The stem of Edith's wineglass snapped in her hand and she screamed terribly. Utch's hand jerked the serving spoon across the platter and sent the squid splattering on the white tablecloth. Severin and I were moving upstairs, Severin ahead of me, moaning as he ran, "Oh God no, no, no—I'm coming!"

I knew what had happened because I knew that bathroom, bathtub and shower as well as Severin; I knew my wet love nest. The crash had been the sliding glass door on the bathtub rim; many nights, Edith and I had precariously opened and closed it. Old-fashioned heavy glass, loose in its rusting metal frame, the door slid in a blackened groove, slimy with old soap slivers and tiny parts from children's bathtub toys. Twice the door had eased out of the groove and Edith and I had clutched it and kept it from falling as we guided it back in its proper track. I'd said to Edith, "Better have Severin fix that. We could get hurt in here." Time and time again, Severin had told *her* to get it fixed. "Call a bathroom man," he said absurdly.

I had always known that if the door fell on Edith

or me, Severin would at least delight in whatever injury it gave me. And if something were to be cut by the falling door, I never doubted what it would be.

"I'm coming!" screamed Severin witlessly. I knew there would be blood but I was unprepared for how much. The bathroom looked like the scene of a gangland slaying. The old door had pitched into the tub and broken over the naked girls, the glass exploding from the frame, sending shards and fragments flying everywhere; it crunched under Severin's shoes as he plunged his arms into the tub. The tub was pink, the water bloody; you could not tell who was cut where. Out the faucet the water still poured, the tub a churning sea of glass and bleeding children. Severin lifted Dorabella out to me; she was quivering, conscious but no longer screaming; she looked nervously all over her body to see where she was wounded. I pulled the shower handle and doused us all so that I could see where her deepest cuts were. Hunting for severed arteries, Severin lifted the bent door frame over Fiordiligi's lovely head and held her under the shower while she howled and wriggled and he examined her body for cuts. Both of them had a multitude of flack-like wounds, boil-sized punctures and swellings on their arms and shoulders. I found one deep cut on Dorabella, in her sodden hair above one ear—a gash that had parted her hair and scalp, nearly as long as my finger but not quite as deep as her skull. It bled richly but slowly; there were no arteries there. Severin tied a towel around Fiordiligi's leg above her knee and twisted it into a fair tourniquet. A wedge of glass, like the head of a broad chisel, protruded from Fiordiligi's kneecap and the blood welled and flowed but never spurted. Both children were perhaps in shock and were in for a tedious and messy glass-picking session at the hospital. It would be long and painful, and there would be stitches, but they would be all right.

I knew that Severin had feared one or both of them would bleed to death in his arms, or be already drowned and bled dry by the time he reached them. "They're all right!" I yelled downstairs, where Utch was holding Edith, who would not move from her chair, sitting as if frozen, Utch said, waiting for the news. "I'll call the hospital," I said, "and tell them you're coming."

Severin took Dorabella from me and carried both nude children down to Edith; white-faced and shaking, she reviewed each wound on each daughter with wonder and pain, as if she had caused them herself.

"Please help yourselves to supper." Edith said vacantly. She did not care. She was only aware of the priority of her children.

Severin suddenly blurted, "It could have happened to you." Clearly he meant, to her and me; he meant *should* have.

With a shock, I realized that I didn't care what they thought. I realized that my Jack and my Bart had taken baths in that hazardous tub; I was thinking only that it could have happened to them, and that it could have been much worse.

We threw their coats around the children and Utch opened the car door for them. Edith never waved or said thank you as she sat with both her slashed daughters against her and let Severin drive them to the hospital, where they were to be picked clean and sewn back together, nearly as good as new. As the car backed out, I was glad to see that Edith was smoking.

Utch insisted that we clean up the bathroom. We agreed that they shouldn't have to see all that blood when they came home. Together we lugged the heavy door frame and few large pieces of glass to the trash pickup; together we vacuumed fragments from every crevice. I found a piece of glass lying across the bristles of a toothbrush; danger was everywhere. We scrubbed that bathroom spotless, drained the blood-filled tub, scrubbed the blood stains on the stairs, put all the stained towels in the washer and started it. With a screwdriver I gouged little slivers of glass out of the vile groove of the glass door. I remembered that Edith had once braced her heels against that door. I knew where the fresh linen was kept (You *would,* said Utch) and we put fresh towels on the racks. I hoped to myself that there might be a slice of glass left behind on the tub floor for Severin to sit on.

When we were done, we weren't hungry. Severin's cold squid was not appealing; it lay dead on the tablecloth, where Utch had slopped it; Edith's spilled wine had bled into it. The dish looked like the terrible debris from an operation.

I hardly said a word as we drove home. Utch broke the silence once: "Your children are more important to you than anything," she said. I didn't answer, but it wasn't because I disagreed.

That night I woke up alone in the damp bed. A window was open and it was raining. I looked everywhere, but Utch was out walking. Where can she go in this weather? I wondered. I checked the children's windows and closed them against the rain. Bart lay sunk in his pillow like a hammer, his fingers bunching the sheet in his sleep. Slim Jack lay in his bed as perfectly as the dream of a dancer. But there was no sleep coming to me, I realized. I checked the children's breathing, regular and deep. I found the umbrella. Utch did not need it where she was. I knew that she had not returned her keys to the gym and wrestling room to Severin.

I thought. If Utch is going to take up walking, I can too. Outside in the rain I greeted insomnia like a peevish mistress neglected for too long.

10

Back to Vienna

"I just go there to be alone," Utch told me. "It's a good place to think—to just rest."

"And you just might run into him up there one night," I said.

"Severin doesn't go there anymore," Utch said. "He's retired, remember?"

"I doubt that he's retired from that."

"Come with me next time," she said. "I know what you think of that whole building but please come with me and see."

"I wouldn't set foot in there at night," I said. "It's just a place full of old jock-itch germs running around in the dark."

"Please. It's special for me, and I want you to see."

"Yes, I'll bet it's special for you," I said.

"It's almost the last place I had an orgasm," Utch said. She was certainly not shy about it. "I thought maybe we might try."

"Oh, no," I said. "I don't go that way. That's not my style."

"Please just try," Utch said. "For me."

I hated Severin Winter for making my wife pathetic in my eyes. But what could I do? I took her to the gym.

In the darkness the great cage hulked like an abandoned beehive, its dangerous sleepers fled from their cells. In the new gym my shin struck an open locker door, and a tin *whang!* echoed among the sweat-stiff socks hung up to dry, the hockey sticks leaning in corners, the kneepads and bandages at rest. Utch said, *"Ssshhh!* Don't let Harvey hear us."

"Harvey?" I thought of a watchdog prowling in the dripping showers.

"The watchman."

"Well, surely he knows *you,*" I said, colliding with a low bench and greeting the cool cement floor with my cheek. There was a film of powder on the floor, a sort of deodorant designed for whole buildings. "For Christ's sake, Utch," I whispered, "hold my hand!"

She led me to the tunnel. Passing the little cave doors, I thought of the squash courts harboring bats. The air was stale. When we emerged into the moonlit cage, the pigeons stirred. Around the groaning board track, I lurched after Utch. "I think I lost the keys," I said.

"I have the keys," she said.

When she slid open the wrestling-room door the rubbery blast from the heaters hit us. I shut the door and she turned on the lights. I knew that from outside one cell of the beehive was brightly lit, like the eye of a domed prehistoric animal.

"Isn't the moonlight enough to see by?" I asked.

She was undressing. "It's not the same," she said. I looked at her strong, round body; she was a ripe, firm woman but she still moved like a young girl. I felt a fresh want for her, like what Severin would have felt if he could only have forgotten himself and let himself go. Maybe he did, I thought. I looked at a stranger watching me undress.

Utch tackled me! By mistake my elbow caught her

236

in the mouth and made her bite her lip; she said, "Not so rough. Be easy, be smooth."

Don't *coach* me, I thought, but wriggled against her. I touched her; she was already wet, and I knew in that instant that there were men—or ideas of men —who could make her come with no effort at all. She slipped me into herself so quickly that I hadn't yet reacted to the mat; it itched; it smelled like a foreigner's refrigerator. She was sliding us across the white-lined inner circle toward a padded wall, and I steered her back to the center, as so often I'd heard Severin holler to his wrestlers, "Don't let him get off the mat!"

Utch was beginning to thrash, to actually bridge under me. She was coming—so quickly—and then I was aware of her keening, a high humming like a bee gone berserk in the hive. I thought of the pigeons in panic, and of Harvey, the watchman, crooning quietly in the darkness, maturbating on the soft dirt floor under the wrestling room. My God, I thought, so it was like *this* for them; Severin Winter knew all this.

We seemed to be jammed into a far corner of the room; we had slid across two mats and were out of bounds, but Utch was still coming. I felt myself grow smaller inside her, and when she was done I had shriveled and completely lost contact.

"I came," Utch said.

"You certainly did," I said, but there was no concealing the jealousy in my voice and she knew that I had shrunk from her.

"You can spoil anything you've made up your mind to," she said. She got up, grabbed a towel from a stack in the corner and covered herself.

"Is it time for a few light calisthenics?" I asked. "Or should we run a few laps?"

She had swept up her clothes and was moving out the sliding door. "Turn off the lights when you leave," she said.

I went after her, around the sloping track. I picked up a splinter in my heel. By the time she reached the tunnel I had caught up; I followed her with my hand on her spine. "Got a splinter," I said. "Damn track."

She sat in the corner of the sauna away from me, her knees drawn up, her head between them, the towel under her. I said nothing. When she went into the pool, I waited for her in the shallow end but she swam a few solitary laps.

I was following her to the showers when she turned and threw something back into the pool. "What was that?" I asked.

"The keys," she said. "I'm not coming here again."

In the green underwater light I saw the key ring settle on the bottom of the pool. I didn't want to leave them there. I would rather have had them sent to Severin for Christmas, packed tightly in a tidy box full of turds. I don't know why I wanted them, frankly, but I dove into the pool and brought them up after Utch had gone into the showers.

Which was how I came to have the keys, and they were in my pocket the night I went walking alone and saw Severin's car parked in the shadow of the gym. The light from the wrestling room shone like the pinhole-opening for a telescope in some mysterious observatory.

So he doesn't go there anymore? I thought. And he hadn't come here alone, I was sure. I looked for cast-off unmatched shoes, but there were no signs. Who was it this time? I wondered. I thought of going to get Edith to show her how much her vengeance had accomplished. Then I thought of Utch at home, still so convinced of Severin's great suffering. She forgave him, but she had not forgiven Edith or me.

All right, Utch, I thought; I'll show you what sort of suffering Severin's up to. As I ran down the foot-path past the library, suddenly it was clear to me:

Severin had been seeing Audrey Cannon all the while; he had never stopped seeing her. Did Edith know?

"Utch is *going* to know!" I cried aloud as I panted past the new science building—wherein, no doubt, George James Bender was breeding fruit flies and pondering the predictable results.

Utch was lying languidly in the bathtub. "Get out," I said. "Put on anything—we'll take the car. Would you like to meet Audrey Cannon?" I held up the keys to the gym and wrestling room and waved them in her face like a gun. "Come on," I said. "I'll show you who's retired."

"Whatever you're doing, stop it," she said. "Please don't be crazy."

"You think he's suffered so much," I said. "Well, come see him suffer. Come see what his whole problem is." I yanked her out of the tub.

"I don't like leaving the children without even telling Jack where we've gone."

"Stop stalling, Utch!" I yelled at her. "Severin is getting laid in the wrestling room! Don't you want to see who he's fucking now?"

"No!" she screamed at me. "I don't want to see him at all."

I snatched up her blouse and handed her my writing pants; they always hung on the bathroom door. "Get dressed," I said; it didn't matter what she wore. I found my jacket with the leather elbow patches and made her put that on. She was barefoot but it wasn't cold outside, and we weren't going to be outside for long. She stopped resisting me, and at the car she slammed the door after herself and sat staring straight ahead while I slipped in beside her. I said, "This is for your own good. When you see what a super bastard he is, you'll feel better about all of this."

"Shut up and drive," she said.

The light was still on in the wrestling room—they

were having a long session—and I insisted that we wait for them at the pool. "It might make him remember something," I said. "Caught twice at the same act! How stupid can he be!"

"I'll look at whatever you want to show me," Utch said, "but just stop talking to me."

I couldn't find my way out of the locker room and through the showers, but Utch knew the way. We went up to the first balcony above the swimming pool and sat where I imagined Edith had once waited. I said, "I should go get Edith too."

"It can't be Audrey Cannon," Utch said. "He's simply incapable of seeing her again."

"Then it's *another* Audrey Cannon," I said. "Don't you see? There's going to be one Audrey Cannon after another for him, because that's how he is. It's probably some volleyball player who's missing four fingers. It's Audrey Cannon again and again, with him. I know."

"You know *you*," said Utch. "That's all you know."

She huddled on the hard bench in her wet blouse, in my jacket with the elbow patches hanging at her wrists, in my pants with the crotch sagging to her knees. She looked like a clown whose house had burned down in the night and had only managed to get dressed in whatever was handy. I put my arms around her, but she struck at me, grabbed my hand and bit it hard so that I had to pull away from her.

"Just wait and see," I said.

"I'm waiting."

We waited a long time.

When I heard Severin singing in German in the shower, I realized that of course Utch would know the song, and that maybe this hadn't been such a good idea. Then the underwater lights flicked on and two naked bodies sprinted, laughing, across the tiles and into the water. Nobody had limped. The short, powerful, seal-like body that broke water at midpool and snorted like a walrus was Severin, of course, and the slim, graceful woman who glided through the green light and slid against him, her hand fondly cupping his balls, was Edith.

"It's Edith," I whispered.

"Of course it is," said Utch.

They saw us as soon as we spoke. Edith swam to the far edge of the pool and hugged the curb. Severin, like a buffalo in his wallow, treaded water in the deep end and stared at us. No one spoke. I took Utch's arm, but she freed herself and walked down the balcony stairs. It took us forever to reach the shower door. My only thought was that our misunderstanding was now complete, because I was sure the Winters thought Utch and I had just finished a ritual of our own.

My last look at Edith was not returned. Her slim back was to me, her wet hair lay on her shoulders, her body was pressed against the side of the pool. Severin still bobbed out in the water, his round face puzzled, apparently finding the coincidence quite funny because he was grinning—or was he just straining to keep afloat? Who knows? Who knows what he ever thought?

At the shower door I turned and flung the key ring at the tempting target of his head. He ducked and I missed.

When we got home, Jack was awake, his narrow body like a knife in the shadow at the top of the stairs. "Why are you wearing Daddy's pants?" he asked Utch. She slipped out of them right there on the stairs and kicked them away.

"I'm not anymore," she said. She led Jack back to his bed, his hand on her naked hip, though I've told her a hundred times that he's getting too old for her to be naked in front of him.

"I didn't know where you were," Jack complained. "What if Bart had woken up? What if he'd had an earache or a bad dream?"

"Well, we're home now," Utch told him.

"I wasn't really worried," he said.

"Have a good dream," Utch said. "We're going to take a trip. Dream about that."

"Who's going to take a trip?"

"You and Bart and me," said Utch.

"Not Daddy?" Jack asked.

"No, not Daddy," Utch said.

"Whatever you're thinking," I said to her later, "there's no need to involve the children, is there? If you want to get away from me, leave the children here. Go off by yourself for a while, if that's what you want."

"You don't understand," she said. "I'm going to leave you."

"Go ahead," I said, "but Jack and Bart stay here."

It had been a wet spring, and a cool beginning to the summer, but the kids were happy to be out of school. When I took them to the University Club pool, I realized that the girl who followed after Jack, teasing him and allowing herself to be shoved in the pool, was Fiordiligi Winter. The scar that marred the knee of one lovely leg was the shape of a chicken's beak and the curious color of a trout's gills. I saw that Dorabella wore a bathing cap; probably her hair had not grown back. I didn't see whether Severin or Edith had brought them; I had a book with me, and I read it.

It was my fifth historical novel, just out, and I was angry at how it was being distributed—as children's literature! My publisher insisted it was not really children's literature and that I had nothing to be upset about; he told me it was being suggested for pre-teens and older. How they could have made such a blunder was beyond me. The book was called *Joya de Nica-*

ragua, and it was about refugee Cuban cigar growers, after Castro, nurturing Havana seeds on plantations in Nicaragua. The book was concerned only with the Cubans who had died in Nicaragua. *Joya de Nicaragua* is the brand name of a quality Nicaraguan cigar. My editor admitted to me that they weren't actually "pushing" the book very hard; my other four historical novels hadn't sold very well; not one of them had been seriously reviewed. A self-fulfilling prophecy if I have ever heard one! And my department chairman had once again failed to list my book among the members' new publications. In fact, my chairman had confided to me that he considered my only publication to be a small article published years ago, a chapter excerpted from my Ph.D. thesis. The thesis was unpublished; it was called "The Application of Bergsonian Time to Clerical Fascism in Austria." *Joya de Nicaragua* is a much better book.

When I brought the kids home from the pool, Utch had finished packing.

"See you in a quick while!" Bart said to me at the airport.

Jack, feeling grown up, wanted to shake hands.

After I'd come home and searched the house for signs of them which Utch might have left me, I discovered Utch had taken my passport with her. That would make it difficult for me to follow her right away.

I found her note pinned to the pillow that night. It was long and entirely in German. She knew very well that I wouldn't be able to read it. I picked over what few isolated words made some kind of sense, but it was clear that I needed a translator. One of the phrases was *"Zurück nach Wien";* I knew that meant "back to Vienna." Another word was "Severin." Who else had she meant for me to use as a translator? Of course she knew I couldn't ask just anybody

243

who spoke the language; the note's contents might be embarrassing. Her intent was obvious.

In the morning I took the note to him. A summer morning. Severin and his daughters were in the kitchen, where he was packing a lunch for them to take to the beach with friends. There was a strange car in the driveway; the car was full of children and the woman driver, whom I didn't recognize, looked like the sort of idiot who could actually have fun in a car full of children. She seemed to think it was uproarious that Severin was packing the lunch and getting the girls off, though everyone who knew the Winters was aware that Edith never did that kind of thing.

"Furthermore," Severin grumbled to me as the car backed, honking, out of the driveway, "it's a better lunch than she's made for her own kids. Drive carefully!" he bellowed suddenly; it sounded like a threat.

"Edith is writing," he told me in the kitchen.

"I came to see you," I said. "I need a little help." I handed him the note.

Still reading it, he said, "I'm sorry. I didn't think she'd leave."

"What's she say?" I asked.

"She's gone to Vienna."

"I know that."

"She'd like you to leave her alone for a while. She'll write you first. She says she's perfectly responsible, and that you shouldn't worry about the children."

It was a longer note than that. "Is that all she says?" I asked.

"That's all she says to you," he said.

There was a long, thin knife spangled with fish scales on the cutting board; it shone in the sunlight through the kitchen windows. He must have been preparing fish for supper. Severin was so singular a sort that he could hack open raw fish in the morning. While I was staring at it he picked up the knife and plunged it into the soapy water in the sink.

"Just give her a little time," he said. "Everything will straighten out."

"There's something in the note about *chickens*," I said. "What is it?"

"That's just a phrase," he said, laughing. "It doesn't have anything to do with the word in English."

"What's it mean?"

"It's just a phrase," Severin said. "It means, 'It's time to move, time to go,' something like that."

I picked up the slimy cutting board and swung it around as if it were a tennis racquet. "What *exactly* is the phrase?" I asked him. "I want a literal translation." I couldn't seem to stop trembling.

" 'Saddle the chickens,' " he said. " 'We're riding out.' "

Staring at him, I kept waving the fish-smeared cutting board. " 'Saddle the chickens, we're riding out'?"

"An old Viennese joke," Severin said.

"Some sense of humor you Viennese have," I said. He held his hand out and I gave him the cutting board.

"If it helps you to know," he said, "Utch hates me."

"Not likely."

"Look," he said, "she just needs to get her pride back. I know, because I have to get my pride back, too. It's really very simple. She knows I didn't really want the whole thing, and she knows you were thinking more about yourself than about her. We were all thinking more about ourselves than about Utch. And you were all thinking more about yourselves than about me. Now you just have to be patient and continue to do as you're doing—only a little less aggressively. Help her to hate me, but do it easy."

"Help her to hate you?"

"Yes," he said. "Edith will hate you too after a while; she'll be sorry about the whole thing. And I'll help her to be sorry. It's already beginning."

"All this hatred isn't necessary," I said.

"Don't be stupid," Severin said. "You're doing it yourself. You're trying to make Utch hate me, and you'll succeed," he said cheerfully. "Just be patient." Severin Winter was at his most obnoxious when he thought he was doing you a favor.

"Where is Edith?" I asked.

"Writing. I told you," he said, but he could see I didn't believe him. He shrugged and led me to the foot of the stairs, where he gestured that I remove my shoes. Silently we crept upstairs, through their tousled, strewn bedroom—the melted candle gave me a strong twinge—to the door of Edith's study. Music was playing. She could never have heard our voices down in the kitchen. Severin pointed to the keyhole and I looked in. She was sitting very still at her desk. Suddenly she typed rapidly three or four lines. Then her movement was again arrested and she seemed to hang above the machine with the perfect concentration of a seagull suspended over water—over its food, its whole life source.

Severin motioned me away and we tiptoed back to the kitchen. "She just sold her novel," he said. He might as well have slapped me with the cutting board, stunned me like a fish and slit me open.

"Her novel?" I said. *"What* novel? I never knew she was working on a novel."

"She didn't show you everything," Severin said.

That night I tried to take up sleeping again. I found an old slip of Utch's in the laundry basket and dressed a pillow in it and slept against it, smelling her smell. But after a few nights it smelled more like me—more like the whole bed and the whole house—and after I washed it, it simply smelled like soap.

The slip became stretched and tore a shoulder strap, but I took to wearing it myself in the mornings because it was nearest me when I woke up. I also found Bart's striped T-shirt with a smiling frog face on it and a silver cowboy jacket that Jack had outgrown. In the mornings while I ate breakfast I hung Bart's T-shirt over the back of one chair and Jack's cowboy jacket over another, and sat down to eat with them in Utch's old torn slip. I was sitting that way the morning Edith rushed in and told me they were all going to Vienna, and did I have any message for Utch?

Vaso Trivanovich and Zivan Knezevich, those diehard Chetnik Olympians, had died within two days of each other. Frau Reiner had cabled. Severin was the executor of their will, which included more awful paintings by Kurt Winter.

"Isn't it ironic?" Edith asked. "Schiele's wife died of the Spanish flu in the 1918 epidemic, and Schiele died just two days later. It's just like Vaso and Zivan. And Schiele's wife's name was Edith, too."

I realized she wasn't making any sense because of *me*. She was staring at the kitchen chairs dressed like children and at Utch's old slip, and I knew that she was embarrassed and couldn't wait to get away from me; that whatever Severin had failed to convince her of about me I was demonstrating for her now.

"No message," I said. I had heard twice from Utch; she'd said the children missed me and that she was doing nothing to make me ashamed of her. In her second letter she had sent me back my passport, but with no invitation.

"I decided to go with Severin because it's summer, after all, and the kids have never seen where their father's really from, and it might be fun to go back," Edith babbled. "No message?" she asked. "Really?" She was scatter-brained. I realized that she could see through Utch's slip, so I remained sitting down. I was embarrassed too, and wanted her to leave. I had to keep myself from asking her about her novel; I wanted to know who published it, and when it would be out, but I didn't want her to know that I wanted to know. She hadn't said a word to me about *Joya de Nicaragua;* I knew she hated it—if she had even read it. She was looking at me as if she thought I was pathetic and there was nothing to say.

"Saddle the chickens," I said, "we're riding out." Which must have convinced her of my lunacy, because she turned and left as quickly as she'd come.

I went into the bedroom, threw Utch's slip in a corner, lay down naked in the bed and thought of Edith until I came in my hand. It would be the last time, I knew, that I could come with Edith on my mind.

A little later, Severin called. I was sure Edith had told him that I was completely crackers and that he ought to check up on me. "Give us Utch's address," he said. "Maybe we can talk to her and tell her you two ought to be together." I didn't hesitate to give him the wrong address. It was the address of the American Church of Christ, where Utch and I had been married. Later, I thought that the trick I had played on Severin was the kind he would play, and that it would somehow please him.

I wrote to Utch that they were coming, and why. "If you see a couple carrying an ugly painting down the street, arguing about what to do with it, stay out of their way," I wrote.

Then the dreams started and I couldn't sleep. They were about my children, and Severin Winter would have understood them. There was one in which Jack is riding in the *Strassenbahn*. He argues with Utch to let him stand on the open platform, and she gives in. The tram comes to a whiplash bend, and when Utch looks back, Jack's gone. Then there's one about Bart, unused to city people. Utch is getting some bread to feed the pigeons in a park, and Bart is standing where he'd been told to wait. The car, which looks like an old Mercedes taxi and reeks of diesel fuel, is not a taxi; it pulls to the curb, motor spluttering, and the driver says, "Little boy?" Because it's a dream the driver speaks English, even in Vienna, and Bart walks over to see what this terrible man wants.

I had to go somewhere; I had to get away. If I was going to Vienna, I needed to borrow a little money from the old source. Oddly, I was even thinking about the Bruegel painting again—about my unidentified character, the lost burgher and that abandoned book. And I owed my parents a repeat of the old ritual. It was better than staying at home.

My mother met me at the Brown Street door. She gushed, "I never knew so many Cubans went to live in Nicaragua, and I never knew what was so special about Havana cigars before. I'm glad you used the foreign title—how do you say *Joya de Nicaragua?*—because it seems, well . . . different. I'm just not sure it's at all suitable for children, but I suppose publishers know who's reading what these days, don't they? Your father, I think, is still finishing it. He seems to be finding it very funny; at least he laughs a lot when he's reading, and I think that's what he's reading. I didn't find it all that funny myself—in fact, it seemed perhaps your bleakest book—but I'm sure he's found something I missed. Where are Utch and the children?"

"On vacation," I said. "Everything's fine."

"It is not, you look simply awful," she said and burst into tears. "Don't try to tell me," she said as she led me down the hall, crying in front of me. "Don't talk. Let's see your father. Then we'll talk."

In the den, the familiar late-afternoon sunlight dappled the open pages spread around my father and in his lap. His head was familiarly bent, his hands typically slack, but when I looked for the glass of Scotch pinched between his knees, I knew immediately. My father's knees were splayed apart and the spilled Scotch puddled the rug at his feet, which were twisted uncomfortably—that is, uncomfortably for anyone who could still feel. My mother was already screaming, and I knew even before I touched his cold cheek that my father had finally finished something, and that once more the particular book responsible for putting him to sleep was not knowable. But it might have been mine.

After the funeral, I was touched that my mother's recovery seemed slowed by her worries about Utch and me. "The best thing you could do for me right now," she told me, "is to get to Vienna immediately and clean up the trouble you're having with Utch." My mother was always a great one for cleaning up everything, and, after all, it's rare when there's something we can do for ourselves which also pleases someone else.

"Remember the good times, can't you?" my mother said to me. "I thought you writers were supposed to have such good memories, but I guess you don't write that sort of thing, do you? Anyway, remember the good times; that's what I'm doing. I think you'll find that once you start the process of remembering, you'll just go on and on."

So. I remember—I will always remember—Severin Winter in his infernal wrestling room on a day we three were supposed to pick him up there. We were all going to the city for an overnight—a movie and a hotel. (Our first hotel and our last.) Severin said he'd wait to shower and change when we reached the hotel.

"God, then he'll sweat all the way in the car," I complained to Utch.

"It's his car," she said.

Edith picked us up. "I'm late," she said. "Severin hates me to be late."

Near the gym I saw Anthony Iacovelli trudging through the snow. He recognized Severin's car and waved.

"An ape loose in a winter resort," said Edith.

We waited, but Severin did not appear. "Thank God, he's probably taking a shower," I said.

Then Tyrone Williams came out of the gym, his black face like a coal moon floating above the snow; he came over and told us that Severin was still up there, wrestling with Bender.

"God, we'll have to carry him to the car," I muttered.

"Let's go up and get him," Edith said. I knew she was thinking that he wouldn't be so angry if we all appeared.

Down on the dark mud floor of the cage a lone shotputter was heaving his ball. It whapped the mud like a body dropped unseen from the board track. An irregular thudding came from the wrestling room. Edith pulled on the door, then pushed it.

"It slides," said Utch, opening it. Inside, the incredible damp heat blew against us. Several wrestlers sagged against the walls, sodden with sweat, watching Severin and George James Bender. Earlier, it might have been a match, but Severin was tired now. He grunted on his elbows and thighs, straining to lift his stomach off the mat; whenever he'd struggle to his hands and knees, Bender would run him forward like a wheelbarrow until Severin's arms buckled and he pitched down on his chest. When Edith said, "Sorry we're late, love," Severin looked too tired to get up again. He raised his head off the mat and looked at us, but Bender pushed it back down; Bender hadn't heard anybody—I doubt if he ever did. Severin fought up to his hands and knees again and Bender drove him forward. Then Severin began to move. He sat sharply under Bender and pivoted so fast that Bender had to scramble to keep behind him. Then he shrugged Bender's weight off his back long enough to stand and grabbed a fistful of the boy's fingers around his waist, peeling them apart and suddenly sprinting across the mat like a halfback breaking a tackle. Bender dove for his ankles but Severin kicked free; his breathing was fierce, great, sucking breaths drawn from some old reservoir of energy, and he crouched, bent double, hands on knees.

Then Bender saw us, and he and the other wrestlers filed from the room as serious as Druids. Edith touched Severin's heaving back, but quickly wiped his sweat off her hand on her coat. Utch gave Severin's drenched chest a hearty smack.

Later I said to Utch that I thought Bender had let him go, but she said I didn't know anything about it. Severin had broken free, she could tell. Whatever, his extra burst had been a special performance for us, so I said, "I didn't know you had it in you, old boy."

He could barely talk; his throat seemed pinched, and the sweat ran in an unbroken rivulet off his bent nose, but he winked at me and gasped, loud enough for the women to hear, "Second wind of the cuckold."

Our first and last night in a hotel, and Severin Winter, as always, provided us with a topic for conversation. His vulgar one-liner kept Edith and me up all night.

"And what did *you* talk about?" I asked Utch in the morning."

"We didn't talk," she said.

Early one morning I took a goodbye walk. I was on hand to see the maintenance men unlock the new gym, unbolt the old cage and air out all the ghosts and germs in there. Behind the tennis courts a young girl was hitting a ball against the backboard; her soft blows made the only sound I could hear. No one was running on the board track. I stood on the dusty floor of the cage, which was beginning its slow summer bake, and in the loose system of nets that keep the baseballs from breaking the skylights. I sensed someone standing, as still as I was standing, at the door of the wrestling room. There was a shadow near his cheek—or was it a hole? I suppose I gasped, because of course I was sure it was Utch's bodyguard come to America to perform a promised slaying: mine. Then the figure seemed discomforted by my stare and moved out from behind the concealing nets. He was too young; there was no hole in his cheek, I realized, merely a black eye.

It was George James Bender; he recognized me and waved. He hadn't been exercising; he was dressed in ordinary clothes. He'd only been standing in the old cage, remembering, like me. I hadn't seen him since his upsetting loss, and suddenly I wanted to ask him if it was true, if he'd slept with Edith, if any of that impossible tale was true.

"Good morning, Professor," he said. "What are you doing here?"

"It's a good place to think," I said.

"Yes, it is," said Bender.

"I was thinking about Severin Winter," I said. "And Edith. I miss them." I watched him closely, but there were no revelations in his dead-gray eyes.

"Where are they?" he asked; he didn't seem interested.

"Vienna."

253

"It must be very nice there," he said.

"Just between you and me," I said, "I'll bet Edith Winter is the best-looking piece of ass in all of Vienna."

His reptile calm was untouched; his face showed only the faintest trace of life as we know it. He looked at me as if he were seriously considering my opinion. Finally he said, "She's kind of skinny, isn't she?" I realized, with revulsion, that George James Bender was actually smiling, but there was nothing about his smile that was any more accessible than his blank eyes. I knew once again that I knew nothing.

So I am going to Vienna, and I'm going to try the Bruegel book again. But of course there are other contributing factors. ("There are always contributing factors," Severin used to say.) It's a way to be near the children, and I admit that I want to assure Utch of my availability. We historical novelists know things take a little time. And Vienna has a fabulous history of treaties; the truces made here over the years run long and deep.

And I'd like to run into Edith and Severin sometime. I'd like to see them in a restaurant, perhaps dining out with another couple. I would know everything about that other couple at a glance. Utch and I would be alone, and I would ask the waiter to send a note from us to that couple. "Watch out," it would say. And the husband would show the note to his wife, and then to Edith and Severin, who would suddenly scan the restaurant and see us. Utch and I would nod, and by then I hope I would be able to smile.

Some other time, there's a question I would like to ask Severin Winter. When it rains or snows, when the heat is unrelenting or the cold profound—whenever the weather strikes him as an adversary—does he think of Audrey Cannon? I'll bet he does.

254

Yesterday Utch wrote that she saw Edith sitting in Demel's eating a pastry. I hope she gets fat.

So. Today I bought a plane ticket. My mother gave me the money. If cuckolds catch a second wind, I am eagerly waiting for mine.

The World of
JOHN
IRVING

"John Irving's talent for storytelling is so bright
and strong he gets down to the truth of his
time."—New York Times

"John Irving moves into the front ranks of
America's young novelists."—Time Magazine

Discover one of America's most exciting writers
with these four books, all published in
paperback by Pocket Books.

THE WORLD ACCORDING TO GARP
_____ 43996-0/$3.95
SETTING FREE THE BEARS
_____ 44001-2/$3.50
THE WATER METHOD MAN
_____44002-0/$3.50
THE 158-POUND MARRIAGE
_____44000-4/$2.95

169